W9-AHF-708

Wish

A NOVEL BY ALEXANDRA BULLEN

For my parents

Copyright © 2010 by Alloy Entertainment.

alloy**entertainment**
Produced by Alloy Entertainment
151 West 26th Street
New York, NY 10001

If you purchased this book without a cover, you should be aware that this book
is stolen property. It was reported as "unsold and destroyed" to the publisher,
and neither the author nor the publisher has received any payment for this
"stripped book."

All rights reserved. Published by Point, an imprint of Scholastic Inc., *Publishers
since 1920*. SCHOLASTIC, POINT, and associated logos are trademarks and/or
registered trademarks of Scholastic Inc.

No part of this publication may be reproduced, stored in a retrieval system, or
transmitted in any form or by any means, electronic, mechanical, photocopying,
recording, or otherwise, without written permission of the publisher. For
information regarding permission, write to Scholastic Inc., Attention:
Permissions Department, 557 Broadway, New York, NY 10012.

ISBN 978-0-545-13906-9

Library of Congress Cataloging-in-Publication Data

Bullen, Alexandra.
Wish : a novel / by Alexandra Bullen. -- 1st ed.
p. cm.
Summary: After her vivacious twin sister dies, a shy teenaged girl moves with
her parents to San Francisco, where she meets a magical seamstress who grants
her one wish.
ISBN-13: 978-0-545-13905-2 (alk. paper)
ISBN-10: 0-545-13905-8 (alk. paper)
I. Title.
PZ7.B91255Wi 2010
[Fic]--dc22

2009022730

12 11 10 9 8 7 6 5 4 3 2 1   10 11 12 13 14 15/0

Printed in the U.S.A.   40
First paperback edition, December 2010

Book design by Andrea C. Uva

Wish

Some girls are wishaholics. You know the type. Forget twinkling stars and shiny copper pennies: These girls stare at a digital clock for the better part of a morning, waiting for 11:11. And when it comes, usually they wish for something, well, less than wish-worthy. A date to the formal. A passing grade. A sudden windfall, or at least enough to buy those jeans that everybody else has.

I don't look for those girls. I look for the ones who know what a wish is worth.

"You must be Olivia."

His shoes came into focus first: squishy loafers with soft raised edges and thick, sensible soles. They reminded Olivia of mushrooms, not only because they were the color of mushrooms—the beige, rubbery, pre-chopped kind usually sold in plastic-wrapped containers—but also because they could easily have been made from some species of fungus.

"It *is* Olivia." Mushroom Foot shifted his weight uncertainly from one toadstool to the other. "Isn't it?"

Olivia Larsen uncrossed her arms and sat up. Had she been sleeping? She remembered finding a hidden spot on the grass by Golden Gate Prep's double-wide doors just as the bell was ringing for lunch. She remembered staring numbly at the sidewalk, getting an ankle's-eye view of her new classmates as they filed in and out. But she could tell by the way the boy was looking at her, sideways from behind a mop of dark, springy hair, an embarrassed little half smile twitching into place, that he'd been standing there for a while.

"Sorry," she said, swatting the seat of her khakis for patches of dirt. That was all she needed: to be paraded around on her first day of school with wet brown splotches all over her butt. "I mean, yeah. I'm Olivia."

As soon as she stood up Olivia felt dizzy, like the insides of her brain were spinning. She squinted, burrowing her fingertips into the sides of her temples, the dull headache that had been with her for months firing up behind blue eyes.

"I'm Miles. I'm supposed to give you a tour. Our moms work together, right?" He thrust one hand forward for her to shake and then quickly pulled it back, as if he'd accidentally touched something hot. "Are you okay?"

Olivia tried to nod, but a full-body yawn stretched her mouth wide open, her eyes reflexively squeezing shut. She hadn't had a solid night's sleep since her family had arrived in San Francisco a few days before. Strange, new city sounds were keeping her awake, and that morning she'd stared restlessly at the digital numbers on her alarm clock, praying it would forget to go off.

"You must be exhausted," Miles warmly allowed, directing a handful of hair away from his forehead.

Olivia swung her saggy backpack over one shoulder. She almost hadn't brought it—what was the point of a book bag when you didn't yet have any books? But it was the same bag she'd carried to school every day since the beginning of seventh grade, a navy blue JanSport with faded nylon straps, and it reminded her of home.

"We can do this another time, if you want," Miles said, shoving his hands into the pockets of his thin-wale, dark green corduroy pants. They were belted below the waist by a fraying piece of rope, tied into a knot and bulging out from under the hem of his muted orange and blue button-down shirt.

"No," Olivia said quickly, feeling bad. It wasn't his fault their moms worked at the same law firm downtown and had arranged for him to show her around at lunch, like some kind of high school playdate. "I'll be fine."

Miles untucked his hands from his pockets, clapping them together and then cringing, like he was surprised by the sound they'd made. "Okay, so," he said, clearing his throat, "are you ready for the grand tour?"

Olivia tried her best to smile as Miles flattened his long fingers against the lobby door and pushed it open.

The lobby was oddly shaped, with an angular roof that jutted out over the entryway and a futuristic front desk built in against one pristine white wall. The receptionist was a young-ish woman with choppy hair the color of a pink highlighter and silver studs in both eyebrows, with a cordless phone wedged between her shoulder and ear.

Miles gestured to her with an open palm. "Olivia, Bess. Bess, Olivia." The receptionist looked up quickly and flashed her a smile as Miles turned on his squishy heels. "Shall we move on?"

Olivia followed Miles around the corner and through a narrow, dark hallway that snaked around the perimeter of the whole school. Golden Gate Prep was a confusing combination of modern and medieval design, with an unassuming slate and glass exterior disguising the labyrinth of hollow corridors and stone archways within. It felt like the building had been renovated from the outside in, and then forgotten.

"It's not so bad once you get used to it," Miles offered, as if reading her mind. Olivia smiled and did her best to keep up, hiding another yawn with the sleeve of her peach-colored cashmere cardigan. It was almost as if basic human functions were beyond her control these days. She was lucky if she managed to string a few intelligible words together in between.

"Sorry if I suck at this," Miles muttered, pushing ahead and dragging one hand along a thick wood panel that split the wall waist-high. "There are people who actually do this here. You know, like, give tours and things," he said apologetically. "But not on a random Thursday after spring break, I guess. . . ."

Olivia nodded, her legs stiff and her muted black boots heavy as cinder blocks as she struggled to keep up.

"Speaking of which," Miles said, pausing at a crossroads where one hallway abruptly bisected another, "what are you doing here, anyway?"

Olivia felt familiar crimson splotches blooming on her face and neck. She had long since accepted the unique dermatological curse of wearing her emotion for all to see, and arranged her mass of strawberry blond curls so that they fell over one shoulder, hoping to hide her blushing profile.

"Er, sorry," Miles stammered. "That sounded way less harsh in my head. It's just, we don't usually get anybody new this late in the term, and all my mom told me is that you moved. She didn't say where from."

"Boston," Olivia offered, digging her fists deeper into the fuzzy pockets of her sweater. This was always her answer, even though it was a lie. Nobody had ever heard of little suburban Willis, which, despite being only twelve miles from the Boston city line, might as well have been in another state for all of the time Olivia had spent there.

"Wow," Miles said, his dark, bushy eyebrows arching skyward. "You didn't drive all the way out, did you?"

"No," Olivia said a little too loudly, recoiling at the idea of a cross-country road trip with her parents. They weren't exactly the word-game-and-trail-mix type of family—at least not anymore. "We flew in over the weekend so my mom could start at work," she explained. "I guess the firm made her an offer she couldn't refuse."

"Right," Miles said, with a careful nod that said he knew there was more to the story. "That would've been a killer commute."

Olivia managed a smile as he pushed through another set of sturdy glass doors and led them outside.

"Welcome to lunch," he announced, letting his recycled-rubber messenger bag fall from his shoulder.

The courtyard was a big open circle, with dappled sunlight playing on the crooked cobblestone. Scattered around clusters of low tables and benches, students were chatting and laughing.

"Where's the cafeteria?" Olivia asked, squinting back through a wall of arched windows.

"There's the Depot, I guess." Miles shrugged, taking an orange from his bag and digging in to peel it with his fingers. "Little café next to the lobby. They have pretty decent coffee, fresh fruit, vegan pastries, whatever. Most kids bring from home. If I have a long enough break, I usually go out."

"Go out?" Back at Willis, the only time they'd been allowed to leave was for field trips or with the occasional forged note.

"The Haight's right around the corner," Miles explained, nodding vaguely behind them. "It's kind of a scene, but there are a couple good coffee shops and burrito places. Of course, you have to look past about a thousand head shops to find them. . . ."

Olivia's eyes wandered from one group of students to another. Lunch at home had been like a road map of the social circles at Willis. The long orange table by the windows was always reserved for Olivia and her group of friends. The theater freaks sat on the floor by the hall. The computer kids played with their newest gadgets by the salad station. The jocks threw greasy handfuls of Cajun fries at each other over by the vending machines. It was the same day after day, year after year, and it was all Olivia knew.

Here there were no designated areas, and to Olivia's untrained eye, it seemed like there weren't really any discernible groups. Everyone was completely unique and somehow also exactly the same. It looked like lunch at the United Nations, if the United Nations' dress code was skinny jeans, vintage dresses, American Apparel sweatshirts, and scrawl-font tees.

"Aren't you hungry?" Miles asked.

Olivia opened her mouth to answer but was silenced by the whir of a skateboard rolling past. She looked up to see the rider: a tallish boy with shaggy, burnt blond hair, and clear green eyes that sparkled in a way that made it difficult for Olivia to look anywhere else.

He smiled when their eyes met, a slow, friendly smile, like he was recognizing her from somewhere else. Olivia felt her cheeks flush as he pushed at the ground with one broad stroke of his navy shell-toed sneaker. He glided down a stone path and behind one of the building's jutting corner wings, and was gone.

"No, thanks," Olivia mumbled dreamily, before snapping to attention. "I mean, not really. I already ate." It was half-true. She hadn't eaten, but she wasn't hungry, and hadn't been for months. Her mother had even started to comment on her collarbones, but Olivia didn't care. She wasn't trying to lose weight—she just wasn't that interested in food anymore.

"So did you find them yet?" Miles asked, pulling a bag of organic pita crisps from his insulated lunch cooler. He popped the bag open and held it out to Olivia.

"Find who?" Olivia asked, politely shaking her head.

"The VIPs," Miles said between crackling bites. "The in crowd. The see-and-be-seens."

Olivia scanned the courtyard again.

"They work hard to blend," he went on. "And they'd never admit to being who they are. But if you look hard enough, you'll find them."

Olivia's gaze landed on a small table nestled against a far wall, partially shaded by the low-hanging branches of a pale pink magnolia. A crew of bohemian-chic hipsters were passing around plastic trays of sushi rolls, fingering chopsticks, and laughing. Lounging on a wooden bench was a thin, ginger-haired guy in a black and tan checkered shirt, his long legs spread out before him. Folded on his lap sat a baby-faced Asian girl, twirling locks of the boy's red curls between purple-polished fingertips.

On the mosaic tabletop another slender girl with dramatic eye makeup and silky dark hair sat in lotus position, carefully sorting through a bag of granola and tossing ingredients up in the air, catching them in her open mouth. She was a study in layers: striped kneesocks over ribbed, solid tights, all tucked snugly into worn, thick-heeled motorcycle boots. A long wool sweater was drawn at the waist over a high-collared dress, and a thin knit scarf wrapped endlessly around her neck and shoulders.

"Ding ding ding!" Miles sang out, jolting Olivia out of her trance.

"Calla Karalekas," he muttered, feigning disinterest. "The planet around which lesser moons revolve. Her father's some kind of ambassador to Greece, and her mother is Japanese royalty."

"She's pretty," Olivia muttered, needlessly. She wasn't pretty. She was possibly the most stunningly gorgeous human being Olivia had ever seen.

"She's all right, I guess." Miles shrugged. "If you're into that kind of thing."

Olivia watched as Miles fidgeted with a faux-leather cuff, rolling it back and forth against the narrow knobs of his wrist. "Which, clearly, you're not," she said.

"Hey," he insisted, straightening his elbows into an exaggerated stretch, "I've gone to school with this crowd since the sixth grade. I've had some time to observe."

"Seems like you do a lot of observing," Olivia pointed out, tucking one thumb into the hole where the sleeve of her sweater had worn thin, and hugging her elbows to keep warm. The late March sun was strong and steady, but every so often a thick breeze would send little quaking shivers up from the base of her spine.

"I learn a lot that way," Miles said, unscrewing the top of his ceramic water bottle and taking a sip. "I've learned a lot about you."

For a moment Olivia leveled her eyes with his, so big and dark that they appeared opaque. "Like what?" she asked.

"Like you're hiding something," he said quickly, settling back against the wall and resting his solid arms against bent knees. "Nobody skips town in the middle of the school year for no reason," he continued, narrowing his eyes into little slits.

Olivia shrugged, crossing and uncrossing her ankles and staring at a patch of weeds pushing up between the crooked stone tiles.

"So what was it?" he demanded. "Messy divorce?"

Olivia shook her head and swallowed.

"Trouble with the law?" His voice was light and easy. A glimmer of a smile was twitching its way across his lips.

She swallowed again. This was the part she hated the most. The fact that no matter what she said, no matter how she said it, that smile would vanish in an instant. She would feel awkward. He would feel like an ass. And they'd finish what was left of their lunch in an uncomfortable silence.

"Come on," he pleaded, as if defying her thoughts. "There has to be some reason you moved all this way. I mean, my mom's firm is good, but it's not *that* good. . . ." Miles waggled his eyebrows, urging her on.

Olivia steadied her shaking hands against the table. "My twin sister died."

Her voice was tiny and unfamiliar. No matter how many times she said those words, she couldn't escape the feeling that it was a line she was repeating from somebody else's life. Maybe the main character in some sappy movie that she and Violet had seen on TV, cracking jokes about the lame acting

11

but secretly feeling unspeakably lucky that nothing so terrible would ever happen to them.

"My mom grew up here," Olivia went on, trying anything to ease the tension of the moment. "Thought it would be good to try something new. Or old, I guess. . . ."

Miles cleared his throat and fidgeted with the empty plastic bag of chips.

Olivia didn't need to look up to know that she'd been right: His easy smile had vanished in an instant. He felt like an ass. And they finished what was left of lunch in an uncomfortable silence.

2

"Dad?" Olivia called into the downstairs hallway, kicking the front door shut. A pane of decorative glass shuddered behind the layers of cardboard her father had taped to one side. The house, a four-story Victorian with canary yellow shingles and lopsided periwinkle shutters, was in various stages of disrepair. Olivia was having a hard time remembering that nothing actually did what it was supposed to do: doors didn't close, windows didn't open, and—

"What the hell?" Olivia swore as one boot dropped straight through a torn-up two-by-four, catching around her ankle and tossing her sideways into the wall.

Apparently, floors weren't floors.

After extracting herself from the subfloor, she dropped her bag in a heap by the stairs and started back toward the kitchen. The commute home from school had been almost more exhausting than the rest of the day combined. She'd had to switch buses and had ended up traveling ten blocks in the wrong direction, ultimately deciding to get off and walk back through the Mission.

"Hey, O," Mac Larsen called as Olivia stepped into the kitchen, turning down the volume on the black-and-white TV balanced precariously over the sink. He was kneeling on the counter, elbow-deep in a ceiling light fixture. A wiry man of average height, Mac was always crunching his knotted limbs into tight, awkward spaces, to get a better look at a leak or a plug.

"Shouldn't you be wearing gloves?" Olivia craned her neck to see her father's hands, twisting free a broken bulb.

"Probably," he grumbled. "How was school?"

Olivia opened the stainless-steel refrigerator, the only new appliance her father had insisted on buying immediately, her eyes scanning rows of containers of half-eaten takeout, two bottles of ketchup, and a lonely onion.

"Fine," Olivia answered, unfolding some leftover Chinese and picking around with her fingers. "What happened to the floor?"

Her father wiped handfuls of dust on his pants, faded jeans he'd had since college, and motioned for her to pass the lo mein. "What floor?"

Olivia handed over the greasy container. "The floor that used to be in the hallway," she said, as he settled on the countertop.

"Had to get in there to look at some pipes," Mac explained through a mouthful of cold noodles.

Olivia grabbed a plastic bottle of water from an opened twelve-pack on the sawdust-covered counter, starting back out into the hallway to her room.

"Mom's gotta stay late at work," he called after her.

Olivia stopped short in the hall. "Again?" she asked, without turning around.

Her father nodded and hopped down from his perch. "Looks like we're on our own for dinner."

"Delivery?" Olivia guessed, slouching back against the molding door frame and feeling it sway dangerously under her weight.

"What do you feel like?"

Olivia shrugged as her father squeezed behind her to get to the fridge. "You know," he said, "that's one thing about this city I might be able to get used to. Anything you want to eat, you got it. Chinese, Italian, Indian, sushi—"

"You hate sushi," Olivia interrupted.

"So what?" her father continued. "I can still get it at midnight. Can't get a piece of toast at midnight back home."

"That's true." Olivia nodded, trying for chipper and starting back into the hall toward her room.

Her dad had always tried to make it better, no matter what "it" was. When Olivia was six and sprained her ankle jumping off dunes at their beach house on Martha's Vineyard, Mac decorated her crutches with iridescent streamers. When their mother, Bridget, was on a case in North Carolina for three weeks, Mac had given the girls leftover cans of house paint, setting them loose in their rooms and, more important, defending their artistic choices (sky blue for Olivia, a Pollock-inspired smattering for Violet) when Bridget returned.

One of the most infuriating parts about Violet being gone was that there wasn't a thing Mac could do to fix it.

"Hey," Mac called again. "School. Was it terrible?" He

15

leaned back against the sink and was gripping the edges of the speckled linoleum countertop with his rough, calloused hands. It was obvious he was trying to lounge, or at least approximate the posture of somebody engaged in casual conversation. But his face was strained and his voice sounded like he'd been swallowing shards of glass.

"Not terrible," she said, forcing softness.

"Make any friends?" he asked.

Olivia's stomach tightened. Of course she hadn't made any friends. She'd gone through her whole life with a built-in social ambassador. Violet had always been a chameleon, able to be anyone at any time, if it meant easy conversation and a fast friend. Olivia thought of herself more like a gecko. Or a newt.

She opened her mouth to speak but stopped when she looked closer into her father's bloodshot eyes, hollow and heavy at the edges. His once-red hair seemed to be attacking itself, and the scruff on his chin was tinged with more gray than before.

He hadn't signed up for this, either.

It had been her mom's idea to pick up and leave Willis in the middle of the school year. Olivia had thought it was a bit of a coincidence that her mother had randomly been offered a top position at a prestigious firm in San Francisco, the same San Francisco where she happened to have access to a house that had been in her family for almost a century. Never mind that up until then the house had been referred to only as "that deathtrap Great-aunt Peggy left us"—all of a sudden, everything was falling into place. Bridget had a new job, Olivia had a new school, and Mac, an out-of-work contractor, had a new project.

A project that, by the looks of things so far, was quickly turning into a thousand little projects, none of which seemed to be approaching any form of completion.

"A couple," Olivia lied. "Everybody's really nice. And the building's cool. Really old, with lots of big windows."

"Yeah?" Her dad had turned to face the sink and was already fidgeting with a stubborn faucet. She could keep talking, if she wanted to, but she knew she'd said enough. He'd gotten what he needed. She'd communicated. She was functioning.

All was well in familyland.

She mumbled something about homework to the back of her father's head, and left him to fix the things he still could.

🦋 🦋 🦋

Olivia collapsed onto her bed after a quick and quiet meal of Indian takeout with Mac, her body sinking into the lavender comforter she'd brought from home. She closed her eyes and inhaled the thick, downy fabric, which still reminded her of Itsy and Bitsy, the twin calico kittens the girls had adopted when they were six. They'd only been allowed to keep the cats for a few months, before Bridget had started breaking out in head-to-toe hives and discovered she was allergic.

Olivia remembered squeezing Violet's hand as they walked up the long driveway back to the MSPCA, tears streaming from Violet's chin and careening onto the gravel. Olivia promised her sister that one day they'd move into a house of their own and have twenty cats and eat nothing but Oreo sundaes and watch all the TV they wanted. This had worked, and Violet had stopped crying, until they got home and she realized that their blankets still smelled like the kittens, who, after much begging, had been allowed to sleep in the girls' room.

Olivia's eyes were closed when a crisp, hair-tickling breeze blew in from the open window, rattling the doors in the room on their loosening hinges. She sat up and saw that one door was slowly creaking open—the narrow, knotted door at the back of her room.

Connected to Olivia's bedroom and facing an overgrown garden at the back of the house was a tiny corner room with a low, garret-style roof. A little bit smaller than Olivia's room, it had two arched bay windows with a cushioned love seat between them. When Olivia had announced she wouldn't be taking this room, but the more ordinary, larger, street-noisy room beside it, her parents hadn't argued. Nobody said anything, but they all knew.

The smaller room was the one Violet would have wanted.

And when the moving trucks arrived and all that was left to unload were several unmarked boxes, nobody said anything then, either. But somehow the boxes—sealed after a silent afternoon spent stowing Violet's things—had ended up in that room, behind two doors that would always stay closed.

Olivia slowly rose to her feet and walked over to the door in the corner. She reached out and held the cold brass knob, lingering for a moment.

It was almost as if she could feel Violet, waiting for her on the other side.

A chill spiked the hairs on the back of her neck and she snapped the door swiftly shut.

The gauzy white curtain ballooned again and Olivia moved to the window. As she tugged it open even wider, sharp city sounds came flooding in—a squealing car alarm, the steady whoosh of wet traffic, boisterous after-dinner voices—as if she'd unmuted a movie she hadn't known she was watching.

Before she knew what she was doing or why, Olivia had maneuvered her narrow limbs through the window and onto the rickety little balcony, slick from an evening drizzle. She carefully pulled herself to her feet and looked down. From four stories up, the city felt formal and strange.

Hugging her sweater close, she used a sleeve to mop a puddle from one side of the railing and settled herself down, looking up toward the sky.

Back at home, after their parents had gone to sleep, she and Violet would climb out of Olivia's bedroom window, swinging up and over an angled eave and leaning flat against the white cedar roof. The girls would whisper whatever new gossip they had to share, which usually meant Violet did most of the whispering. Gazing up at the clear night sky, Olivia would redraw constellations with her finger, and Violet would hold her breath, searching for shooting stars to wish on. It was the kind of quiet that was almost scary, like they were the only two people left on the entire planet.

On her new balcony, Olivia tried to block out the rhythm of cars and snippets of conversation floating up from street level. Yellow sidewalk lanterns blurred in her vision as she made out the shadows of low town houses stretching back toward the horizon. The pointed rooftops blended together against a blue-black blanket of sky, a layer of dark fog and heavy clouds obscuring any stars that might have been hiding behind them.

Olivia wanted to feel disappointed. She actually *tried* to miss home. But really, she didn't.

She couldn't.

It was around February when Mac and Bridget sat Olivia down at the dining room table and told her she wouldn't be going back to Willis High after spring break. Olivia remembered staring through a square, crystal vase at the shape of her father's knuckles, thick and distorted as they rapped against the faded oak. Predictably, Bridget did most of the talking, her voice careful and composed, as if she were bracing herself for outrage or, at the very least, impassioned dissent.

Olivia couldn't remember if she'd actually said anything at all. Probably a question or two about logistics—had they already booked a flight? When would they be leaving?—but any words she'd spoken would have been muttered in the cold, empty voice of somebody who didn't have enough left in her to care.

That night, she lay awake in her old canopied bed, trying to convince herself to feel *something*. She'd done the same thing after Violet's funeral—the whole afternoon she'd moved from room to room in their house like a robot, her features frozen, her body aching and hollow. She hadn't cried once, and, staring at her reflection in the oval-shaped mirror hanging in the downstairs hallway, she'd wondered if forcing herself to conjure up specific details about her sister would remind her body how to feel again.

She remembered the way Violet's nose twitched and wrinkled at the bridge when she was confused. The way her laugh, her real laugh, reserved for when something was truly, actually funny, caught in the back of her throat, and sounded a little like snoring.

But still, no tears.

And again, when Olivia learned she'd be leaving her house, her school, all of her friends at once, she knew the appropriate reaction would have involved some kind of resistance. But no matter how hard she tried, she couldn't access anything inside of her that resembled a nostalgic twinge.

Since Violet's death, the house had felt too big and silent, anyway. And at school, she wasn't sure what was worse—being the new girl, or being the girl who looked exactly like the other girl who'd died over the summer, the girl who loved everyone and whom everybody loved.

The girl who was so much fun.

Olivia had packed all of her things a week early, living out of one suitcase and sleeping on spare sheets. As far as she was concerned, she'd already left. No place would ever be home again, no matter where it was or how much of her own stuff she had around her.

And now, looking up at the foggy sky, she *tried* to feel sad that she couldn't see any stars. She *wanted* to want something that reminded her of Violet. She *wished* she could feel something, anything, standing in the darkness, alone.

But all she felt was cold.

Olivia shivered, crawled back inside the window, and drew the curtains tightly shut.

3

er eyes still blurry with sleep, Olivia fumbled her way to the kitchen early Friday morning, feeling automatically for the pot of coffee her father always brewed before going out for the paper—i.e., to sneak an illicit donut and cigarette. Usually, Olivia wished he would give these indulgences a rest, but secretly she loved that her dad was consistently less undercover than he thought, always returning with telltale crumbs on his collar, or the subtle musk of stale smoke in his hair.

Olivia tipped the solid metal urn over the lip of her favorite Red Sox mug, watching with muted frustration as the last lukewarm drops of grainy liquid sputtered out. Olivia had only recently inherited her parents' caffeine addiction, and whether it was out of conscious resolve or absentminded oversight, Mac had yet to adjust his morning measurements accordingly.

Too foggy-brained to fathom brewing another pot, Olivia filled the teakettle with water instead. Violet had detested Olivia's growing coffee habit, insisting that green tea was a healthier alternative. Olivia thought green tea tasted like gunmetal, but had saved the economy-size box Violet had ordered online from some healthy-living website, just in case.

Olivia leaned against the sink, waiting for the water to boil and staring vacantly at the sloping kitchen table in the center of the room. The house had been partially furnished when the Larsens moved in, with a few worn, antique pieces covered with drop cloths and wedged awkwardly under stairwells. Mac claimed he would refurbish them all, explaining how easy it would be to polish here, reupholster there. But Bridget had insisted that Mac haul just about everything to the Salvation Army, in order to make room for the new dining set and leather sofa she'd picked out from a Crate and Barrel catalogue on the plane.

The kitchen table, with one floppy leaf and a huge, branch-like crack twisting across its middle, was the one piece Mac had managed to hold on to, most likely due to the fact that the only time Bridget spent anywhere near the kitchen was early in the morning, before she was awake enough to complain.

The kettle squealed and Olivia poured herself a cup of tea before shuffling upstairs to get ready for school. From the back room on the second floor, envisioned as a full-service gym but now doubling as a storage space/living area, Olivia heard the hushed dialogue of the television and the slow, methodic thumping of her mother on the treadmill.

A track star in high school and college, with yearbooks and scrapbooks to prove it, Bridget spent an hour every day, no matter the day, no matter the hour, chugging on the treadmill and watching the trashy daytime soaps she had TiVo'd the afternoon before.

"Olivia, is that you?" Bridget's sturdy voice called out, midstride.

Olivia stalled on the landing, bringing the mug close to her nose and inhaling a wet cloud of herbal steam. She closed her eyes for a moment and leaned back against the wobbly banister before turning and making her way back down the hall.

Bridget's routinely frosted dark blond hair was pulled up in a tight, high ponytail, her prominent cheekbones dotted with little patches of red—the only sign that she was working at all. Her slender arms pumped almost imperceptibly at her sides, her gaze fixed on the small TV nestled precariously in the middle of an empty bookshelf.

"Morning," Olivia said quietly, resting the angle of her hip on the doorjamb and tilting her head toward the set, wondering which disgruntled housewife or conniving stepfather was holding court today. She could never understand how her mother, who spent thirteen hours a day deposing white-collar witnesses and decoding multimillion-dollar contracts, could lose herself so thoroughly in the melodrama of overacted soaps.

"Good morning," Bridget huffed, wiping her forehead with the back of one slim wrist. "I thought we might go shopping later."

Olivia turned her head from the television back to the treadmill, her eyes wide with scrambled alarm. "What?" she asked, trying to remember the last time her mother had proposed that they do anything together. "I mean, why?"

Bridget jabbed at the electronic buttons on the dash, lowering the incline and slowing her pace to a brisk walk. "There's an event Saturday night," she said, gripping the handles, her manicured fingernails wrapping delicately around the shiny metal bars. "A cocktail party at the office, to welcome me—all of us—into town."

"Tomorrow?" Olivia asked, as if she might already have plans. It seemed the only possible way out.

Bridget nodded. "All of my nice things are still in boxes." She sighed. "And it's been a while since we've shopped for you. What do you think?"

Olivia tucked one bare foot back behind the other, her eyes blurring over the hypnotically cycling mechanical belt. It hadn't been a *while*. It had been exactly seven months, two weeks, and three days.

The only thing Violet and their mother had ever agreed on had been the overwhelming satisfaction achieved by touching things in fancy stores, trying them on, wrapping them up, and bringing them home. Although it was not a pastime Olivia had much interest in, she often tagged along, if only to watch Violet veto Bridget's more conservative selections. It was the one occasion on which Bridget deferred to her eccentric daughter's expertise, and Olivia loved to see her mother, for once, in the position of asking for help.

Now the idea of the two of them wandering aimlessly in and out of boutiques, not only strangers in a new city but doubly lost without the guidance of their shopping guru, was enough to make Olivia's inner ears ache.

"I don't know," she said. "I don't really feel like going to a party."

Bridget's light eyes were sharp and focused as she slowed to a stop and stepped off the machine. "Well, you don't have to come," she spoke evenly. "But it might be fun."

Olivia shifted her weight from one bare foot to the other,

every cell in her body begging to be released and allowed to run back upstairs to her room, where nobody asked her to do things like shop or be polite.

"Phoebe Greer will be there with her son," Bridget continued. "Miles, I think. I asked her to arrange for him to show you around yesterday. Did he find you?"

"Yeah," Olivia managed. "He found me."

"Good," Bridget confirmed. "Then you'll have somebody to talk to at the party." She laid a firm hand on Olivia's shoulder as she squeezed past her into the narrow hall. "But," she said, with a tight, awkward smile, "only if you feel up to it."

Just about the last thing Olivia felt up to doing was getting dressed up and standing awkwardly with plastic cups and tiny plates of hors d'oeuvres and not enough hands to eat them. But she knew that smile. And she knew where arguing would get her. This was her mother's game, and Olivia's only option was to play along.

"Fine," she grumbled. "But I don't need to go shopping. I'm sure I can find something in my closet to wear."

Bridget nodded and gave Olivia's shoulder a tiny squeeze. "It's up to you." She shrugged, smiling coolly and inching past her daughter toward the stairs.

🦋 🦋 🦋

That afternoon, Olivia stood with her hands on her hips, staring vacantly into the open closet.

Her second day at Golden Gate had been interminably long and deafeningly quiet, and she'd somehow managed to get by without uttering more than forty-eight words. She'd gotten to each of her classes early, introduced herself to the teacher (*Olivia Larsen, I'm new here; nice to meet you* = 9 words x 5 classes = 45 words), said, "Excuse me," when she'd stepped on somebody's toe, rushing on her way to AP Calculus (two words), muttered a curt and hurried, "Hey," when she'd spotted Miles in the courtyard (one word), and smiled tightly when she'd clumsily bumped into the mysterious, green-eyed skater boy in the hall (zero words).

She'd been slowly unpacking since she got off the bus, starting with the boxes full of her favorite books and collection of tattered journals. But the new bookshelves her father was supposedly building were still in pieces in his shop in the basement, and she hadn't felt much like writing in her journal lately. She'd moved on to the unopened boxes of clothing, stuffing sweaters into the bottom drawers of the clean, white armoire her mother had picked out at Pottery Barn. The last thing she wanted to think about was finding a dress for the stupid cocktail event tomorrow night, mostly because she didn't want to go, but also because her collection of formal wear, recently unfolded and draped on a few sad wire hangers in the closet, was officially pathetic.

There was the thick, strapless gown she'd worn to the sophomore semiformal, which had made her feel glamorous at the time, but weighed about two hundred pounds and was way too fancy for the office. There were a few flowery cotton sundresses, sleeveless and not at all appropriate for any place other than the beach. And of course the mauve taffeta number she'd worn as a junior bridesmaid in her cousin Lorelei's wedding, with puffy sleeves and a high, cinched waist that had made her feel like an Oompa-Loompa on the one occasion she was forced to wear it.

Olivia groaned and fell back onto her bed, covering her face with a pillow.

Shopping had been Violet's number one extracurricular. When Olivia and her mother had gone through Violet's things, even they had been astonished to discover the amount of clothing she'd managed to amass over the years. She hadn't been a spree-shopper, coming home weighted down with bags from Saks or Nordstrom. It was all done piecemeal—a soft cotton tunic from that little boutique in Wellesley Center; a pair of enormous sunglasses from a flea market in Harvard Square; the vintage Pucci dress she'd found in a Somerville consignment shop and was planning on wearing to the junior prom. . . .

It was smooth satin, almost liquid to the touch, and swirled with bright concentric circles. It had originally been astronomically expensive, but had been marked down to just within her budget because of an enormous, side-baring tear at the zipper.

Violet didn't care. She'd had to have it, claiming that a seamstress would be able to fix it, no problem. But she'd never gotten the chance to find one.

Olivia sat up on her bed, her feet landing heavily on the carpet.

The dress.

Slowly, she stood and walked across the room to the door in the corner. Before she had time to change her mind, she took the knob in her hand and turned it, pulling the creaky door open and stepping inside.

The room was flooded with hazy sunlight and stale, trapped air. There was no furniture, only the windows, the built-in love seat, and a sad row of boxes against the far wall. Olivia held her breath and walked purposefully toward the boxes. She knelt beside them, running her hands along the masking tape.

Carefully, afraid of making a sound, Olivia pulled back the cardboard flaps. Her nostrils immediately tingled at the familiar scent, a mix of sea salt and strawberry-kiwi shampoo.

She plunged her hands into the first box, digging around pairs of cowboy boots and metallic ballet flats. The second box was accessories, mostly chunky charm necklaces and printed scarves. It was in the third box that she found the dress, folded neatly near the top.

She let her fingers graze the soft, cool satin, the dizzying print starting to blur behind her clouding eyes. Her fingers caught in the hanging threads by the zipper, poking through the gaping hole down the side. All she needed now was a seamstress.

Crawling to her feet, she brought the dress out in front of her, held the fabric against her skin.

Of course.

Violet had had the answer all along.

_4_

The rain just wouldn't let up.

It was a familiar refrain, and everyone from the punky receptionist at school to the perky weather blonde on the six o'clock news seemed to have an opinion about when the rainy season would finally end.

Before the move, Olivia's mother had enthusiastically reminded her daughter that they couldn't be arriving at a better time of year. "You won't see a drop of rain from March to October," she'd said.

So far, it had rained at least once a day. And not always just sprinkles. Heavy, sky-splitting downpours, the kind that made wearing jeans or getting out of the car a gamble.

Olivia had left her stoop and started down Dolores just as Friday evening's downpour was getting under way, a single, fat drop splattering on the sidewalk beside her boot. Almost an hour of sloshing through puddles of murky curb water later, she'd decided that searching for a seamstress in the rain wasn't one of her most brilliant ideas. After trudging from one soaked corner to another, scanning the hodgepodge of window displays—a cute little antique furniture shop, a watch repair store, and about ten yoga studios in a six-block radius—she was fairly certain that she wasn't going to find a tailor in her neighborhood.

She was pulling the collar of her black Windbreaker tighter around her neck when a dim light in a dark corner storefront caught her eye. It was in a building on the corner across from the manicured median of palm trees, a building she walked past every day on her way to the bus stop. A burgundy awning jutted out from the dirty concrete wall, and Olivia had always assumed the space was empty. There was even a laminated sign in the window, one that she could have sworn used to say FOR RENT. But as Olivia walked closer, ducking under the awning, which flapped wildly in the wind, she saw that the sign was actually a handwritten note:

Mariposa of the Mission.

Olivia cupped her hands to the glass and peered inside. The glare from a yellow streetlight floating overhead made it hard to see anything, and she could just barely make out the hulking shadows of garment bags and sewing machines. It looked like an abandoned dry cleaner's, minus the mechanically rotating shirts.

Olivia blinked, her eyes traveling across the room. In the far corner, lounging on a threadbare divan, was a small, dark-haired girl. She glanced up from the paperback book open in her lap, and looked pointedly through the window at Olivia, almost as if she'd been waiting for her.

Olivia quickly dropped her hands to her side and hopped back, startled. Was it possible that all this time, the very thing she was looking for had been around the corner from where she'd started, just a few hundred feet from her own front door? Why hadn't she seen it before?

Olivia took a deep breath, remembering the dress she'd stuffed inside her purse, and pushed carefully through the heavy glass door.

Tinny chimes rang out as soon as she stepped onto a straw welcome mat, and Olivia let the door shut quietly behind her. The girl in the corner had gone back to her book, and Olivia stood awkwardly at the entrance. Half-dressed mannequins haunted every corner of the small space, staring down from high perches with blank faces. Folds of fabric were layered on low wooden tables, and hidden in each nook and darkened corner were miniature glass butterfly figurines of varying shapes and colors. A soft yellow light fell in shafts from two tasseled lamps, cutting rays of swimming dust across the floor.

Olivia cleared her throat, but the girl continued reading, her thick, dark brows furrowed to a bushy point. "Excuse me," Olivia gingerly began. "Do you—?"

"We're closed," the girl said, noisily flipping a page. She was remarkably tiny, with sticklike limbs that were swallowed by the round crimson cushions of a vintage love seat. The love seat itself was missing two legs, and had been propped up on one end against a broken, boxy record player.

"Closed?" Olivia quietly repeated, her shoulders sinking. She glanced back through the darkening window, already imagining a night of mauve taffeta travesties, the itchy lining, the horrific swishing sound it made around her knees when she walked. She was reaching one hand to the door when a sharp voice called out from behind her.

"Wait!"

Olivia looked back to see that the girl had abandoned her book, which now lay open facedown in her lap. It was one of those steamy romance novels usually buried deep in the dollar bin outside used bookstores, with a half-naked couple swooning across the cover.

"I've seen you before," the girl said, staring at Olivia with tight, beady eyes. "You live nearby?"

Olivia nodded and swallowed. "Yeah," she answered, her mouth dry and her tongue slow. "We just moved in down the street. I was just, um, on my way home and I thought . . . I mean, I was just looking—"

"Looking is allowed." The girl smiled, revealing a crowded row of what looked like baby teeth and pulling herself up to her feet. She spoke with a slight and indistinguishable accent, cleanly articulating each syllable and sound. Olivia wondered if she was foreign, or just one of those people who talk funny to be different.

"I know that," Olivia said, suddenly defensive.

The girl reached behind a patchwork quilt that was hanging from a clothesline strung across one corner of the room, and pulled an old broom from where it had been leaning against a wobbly chest of drawers. Much like the girl, all of the furniture in the shop appeared arthritic, like it might buckle or fall if you sneezed in its general direction.

"I'm Posey," she said, lazily swatting the broom across a patch of dusty red tiles.

Olivia took a step closer. "Olivia," she said, her hand hanging awkwardly between them. Posey hesitated before extending her own hand, which was so small and spindly Olivia worried it might shatter into pieces. From close up, Posey's brown eyes were flecked with bits of yellow-orange, and blinked curiously through dark, crooked bangs. There was something about the way she stared that made Olivia uncomfortable, like she suddenly wanted to put on another layer of clothes.

"Nice to meet you, Olivia," Posey said, spotting a toppled pile of fabric swatches at her feet and bending over to straighten it. As she stood, the corner of her shoulder bumped up against a table leg, and one of the small butterfly figurines tottered from side to side. Posey hurried to keep it from falling, delicately steadying its trembling wings to stillness.

"I like your butterflies," Olivia said, realizing immediately how lame it sounded. "I mean, they're nice. I like butterflies, you know; they're—"

Posey smiled. "Thanks," she said. "They were my grand-mother's."

As Posey carefully lifted her hand from the ornament and went back to sweeping the floor, Olivia recognized a familiar flash across her eyes. *They* were *my grandmother's*. It was the look of someone who had lost something she'd never get back.

"Was this her shop?" Olivia inquired.

Posey nodded. "She started doing alterations for people in the basement," she explained. "Pretty soon, she had a following. There were articles in magazines, the Style section of the paper . . ."

"She must have been talented," Olivia ventured.

"She was," Posey said, the lost look in her eyes lingering as she continued sweeping the same superclean spot on the floor. "I've tried to keep it going without her, but . . ." Her voice trailed off as she gestured with her eyes at the empty, run-down shop, before vigorously tossing her head from side to side, as if to shake out something that hurt too much to remember.

"So what can I do for you?" Posey asked abruptly, tilting the broom back against the corner and settling her petite frame onto a wooden rocking chair.

"Oh," Olivia said, dropping one hand into her bag and searching for the soft folds of fabric inside. "I have this dress, and it has a really big rip up one side. . . ."

Posey gestured for Olivia to spread the dress out over her knees. She searched the material lovingly with her hands, her small, agile fingers quickly landing on the torn zipper. "It's a beauty," she said. "Vintage?"

Olivia smiled uncertainly. "I really have no idea; it's—it was—my sister's."

Posey nodded, staring past Olivia, or through her.

"Great style," she remarked approvingly, hoisting herself up and laying the dress over the back of an empty chair. "Definitely a dress for someone who knows how to have a good time."

"Yeah," Olivia said. "That was Violet."

She hadn't meant to sound so sad, but she could tell as soon as the words escaped that they had landed hard.

Posey smiled, her eyes now light and twinkling. "Come back next week," she said, folding the dress back up and placing it on top of her book. "Is Thursday good for you?"

Olivia anxiously chewed at the inside of her cheek and crossed her arms. "That's the thing," she said. "I kind of need it by tomorrow."

Posey froze, one hand still resting on the couch, the other curling into a tight little ball in her lap.

"I know it's short notice," Olivia apologized. "My mom is making us go to this reception thing, and I don't really have a choice. It's not really a big deal. I mean, I'll just be standing in a corner all night, probably, so it doesn't matter what I wear. I just thought, I don't know, if there was any way . . ."

Posey looked up with her head tilted to one side. Her eyes held Olivia's for a long moment before shifting across the room. In between two bare windows was a child-size wooden desk, scratched and complete with a built-in seat. The surface was bare except for a single spiral-bound notebook, lying open with a pencil beside it. "Leave your address," she said softly. "I can drop it off tomorrow."

It wasn't until Olivia exhaled a heavy sigh of relief that she realized she hadn't been breathing. She hadn't thought the dress was so important, but something about the look in Posey's eyes sent a flood of raw emotion washing over her body, like standing under a bitter-cold waterfall, with the sun at your back.

Olivia nodded once and walked to the desk, writing her address in careful print at the top corner of the open page.

She turned to the door. The sky was streaked with a cloudy pink trail, the sun disappearing behind a row of pastel houses at the top of the hill.

Olivia turned back to wave good-bye, but Posey was already lost again in her book. She wanted to say thank-you, or something like it, but feared the words would be too plain, too loud to mean what she wanted them to.

Olivia smiled and stepped out onto the sidewalk, where the air was moist and thick enough to bottle.

At last, the rain had stopped.

5

"Olivia, are you in there?"

Olivia sat wrapped in a fluffy white bath towel at the foot of her bed, staring dumbly at the garment bag lying open beside her.

"Your father went to get the car," her mom continued from the hall. "Meet us out front in a minute?"

"Sure," Olivia said flatly. "I'll be right there."

Just as Posey had promised, a floppy garment bag with Olivia's name safety-pinned to one side had arrived on her stoop that afternoon. Olivia reached for the zipper and pulled it down slowly, careful not to catch any loose fabric in its wake. She tugged the front flap open, angling the hanger to free the material, and gasped. Sinking backward onto the bed, Olivia dropped her eyes to the floor, then brought them back up for a second look, which only confirmed what she had known from the moment the dark, heavy fabric had peeked through the side of the bag.

This was not Violet's dress.

First of all, this dress was black. All black. No spiral satin prints, no contrasting colored circles. The empire waist had become a drop, and the narrow, delicate straps had been replaced with a thick halter, plunging into a deep V at the neck. It wasn't that the dress was ugly—it was simply, in fact, not hers.

Olivia sprang to her feet. "It must be a mistake," she concluded out loud, opening the bag wide and angling the gown back in place. She was tugging the stubborn zipper back across the front, when a crumpled piece of paper fluttered onto the floor.

She bent down to pick it up, unfolding what looked like a business card. The words *Mariposa of the Mission* were typed on the front, above a stark, rudimentary graphic of a small golden butterfly. Olivia flipped the card over and saw that a note had been scrawled on the back. She stared at the sloppy, childlike handwriting, her eyes blurring the six little words and setting them swirling. Part of her hoped that if she stared long enough, they might morph into something not so devastatingly useless, like a shopping list or a recipe for lasagna.

OLIVIA: TRY IT ON FIRST. POSEY.

She balled the card up in her palm and tossed it at the wall. "Do you need any help?"

Olivia jumped in place. Her mother was still standing on the other side of the door. "No," she called out. "I'm fine."

Silence, then the staccato clatter of high heels disappearing down the hall.

Olivia sat down on her bed and put her head in her hands. She could say she didn't feel well, which was certainly the truth. But even before she'd fully played out the scenario in her mind, she knew it wasn't an option. Her parents wouldn't buy it. They'd see it only as a sign that something was *wrong*, which would initiate a chain of events involving probing but meaningless questions from her mom, and sidelong, uncomfortable glances from her dad.

"Fine," she grunted. She hauled herself up from the bed and in one swift motion unhooked the dress, lifted it over her head, and slipped it down over her bare shoulders.

A full-body shiver started up from the base of her spine, and tiny blond hairs stood up all over her arms and at the back of her neck. Olivia arched one foot and nudged the closet door all the way open, turning to face the full-length mirror that had been left hanging inside by whoever had lived there before. She watched her reflection, her mouth moving slowly into the shape of a perfectly rounded O.

If she hadn't been the one to take the dress out of the bag, she never would've believed it was the same gown. Where on the hanger it fell shapeless and heavy, on her body it seemed suspended in air. Where it had looked boring and simple in the bag, it now exuded sophistication and elegance. It was as if Posey had molded the fabric with her inside of it.

A long, blaring honk rose up from the street outside her window. Her parents were waiting.

Olivia took a deep breath and stuck her feet in a pair of old patent-leather high heels. As she bent down to guide one heel with her fingers, a flash of color caught her eye. Tucked near the inseam, at the very bottom of the dress, was a tiny, embroidered butterfly. Olivia pressed her finger against it, as if maybe she could flick it off.

But it was there to stay.

Olivia leaned against one of the high, round tables that had been arranged in an open semicircle around the lobby of Bridget's office building downtown. The building itself wasn't very big, dwarfed by the skyscrapers huddled together a few blocks in from the water. But the lobby had an elegant, old-world feel, complete with low-hanging chandeliers and pivoting brass arrows over mirrored elevator doors.

When they'd first arrived, Bridget had paraded Mac and Olivia around the room's perimeter, making introductions and prompting Olivia to deliver sound bites about her new school and the transition from East to West Coast. But Mac had quickly found the bar, and Bridget had been swallowed into a crowd of coworkers. Olivia had had no choice but to stake out a table in the corner, already piled high with discarded cocktail napkins littered with shrimp tails and toothpicks.

Before, when Bridget had dragged the girls to functions or events, Olivia and Violet would find ways to entertain themselves, stealing sips of their dad's Stella Artois and making fun of the stuffy suits trying to impress each other. As long as they were in it together, even a boring cocktail reception could be almost fun.

Now, with nobody to laugh with, Olivia felt more alone than ever.

"Killer dress." A raspy voice spoke suddenly from over her shoulder. "Is it Prada?"

Olivia turned to find a girl at her elbow blinking behind tortoiseshell glasses. She looked a couple of years younger than Olivia, and a couple of heads shorter, too. Her hair was fine and white blond, arrayed around her head in tiny little buns that stuck out in frantic points.

Olivia smiled politely, glancing carefully from side to side, hoping to see her father flagging her down from somewhere across the room.

"Seriously." The girl was nodding vigorously and maintaining eye contact for just a bit longer than Olivia was comfortable returning. Her bright blue eyes were heavily lined in wet-looking charcoal, with shimmery gray shadow stuck to the corners of the lids. "Like, *really* hot," she added, for effect.

Despite the girl's elastic gold miniskirt, black fishnets, and a fuzzy mohair sweater, there was something soft about her, the way her pint-size feet seemed to swim in her metallic ankle boots, or the dimples in her pink, chubby cheeks.

"Thank you," Olivia said softly to the plastic cup of raspberry seltzer squeezed between her palms.

"I'm Bowie," the girl said, nudging Olivia's torso with her shoulder, as if this was an alternative to hand-shaking Olivia was not aware of. "Bowen, technically, but it sounds too much like an airplane, I think. And besides, my dad was a Ziggy Stardust fanatic."

Olivia nodded, still secretly scouting the lobby for an excuse to duck away.

"Or so I've heard," Bowie added with a knowing laugh. "Man, what is taking Miles so long?"

Olivia looked up sharply as Bowie waved one hand wildly in the air above them.

"Miles!" she called, pointing with exaggerated movements at the top of Olivia's head. "Look what I found!"

Miles emerged, walking toward them from the crowded makeshift bar set up at the lobby's front desk. He was easy to spot among the sea of suits, in wrinkled linen pants and the same threadbare, tangerine and blue checkered button-down he'd worn to school the day before. And, of course, the mushroom loafers.

"I could hear you screeching from across the room," Miles hissed, awkwardly clutching two glasses slosh-full of red wine and lowering them to the table. "*Please* don't get us thrown out again."

Olivia looked quickly back and forth from Miles to Bowie, confused.

"Hi there," Miles said, holding up a glass for Olivia to take. "Sorry about her. She's under the impression that her life is being filmed for the outtakes."

Olivia took the glass and managed a smile.

"Oh, Miles, lighten up," Bowie sang, throwing down a hefty sip of the purplish wine before gagging half of it back up. "Is this merlot?"

Miles rolled his eyes. "Yes, and it's not for you," he barked, wrenching the glass free from the viselike clutches of her fist.

Olivia smiled and took a measured sip from her glass. She hadn't had a drop to drink since last summer, and the fruity sweetness pooled at the back of her throat, swimming around her insides and quickly fogging up her head.

"I hear we're neighbors," Bowie said, dropping her hand to the crook of Olivia's arm. Her nails were stubby and painted black.

"Really?" Olivia managed. *It's called conversation,* she reminded herself, like a visitor from a foreign planet. *Answer one question, ask another.* "Where do you live?"

"We're on the other side of Dolores Park," Miles interjected.

Olivia's eyebrows cinched as she considered this. Were they related? With Miles's dark features and multiracial complexion, and Bowie's, well, Bowie-ness . . . Olivia couldn't imagine how it could be true.

"She's my stepsister," Miles clarified. "I told her about the tour my mom made me give you the other day."

Olivia felt her cheeks flushing and looked away. Somehow she'd forgotten that her mother was the reason she had anybody to talk to at this lame reception in the first place.

"I mean, not that I minded." Miles smiled with considerable effort, needlessly clearing his throat. "It wasn't a big deal or anything."

Bowie rolled her eyes. "Smooth, Miles," she said. "Way to make a girl feel welcome. Even *I* wouldn't say something that awkward, and I'm a freshman."

Olivia took another, heartier sip of her wine and tapped the rounded toe of her shoe against the polished travertine floor. "Which one's your mother?" she asked, less because she cared about the answer and more because she didn't want Miles to think she was upset.

Miles swayed back on the heels of his mushroom shoes and scanned the mingling crowd of San Francisco's legal elite. "There she is," he said, pointing toward a large oval window, beneath which stood a striking African-American woman, talking to a group of enraptured male attorneys. She was wearing a pin-striped suit, softened by stilettos and a chartreuse silk scarf, tied in a perfect knot at her neck.

"And she's remarried to the David Bowie guy?" Olivia

asked. She was straightening out facts and hadn't meant to be funny, but Bowie was suddenly laughing so violently that it appeared she might choke.

"Not exactly," Bowie said after catching her breath, gesturing back to where Miles's mom was standing. Another woman had joined the small group, younger looking, with angular features, a sleek black bob, and rimmed eyeglasses similar to Bowie's own. The two women slipped into each other's outstretched arms, sharing a quick but comfortable kiss before turning back to the men, who were pretending to study the labels on their bottles of imported beer.

"Oh," Olivia said, gradually registering the scene. "So they're—"

"Gay, gay, gay!" Bowie crooned, stealing Miles's cup and waving it in the air as if leading a chant.

Miles narrowed his eyes and snagged back his glass.

"But don't tell Miles," she whispered, leaning in closer to Olivia. "He still thinks they're just really good friends."

A laugh escaped Olivia's lips, surprising them all, and she took another healthy sip.

"Ready?" Bowie asked, finishing the last of Olivia's seltzer and slapping the empty cup on the table.

Miles looked to Olivia and raised an eyebrow. "Ready for what?" he asked, looking like he might be afraid of the answer.

Bowie threw her hands up dramatically and tugged at Miles's unbuttoned sleeve. "Come on," she whined. "You said you'd take me to that spring break after-party in Sea Cliff. There's going to be live music and everything. You know they'll never let me go by myself."

Olivia suddenly felt like she had been eavesdropping. She began fidgeting with items in her purse, checking the time on her phone as if there were somewhere else she needed to be.

"I don't know," Miles said. "I'm not sure I can handle another White Stripes cover band."

Olivia reached to the back of a tall chair for the ugly, tasseled shawl her mother had insisted she throw over her shoulders as they were walking out the door.

"Let's go. We can even bring this one," Bowie said, grabbing Olivia's wrist and shaking it. "It would be the *neighborly* thing to do."

"Oh, thanks," Olivia said, "but I should probably go keep my dad company." She gestured across the lobby to the bar. Bowie followed her gaze, to where Mac sat hunched over a bar stool with an empty seat beside him.

"That's your dad?" Bowie asked. "He's hot."

It was not the first time Olivia had heard this about her father, but it still made her fidget and blush.

"Fine," Miles groaned and grabbed Bowie by the shoulders. "Let's go before you get us all arrested. I guess this *is* my last chance to watch Graham have a tantrum when his disco ball turns into a piñata."

Bowie cheered and clapped Miles hard on the back. "That's more like it," she said, linking arms with Olivia. "Now let's go say some good-byes."

6

"You are going to *die* when you see this."

After a stomach-churning ride up and down roller-coaster hills in Miles's moss green Volkswagen Rabbit, Bowie pulled Olivia out of the parked car and onto the sparkling sidewalk. Sea Cliff was far more glamorous than any neighborhood Olivia had yet seen, with boxy mansions surrounded by artful topiaries and imposing statues of lions flanking the columned front doors. Miles lingered by a high, wrought-iron gate that was set back from the road, and waited for the girls to catch up.

"Whose house is this again?" Olivia asked, following Bowie along the sidewalk.

"Graham Potter," Bowie said, the heel of her boot catching in a crack and rocking her toward the curb. "He has this party every year. It's sort of a spring tradition. Everybody meets at the community gardens in the morning and gets the ground ready for planting. And then they all come back to Graham's, because it's basically the most amazing house in the universe."

She gestured up a winding stone path illuminated by dim bulbs embedded in the ground.

Tall hedges lined the property, and a few small bubbling fountains were scattered across the lawn, complete with back-lit cherubic sculptures, naked and spitting into clear, shallow pools. "Graham's dad invented some kind of software, I think," Miles told her, digging his hands into his pockets and shuffling ahead. "Something computer related."

Olivia's jaw dropped as the house came into view. It was literally dug into the side of a cliff, with square, stucco boxes jutting every which way. The roof was covered in arched Spanish tiles, and floor-to-ceiling windows revealed a sparkling modern interior, straight from the pages of one of the design magazines Olivia's mother had bought at the airport and never gotten around to reading. "Are you sure he didn't invent the computer?" she asked, dumbfounded.

"I know, right?" Bowie laughed, dragging Olivia up onto the pristinely clipped lawn. Olivia expected an alarm to go off, or a pack of dogs to start howling at her heels, but Bowie seemed to know where she was going.

Miles and Olivia followed Bowie through a sliding glass door and into the brightly lit kitchen, where a group of kids was huddled around a high center island, balancing eggs on its butcher-block top. A few of them wore white cotton sheets tied around one shoulder, with lopsided floral crowns circling their heads.

"It's the equinox," Bowie explained, gesturing to the eggs. "You're supposed to be able to balance an egg on its end. Pagans, togas . . . you know."

Olivia swallowed and forced a smile, tucking the folds of

her long black gown behind her as if to make it disappear. She couldn't have felt more out of place. The half of the party that *wasn't* dressed in sheets and garlands wore ratty old jeans and printed T-shirts over long-sleeved waffle tees. Olivia crumpled her scarf into a ball and tucked it into her purse, and wished she could flush both of them down the nearest toilet.

Bowie grabbed a handful of cups from the marble countertop and ducked back through the door onto the redwood porch, where a crowd of guys in homemade togas stood around a keg. Bowie held up a finger to say that she'd be right back, and gestured to Miles, who was talking to a girl in overalls by the breakfast nook.

Olivia's eyes flitted anxiously around the kitchen, a tight, twisting feeling clenching at her insides. Even at home, she'd never felt 100 percent comfortable at parties. She never knew what she was supposed to be doing or saying, or how she should be standing to look like she was having a good time. But Violet was always there to save her a seat, or bring her a drink in a red plastic cup.

After the summer, she'd pretty much stopped going out altogether. And when school started up in the fall, their friends had tried to include her, calling her on Friday nights to hang out in Morgan Jennings's basement when his parents were out of town. But they had quickly given up. Which only proved to Olivia what she'd feared all along: They weren't really *their* friends at all. They were Violet's friends. And Violet was gone.

"Here," Bowie said, passing Olivia a cup of foamy beer. "Come on, we have to save that poor girl from Miles. He turns into an eco-crusader at these things. It's not pretty."

Bowie maneuvered through a crowd of girls by the industrial-size kitchen sink, joining Miles and the girl he'd cornered in the pantry.

"Let's go, Al Bore," Bowie murmured, linking her arm into Miles's elbow and dragging him through a high-ceilinged hallway, beckoning for Olivia to follow along. "The music's this way."

They shouldered their way through an endless, narrow hall, the insistent plodding of a bass guitar beckoning them into a sunken living room on the other side of the house. The space had been cleared of all furniture, save the tree-size potted plants sandwiching a wide brick fireplace. Against one windowed wall at the back of the room, with the lights of the Golden Gate Bridge twinkling in the background, a band was playing on an improvised stage.

"These guys rock," Bowie said, as Miles sulked against the mantel, a floppy palm frond sticking out from behind his frazzled hair. "That's Graham singing. Don't they kind of remind you of Kings of Leon?"

Olivia squinted at the stage and nodded, even though Bowie might as well have been speaking in tongues. The music sounded like just about every indie band Violet had been obsessed with over the past two years, and Olivia struggled to remember her sister cutting out photo spreads from the pages of *Nylon* and plastering them onto her notebooks and locker. Basically, the recipe for Violet's approval involved long, shaggy hair, skinny jeans, altered vocals, and heavy bass.

Graham's band passed with flying colors on all counts.

Bowie squeezed into the crowd, tossing the points of her hair from side to side, her shoulders dipping up and down to the beat. All around her, kids were laughing, dancing, toasting each other with easy smiles and half-empty glasses of color-ful drinks. Bowie motioned for Olivia to join her, but Olivia pretended to be lost in the music, staring intently at the band as if she were studying the complexities of their compositional arrangements or instrumental breaks.

Onstage, Graham, whom she quickly recognized as one of the lounging hipsters from the courtyard, was sing-screeching into a handheld microphone, his damp, orange hair sticking to his face. He stood on the tips of his sneakers for one last earsplitting wail, before dropping dramatically to his knees and bowing toward the back of the stage, in a gesture that said either (A) *I'm praying to Mecca; please don't interrupt,* or (B) *It's time for a drum solo. I'm spent.*

And that's when Olivia saw him.

All inverted elbows and flying drumsticks was the skater boy from school. His face was flushed in an expression of bliss-ful concentration, his green eyes blinking ferociously as loose locks of sandy blond hair flew spastically around his head. It was an impressive performance, equal parts exciting and terri-fying, and Olivia's eyes were glued to every heavy bass-drum thump, every shattered attack of the hi-hat. She'd never seen anybody look so free or alive. It was beautiful.

Somewhere in her periphery she saw Miles hovering by her elbow and heard him mutter something about another drink. She thought about nodding, but probably didn't. It wasn't until the drum solo ended and Graham had belted out another anthem-rowdy chorus, ending in a sweeping clash of cymbals and raucous applause, that Olivia remembered to try breath-ing again.

"Thanks for coming," Graham panted into the mic when

the whooping shouts and whistles had finally started to fade. "We're taking a little break, but we'll be back for the count-down, so don't anybody move, all right?"

The crowd responded in happy unison as Graham shoved the mic in their direction before flinging it to the hardwood floor with a muffled *thwap*, rock-star style.

Skater/Drummer Boy reached his long, wiry arms up over-head. His soft blue undershirt hiked an inch or so above a crackled leather belt, just enough to expose a section of his waist, the sharp line of muscle cutting down across one hip. Olivia felt the back of her neck getting hot, and she worried that she was actually sweating.

"So?" Bowie had reappeared at Olivia's side and was strip-ping off her sweater, revealing a tiny black tube top, felted in clingy mohair fuzz. "What'd you think?"

"Do you know where the bathroom is?" Olivia asked. She felt vaguely dizzy, a deafening rhythm in her heart and her head, an anxious flutter at the base of her throat. She needed to run some cold water over her wrists.

Bowie pointed to where a short line was snaking back around a cast-aside armoire full of expensive-looking figurines and black-and-white photos in frames. Olivia took off through the crowd. As soon as she cleared a cluster of kids knocking back shots by the fireplace, she froze abruptly in place. There he was, waiting at the back of the line, propped up against a thick-framed map of the world.

It was too late to turn around. She took a deep breath and planted herself beside him. He wasn't nearly as tall up close, and, sneaking glances of his profile, she spotted a neat little row of tiny round scars, barely hidden underneath a thin layer of stubble at his jaw. Olivia's heart thumped, and she clenched her hands behind her back.

"Is this the line for the bathroom?" she asked, and instantly regretted it.

No, this is just the way we stand, all lined up in a row for no reason. Welcome to California!

He turned abruptly toward her, shaggy hair falling over his sea green eyes and sticking to the slope of his nose. "Yup." He nodded with a smile, pushing back at the hair that had fallen, as if to get a better look. His teeth were big and adorably crooked.

"Cool," she said. *Cool.* She glanced at the floor for a trapdoor to fall through, hoping for at least a small fight to break out somewhere across the room. Anything to stop the uncontrollable fountain of lameness that was pouring out of her mouth.

"I keep seeing you," he said. "In the courtyard, right? At school?"

And . . . now she was a stalker. She hadn't been in school one week, and already she'd turned into the overdressed girl who stared too long and tried too hard.

Olivia swallowed and nodded, racking her brain for something officially not-psychotic to say back.

"I'm Soren," he went on, extending a hand. "What's your name?"

"Olivia," she answered, taking his hand. It was warm and sweaty and strong. "I'm new."

"Yeah, I caught that," Soren joked, and then, through another heart-wringing grin, he whispered, "Welcome to Hippie High."

Olivia squeezed her damp fingers tighter together and

harnessed enough courage to steal a glance back up at him. Which was about when she realized that he was looking at her. And not in a way that made her feel crazy, or like maybe she had arugula wedged between her teeth. Really *looking* at her. Like for one reason or another she'd caught his eye, and he couldn't figure out how to look away. Like maybe he'd run out of things to say, not because he wasn't interested. But maybe because he was nervous, too?

The bathroom door swung open and Graham stepped out, clapping Soren on the back as he passed.

"I should . . ." Soren pointed at the bathroom and Olivia nodded vigorously.

"Right, so," she said, gesturing for him to go ahead. "Good luck!"

He smiled, a sweet, lopsided little grin, and closed the door between them.

Olivia nestled herself against the wall on the other side of the bathroom door. It wasn't until the band was back onstage a few minutes later that she realized it had sounded like she'd wished him good luck with the toilet.

Graham was already gripping the mic and hushing the noisy crowd as Soren snuck out of the bathroom and headed back for the stage.

"So, since this year's party fell right on the equinox, we thought we'd do a little countdown to spring," he explained, wrapping his guitar strap over his chest and plucking out a few notes. "Can I get some help up here, Eve?"

From across the room, the miniature girl with purple fingernails Olivia had first seen sitting on Graham's lap in the courtyard appeared and bounded up to join the band. She was dressed in a candy red skirt with a hedgehog embroidered on one side, leggings, and an oversize black sweatshirt that had been cut at the collar. Her feet were bare and dirty from working outside.

"Who's ready for some sun?"

The crowd roared. Soren leaned forward over his drums, peering out into the crowd and squinting. He was clearly looking for someone, his neck craning sideways and swiveling around the room. Until he was looking directly at Olivia. His mouth was open and he gave her a little beckoning wave, one hand now shielding his eyes from the halogen-lamp spotlight that hung from a crossbeam in the ceiling.

The little veins in Olivia's neck pulsed and fuzzy black spots appeared in the corner of her eyes. Could this really be happening?

The other band members, a beefy kid with long, blond dreadlocks playing the bass, and a balding guy at the keyboards who looked at least thirty, were each joined by girls from the crowd, and Soren was still smiling. And waving. *At her.*

Olivia inhaled, fueling the Jell-O-like wobble in her belly, and took a step forward. Just then, rustling footsteps approached from behind her, a cascade of silky, jet-black hair whipping her in the face as a blurry figure hustled by.

"I'm coming, I'm coming," the girl called out as she ran up onto the stage, hopping next to Soren. He wrapped an arm around her waist and pulled her tight to his side.

Calla. The glowing earth goddess Miles had pointed out at lunch. And, if possible, she looked even more naturally beautiful than she had before, in dark, faded jeans, a ribbed white tank top, and chocolate brown flip-flops, her glossy, tanned skin glistening in the spotlight, her almond eyes dark and mysterious.

"Five . . . four . . . three . . ."

Graham was counting, people were yelling, the world was spinning. . . .

Olivia's face felt like it was about to explode. All around her, people were hugging and clapping, so she clapped, too. Until she realized that the band had started to play and she was still clapping, and now she was the new girl in the fancy dress, clapping to herself in the corner.

The bathroom was empty when she peeked behind the door, and so she locked herself inside, wondering if she'd survive a jump from the window.

And wondering if she cared.

🦋 🦋 🦋

"No throw up."

Olivia was slumped in the back of the cab she'd flagged at the end of Graham's block, her head bobbing against the cool, foggy glass. The bearded driver squinted at her through the rearview mirror, carefully evaluating her puke potential.

"I just have seats reupholstered. Very expensive." He wagged a finger. "You throw up, you pay."

Olivia nodded and immediately felt dizzy from the effort. She let her head fall back against the seat and folded her arms over her face.

It had started as a bit of a slosh in her belly. And then the room had started to spin. She couldn't remember exactly what she'd had to drink, after the first glass of wine at the office party, half of a beer, and the shots of something fruity she'd been offered on her way back from the bathroom, after . . .

Olivia cringed, a sudden flash of Soren's lopsided smile onstage blurring in her mind's eye. Then Calla falling into his lap as Graham counted backward from ten, her hands around Soren's neck, leaning in for a midnight kiss.

A hollow feeling grew in the pit of her stomach, and Olivia fumbled for the window, opening it a crack. The crisp night air filtered in, drying the damp sweat on her forehead. As much as she'd hated it while she was there, she missed Willis, her old school and friends, the lame parties, the drunken jocks, the girls who were superficial and fake, fine, but at least they knew who she was.

Mostly, she missed Violet.

Olivia squeezed back hot tears too late, and a few escaped, falling heavily onto her dress.

This isn't how it was supposed to be, she thought. *Violet would never have let this happen. I want my sister. I want my sister. I want my sister.*

"I just wish I had my sister back," she whispered out loud, her hands over her eyes, pressing the tears against her wet cheeks.

It happened so fast that later on she'd wonder if she was hallucinating. But as soon as she'd opened her eyes, a strong, sturdy breeze whipped through the cracked window, carrying with it what looked, at first, like a lightning bug.

It swirled around the back of the cab, frantic and confused. Olivia quickly figured it was trying to get out, and reached across the seat to open the window. But instead of immediately flying through, the neon insect slowed the flapping of its wings, settling gently on Olivia's knee before taking flight and disappearing back into the night sky.

The bug had only been still for a second, but it had been long enough for Olivia to realize it wasn't a lightning bug at all. It was just as tiny, and just as bright, but its wings were wide and broad and swirled with silver and gold.

It was a butterfly.

7

*O*livia woke in the middle of the night with what felt like battery acid coating her mouth, gripped by a sudden, mind-numbing thirst.

Water.

She squinted one eye open, gathering up the strength to lift her heavy head from the pillow, and reached across to her bedside table. She fumbled for a glass of stale tap water and gulped it down, oblivious to the tiny particles of dust that had settled on the surface. Hauling herself onto her elbows, she gripped her head in her hands to lessen the intense pounding, which seemed to be reverberating all the way down to the ligaments in her ankles. Slowly, she opened her eyes, allowing them to drift to the floor, where a shadowy heap of dark material lay next to the foot of her bed.

The dress.

Olivia groaned out loud, the events of the night before rushing back like the incoming tide. Like it wasn't bad enough she'd made a complete jerk of herself, wearing a ball gown to a toga party and stalking Soren by the bathroom, but she was hallucinating now, too? A fluorescent butterfly?

"Am I losing my mind?" she whispered out loud.

"Basically, but what else is new." A crisp, mocking voice came from somewhere nearby.

Olivia whipped her head around, looking back toward the hulking headboard, then out through the gently blowing curtains.

"Hello?" she called quietly out into the darkness, feeling ridiculous.

Nothing.

"Awesome," she muttered. "Now I'm hearing voices."

"Oh, would you calm down?" the laughing voice ridiculed. *"You may be crazy, but you're not schizophrenic."*

Olivia's heart jumped, landing somewhere up around the middle of her throat. She threw the covers back and hurriedly tiptoed to the door, pulling it open and craning her neck to see up and down the hall. It was empty and silent. She shivered and hugged her elbows, closing herself back inside.

Nobody.

Her nose twitched and tickled. What was that smell?

A thin stream of cigarette smoke swirled from behind her. Olivia looked down and followed the curling, smoky trail past her bed, past the window, all the way to the small, crooked door at the back of her room. The door was open just a crack and spilling a shaft of cool blue light onto the floor.

Olivia put her hand to the knob and took a deep, steadying breath before pulling the door open and peering inside. There, lounging on the windowsill, smoking a cigarette and backlit by the eerie glow of a full moon, was her sister.

"Violet?" Olivia whispered into the darkness, stepping through the door and slowly making her way across the room. She felt as if she were gliding, her feet floating inches above the crooked floorboards. It was as if the rest of the world disappeared and all she could see was her sister, her milky-skinned, freckle-faced, beautiful sister, waiting for her across the room.

"You forgot my name already?" Violet laughed, hopping down from the sill and opening her arms wide on either side, an invitation.

Olivia stood frozen in the middle of the room, arms heavy as cement by her sides.

Violet took another step forward and waved one hand in front of her sister's blank face.

"Hello?" Violet prompted, her pale blue eyes sparkling as she shook her sister gently by the elbows. "Can a girl get a hug, please?"

Olivia swallowed the lump that was throbbing in her throat. "What . . . but . . ." she stammered. "I . . . I don't understand."

Violet huffed an impatient sigh and shook Olivia's elbows, pulling her sister in to her chest. "It's a simple concept, O," she joked, squeezing her sister tight. "I hug you. You hug me. See?"

Olivia's eyes burned and she felt herself slowly melting into her sister's arms, burying her face in the waves of Violet's perfect, loose curls.

Sea salt and strawberry-kiwi shampoo.

"It's you," Olivia whispered into the side of Violet's neck. "It's really you?"

"Last time I checked, there were only two of us," Violet laughed, pushing Olivia away and separating entangled strands of their matching cinnamon red locks.

"But, what . . ." Olivia started, shaking her head. "I mean, you're . . ."

Violet took a long, exaggerated drag from her cigarette before ashing it outside.

"You don't smoke," Olivia announced. "I mean, you never used to—"

"One of the perks." Violet smiled, waving the flickering butt in front of her face. "Cigarettes can't kill you if you're already dead."

Olivia slowly walked toward the window. "So, you are . . ." she stuttered. "I mean, you're still—"

"As a doornail, I'm afraid." Violet nodded and took another exaggerated drag.

Olivia looked back through the open door toward the shadow of her bed, the rumpled pile of blankets leaning in a heap to one side. She stared long and hard at her sister before shaking her head and marching back across the room.

Collapsing with a sigh onto the edge of her bed and falling back against the pillows, Olivia pulled the blankets up and over her face. She took a few shallow, labored breaths, her eyes pressed shut.

It had to be a dream.

Olivia took one more breath before squeezing handfuls of soft fabric up by her ears, and flinging the comforter back down to her lap.

"Ta-da!" Violet exclaimed, standing over her on top of the bed. "Still here."

Olivia curled her legs up underneath her body and scooted back against the headboard. "Okay," she spoke, her voice calm and reasonable. "Okay. So, you're—"

"Dead," Violet said flatly, flopping to cross-legs on the bed beside her sister. "Dead, O, you can say it. It won't make me any deader to say it out loud."

"Right," Olivia said. "Sorry. You're dead. But also . . ."

Violet smiled, the cigarette perched casually at the corner of her lips.

"You're here?" Olivia asked quietly.

Violet took the burning filter from her mouth and flicked it across the room and through the open window.

"Either that," she said, placing a gentle hand on Olivia's trembling knee, "or this is one hell of a hangover."

8

"**O**f course they wait until I'm dead to do something like this."

Violet and Olivia were crouched on the balcony outside of Olivia's room, knees hugged tightly into their shirts to keep warm in the chilly predawn air. Across the street, Dolores Park was covered in half shadows, the tall row of trees cutting a ragged silhouette against the lifting curtain of night.

"Like what?" Olivia asked. The pounding in her head had somewhat lessened and had been quickly replaced by a jumble of cloudy memories and frantic questions.

Starting with: Was it possible that one of her drinks last night had been laced with a hallucinogenic drug?

"Like this!" Violet flung her arms wide, indicating the picturesque city skyline that was just beginning to assert itself from beneath the darkness. From up here, the rows of pastel houses looked like a page from a pop-up book. It was a stunning view, but Olivia couldn't take her eyes off of her sister.

"Do you have any idea how lucky you are to live here?" Violet asked, snapping another cigarette free from a pack in her pocket.

Olivia kept staring at her sister's profile. *Violet.* Violet was back. Violet was sitting right beside her. She looked a little paler, maybe, and a little thinner, too—Olivia noticed a trail of blue veins crisscrossing the insides of her sister's wrists, veins she didn't remember ever seeing before. But other than that, it was the same old Violet. The same wild, copper-colored hair; the same sparkling, impish eyes.

She was even wearing the same knee-length jean cutoffs, the ones she'd made from an old pair of Sevens, which fit perfectly up top but had been about two inches two short at the ankles. And the same apple green lace camisole she always wore under dresses in the summer.

It was exactly the outfit Violet had been wearing the last time Olivia had seen her, on the beach that night. . . .

"What's up?" Violet asked, inhaling deeply as she struck a match.

Olivia shook her head, mute. If she started asking questions, it would mean she was starting to believe. It would mean she'd accepted that this was actually happening.

"You still don't believe this is actually happening, do you?"

Olivia's eyes shot up to her sister's face.

Violet smiled and rocked on her hips, nudging Olivia's side and shoulder. "Don't look so horrified!" she shouted. "It's not like we couldn't read each other's minds when I was alive. Why should it be any different now?"

Olivia chewed at the inside of her lip. Violet, or the ghost of Violet, or the drug-induced apparition Olivia had accidentally conjured that looked a lot like Violet . . . *Whoever* she was, she did have a point. "But," Olivia quietly began, "how?"

Violet shrugged. "Does it matter?" she asked, flashing her sister a tricky smile.

Olivia rolled her eyes. Violet had been back for less than an hour and already she was being difficult. "Kind of," Olivia hissed. "I mean, you go to sleep and your sister is dead. You wake up, and she's smoking butts on the balcony. It's not exactly your average turn of events."

Violet took a deep drag off her cigarette and ashed it between the chipped-white bars of the painted iron railing. "Well," she said, "you know how I feel about average."

Without thinking, Olivia reached forward and pinched the glowing cigarette from between her sister's lips. "True," she said, flicking the stub out over the balcony. "And you know how *I* feel about smoking."

Violet watched with wide eyes as the cigarette sailed to the sidewalk below.

"Fine," she huffed. "But you don't have to be such a grump. It's not like any of this was up to me."

"Then who?!" Olivia demanded, her voice suddenly loud and brash.

"Easy." Violet flinched. "Just because I'm a ghost doesn't mean people can't still hear *you*."

"Then *who*?" Olivia repeated in a stern whisper. "Who was it up to? How did you get back here? And where have you been? And . . . what the hell is going on?"

Violet looked long and hard into her sister's eyes before opening her face into her trademark silly grin and tossing off yet another infuriating shrug.

Olivia groaned, a familiar swell of frustration rising up from the pit of her stomach. It was a feeling as old and comfortable as any other she'd known, and one that usually resulted in the overwhelming desire to take Violet by the arms and shake her silly.

And now, Olivia thought with a sudden pang to her heart, she could.

She turned quickly to her sister and reached out her hands, laying one gently on each of Violet's shoulders.

They felt like Violet's shoulders.

Olivia cupped her hands firmly against the backs of her sister's triceps, the tiny little bumps both girls had always shared, tickling the pads of her fingers like Braille. She pressed her palms over the bony mounds of Violet's shoulders, and shook.

Violet's head waggled back and forth, her jaw shuddering, her eyes wide with alarm. "What the hell?" she demanded, wriggling free.

Olivia slowly took her hands away and brought them back to her lap, shaking her head, a small smile creeping its way to the corners of her lips. "Just checking," she said.

Violet stood and looked out over the railing, heaving an exhausted sigh. "Fine," she surrendered. "I can tell we're not going to have any fun here until we get you some answers."

"That's right." Olivia nodded.

"So . . ." Violet clapped her hands together. "Let's retrace our steps!"

Olivia smiled. This was one of their mother's favorite games. Whenever Violet lost something—which was often—Bridget would appear out of nowhere to lead her through a step-by-step reenactment of the events leading up to the forsaken object's disappearance. Violet would stomp around, refusing to participate, but without fail, their mother's thorough investigation would always produce the missing item—keys in the cushion of the couch, cell phone on top of the toilet—and Violet would be forced to admit defeat.

"Okay," Olivia said, closing her eyes. "I was at Mom's cocktail reception."

"Yeah, too bad I didn't make it back in time for that," Violet deadpanned.

Olivia shot her sister a withering glare.

"Sorry," Violet said. "Proceed."

"Okay, then I was at the party." Olivia's voice shrank. "I was really upset."

"About what?" Violet asked.

"About *everything*," Olivia said softly. "The night was a disaster without you. I drank too much, I didn't really have anybody to talk to, I was a total loser. I wished you were there."

Violet nodded, waiting for more.

"No," Olivia said, straightening her legs out toward the railing and turning to face Violet head-on. "Seriously. I *wished* for you. Out loud. In the cab."

Violet looked down at her sideways. "You mean, like . . ." Violet paused, scrunching her features together, the way she did when she had been called on in class and didn't know the answer. "Fairy-tale style?"

Olivia shrugged. "I guess," she said, trembling panic seeping back into her voice. "I don't know. All I know is that I wished for you, the glowing butterfly flew out of my dress and into the night . . . and now you're here."

Olivia reached back for a few strands of hair, twirling them together around one finger and inspecting their dry, fraying ends. She kept her eyes on the sidewalk below. The sun was just coming up, and a few hard-core bikers were already zipping across the pavement. If she looked back at her sister, Olivia knew she'd start crying, or laughing, or both, and that wouldn't get them anywhere.

Violet cleared her throat. "Um, Olivia," she began slowly, "what butterfly?"

Olivia rolled her eyes. It was bad enough she had to see it, but saying it out loud was like pouring a box of salt over a bloody, open wound. "There was this butterfly," she said heavily. "I guess it was like a tag, or something, sewn into my dress—"

"What dress?"

"The dress the girl in the Mission made me," Olivia explained. "After I took yours in to have it fixed."

Violet just stared at her. "Okay, so what happened to the butterfly?"

Olivia threw up her hands. "I told you!" she huffed. "It flew away. Into the night. Bye-bye, butterfly. Hello, sister-ghost."

Violet didn't waste any time with dramatic pauses, immediately erupting into a fit of hysterical laughter, kicking her bare feet against the iron balcony, her long, bright curls shaking out around her face.

"Stop it!" Olivia commanded. "This isn't funny. This is my *life*, okay? I have no idea what's going on. You asked me what happened, and that's what happened. All right?"

Violet composed herself and looked hard into Olivia's jumping blue eyes. "All right," she said. "So then what? The wish, the magical butterfly, and what happens next?"

Olivia searched the deepest spaces in her memory, trying to come up with something, *anything*, that could possibly explain even part of what had occurred since then. "And that's it," she gave up. "I woke up, and you were here."

Violet stared at her for a long moment, her blue eyes squinting and serious. "Okay." She nodded. "I think we need to talk about this dress."

🦋   🦋   🦋

"We're closed."

The tinny chimes were still ringing overhead as Olivia stepped carefully into Mariposa of the Mission.

"She always says that," Olivia whispered under her breath to Violet, who was as dumbstruck as Olivia had been that first rainy afternoon, eyes darting from one bald and haphazardly attired mannequin to another.

During the walk over, Violet had coached Olivia on what to say when they got there, and Olivia had pretended to listen, but she'd been too distracted searching the early-morning faces of everybody they passed. Could they see Violet? Could they hear her? Or did Olivia just look like a lunatic, nodding to herself as she hurried along the sidewalk? After a few sideways glances from a homeless guy pushing a shopping cart, she was pretty sure the latter was the case.

Inside the shop, Posey was spread out on the couch, her back to Olivia, with a new paperback open in her lap. This one had a tropical theme, with a brawny guy lounging against a palm tree and a busty bikini model straddling his lap in the sand.

"Hi." Olivia spoke tentatively.

"What part of *closed* was confusing?" Posey closed the book quickly and looked up.

"Oh." She started. "It's you."

Olivia nodded.

Violet's instructions had been simple: Olivia would explain about the dress. And the butterfly. And, without going into too much detail, she'd *suggest* that something, well, even stranger had happened overnight. And then they'd wait, for what was sure to be a logical explanation.

But now that she was here, in the shop—which, the more Olivia looked around, was really just an old, grimy seamstress's studio—the whole plan sounded a little, well . . . insane.

"Hi," Olivia repeated, exhaling and playing with the tips of her nails. "I was just . . . I mean, I just came to—" She could feel Violet's eyes burning into the side of her face. "I mean . . . I thought I should . . . pay you!" Olivia spat suddenly. "For the dress! I forgot before, and then I remembered. So here I am!"

Violet flopped her arms to her side and groaned.

This had not been part of the plan.

"Okay," Posey said cautiously, standing and heading toward the register.

Olivia reached for her wallet as Posey snapped open the drawer, which clanked and trembled into place.

"You know," Posey began, rifling through a pile of receipts, "I wasn't actually worried about not seeing you again."

Olivia's eyebrows wrinkled, and she wasn't sure, but she thought maybe she saw the beginnings of a sly smile playing across Posey's lips.

"What do you mean?" Olivia asked. Violet nudged her eagerly.

"I don't know." Posey shrugged. "Something just told me that you might have some . . . questions."

"Oh," Olivia stammered. "Well, I mean, I'm not sure I know how to—"

"For the love of God," Violet whispered. "Just tell her!"

Olivia shot Violet a stern look before turning to Posey. She was about to return to her broken explanation when she realized that something in Posey's posture had changed. She looked somehow taller, like her neck was stretching farther away from her body.

She looked like she was trying to listen.

"Posey?" Olivia asked.

Posey glanced quickly back in Olivia's direction. "Yeah, I just . . ." Posey swatted the air. "I just thought I heard something. That's all."

Olivia's heart was thumping so violently in her chest she was positive her whole body was vibrating.

"You were saying?" Posey asked.

"Well," Olivia continued, "about the dress. Something kind of . . . out of the ordinary . . . did happen while I was wearing it."

"Really?" Posey asked, shoving the register drawer shut noisily. "Like what?"

"You know, I mean, nothing too weird, but just"—Olivia talked in circles, buying time—"I think I saw a butterfly."

Posey stared at her blankly.

Olivia felt small beads of sweat forming at the nape of her neck, and her tongue flicked anxiously at the corners of her mouth.

"Was it a monarch?" Posey asked, making her way back to

the couch and lowering herself into one corner. "I haven't seen many yet myself. Usually the city is just swarming by now." She picked up a piece of loose fabric and began folding it into quarters.

Olivia cleared her throat, searching for Violet out of the corner of her eye. Violet made a rolling gesture with her hands, cocking her head toward Posey and urging Olivia on. "Um, no." Olivia took a deep, musty breath. "It was glowing. It was a glowing butterfly. And I think it came from my dress."

Posey continued folding, smoothing out the creases with her hands and placing the fabric on the arm of the sofa. "And?" she asked, almost impatiently.

Olivia looked to Violet, who shrugged. "And . . ." Olivia continued, unsure of where to go next.

Posey picked up another swath of fabric and lined up the edges, the corners of her mouth pursing as she began to whistle softly.

Suddenly, Olivia's cheeks were burning and her hands shook at her sides. "'And'?" she repeated, her voice cracking as it grew more intense. "What do you mean, 'and'?! I just told you that a butterfly, a *glowing butterfly*, flew out of my dress. The dress *you* made me. I was in a cab, I was crying, and there it was. And something tells me you know why. *And*. You're going to tell me about it." When Olivia had finished, her mouth was dry, and the throbbing was back behind her eyes. Violet was standing, mouth agape, and inching a bit toward the door.

This was not part of the plan, either.

Posey stared up at Olivia, her narrow yellow-specked eyes blinking furiously. Her thin, pale lips were still pursed, the memory of a whistle between them, when suddenly they parted, and a wide, toothy grin divided her face. "All right," she said.

Olivia stared at her. "All right?"

Posey nodded. "I guess there are some things I could tell you," she said. "Like, for starters, I was just messing with you about the monarchs."

Violet chuckled from over Olivia's shoulder.

Posey gestured to a chair in the corner, piled high with thumbed-through pattern books. "Have a seat," she offered. "You can put those anywhere."

"I'm okay," Olivia insisted, planting herself firmly on two feet.

Posey gave her a look and shrugged.

"Okay," she began, "but you're probably going to want to sit down for this."

9

"Any questions?"

Olivia sat tall in a straight-backed wooden chair, her hands poised lightly on her kneecaps, her eyes trained on the foggy storefront window. The neighborhood was waking up around them, already teeming with morning errand-runners and the trendy Sunday brunch set. Everybody—hipsters; stroller-pushing young moms; grumpy, haggling homeless men—seemed to walk past the shop without even seeing it.

Olivia wondered, not for the first time that day, if she was dreaming.

After all, Posey, who was curled into a ball on the couch, using her small, nimble hands for emphasis, had just finished explaining to Olivia that she—Posey, Mariposa of the Mission—was magic.

A magical seamstress.

And now the magical seamstress, maker of magical dresses, weaver of mystical fabric that spat out glowing butterflies, granting a single wish to its wearer, wondered if Olivia had any *questions*.

Violet was crouched over the kiddie desk by the door, leaning forward on her elbows. Olivia stole a glance in her sister's direction and saw that, for the first memorable time in the history of their lives, Violet was speechless.

Olivia felt a laugh escaping, a sort of guttural reaction to the complete absurdity of the situation. But it had been so long since she'd made a sound, or even swallowed, that a low gurgle caught in the back of her throat, eventually working its way up to a powerful cough.

"Would you like some tea?" Posey asked, making as though to stand.

"No!" Olivia said, and then realized that she was yelling. "Sorry, no. I'm fine, thanks."

"Okay." Posey nodded. "Look, I know it sounds crazy. And I don't really have any explanation for it. My grandmother didn't, either. It's just something we've always been able to do. Sometimes, some people, we just *know* when we see them. That we have to help."

"So you knew," Olivia said, whispering now. "When I came in with the dress?"

Posey shook her head, her short, crooked bangs falling down over her eyes. "I knew before you walked into the shop."

"What does that mean?" Violet asked, looking up from the tiny desk, her head cocked to one side.

And then, as if in direct response to a question Violet hadn't asked—because Violet technically wasn't there—Posey continued:

"It means I've seen her around. I knew before she ever came inside."

Posey looked directly at Olivia as she spoke, and Violet hopped up from the desk. "Can she hear me?" Violet whispered.

Olivia looked back at Posey. "Can you . . ." Olivia started carefully. "Who were you talking to, just then?"

Posey spread her sticklike legs out in front of her on the couch. She was wearing old, faded jeans that fell short of her ankles, but not in an intentionally stylish way. More like they were old favorites she couldn't bear to throw out.

"Your sister," Posey said flatly. "She's here, isn't she?"

Olivia looked from Violet to Posey, Posey to Violet. "But you can't—"

"I can't see her, no," Posey said, pointing and flexing first one foot, then the other. "*I* didn't wish for her, did I?"

"But how did you know that I did?" Olivia asked.

Posey threw up her hands. "Your sister dies. You have a magical, wish-granting dress," she said, laying out the ingredients. "What else are you going to wish for?"

"But you didn't know it was magic," Violet prompted Olivia from the corner.

"Yeah," Olivia agreed. "I didn't know it was magic when I made the wish."

"So?" Posey asked.

"So how could you know that I *accidentally* wished for Violet back?"

"You mean, other than the fact that you've been taking cues from the corner of the room since you got here?"

Violet and Olivia looked at each other, before Olivia hurriedly looked away.

"Regardless," Posey continued, swinging her legs down and walking slowly to the other side of the room. "There are some things we need to talk about."

"Okay," Olivia said, following Posey behind the hanging quilt in the corner. "Like what?"

"Like rules," Posey said, crouching down and opening a hidden, rounded door. Cool, damp air rushed out, encircling Olivia's feet, as Posey reached into what appeared to be a neglected crawl space. She fumbled around with one arm before pulling out a heavy, leather-bound notebook and plopping it onto the floor.

Olivia knelt beside Posey to get a closer look. Loose, yellowing pages shuffled out from one side, and a cloud of dust escaped in a *poof* around their faces.

"Hold on," Violet, who was standing over Olivia's shoulder, interrupted. "Does Harry Potter know she stole his diary?"

"Sorry about the dust," Posey said, squinting and waving her hand through floating particles. "I haven't opened this since, well since my *abuela* died, I guess."

Olivia nodded and shifted her weight forward. The aged brown leather was embossed with the initials *M.M.* in shiny gold print. Posey flipped open the cover, which was slowly pulling away from the thick, frayed binding, and carefully turned through the pages.

"This is just the record book," Posey said, running her finger down a list of names, scrawled in the same elegant script. "I need to sign you in."

Olivia looked up at Violet.

"Maybe she wants to send thank-you notes?" Violet offered.

Olivia rolled her eyes. "So." She turned back to Posey. "The rules?"

"Right," Posey said. "Rules. There are only a few, but they're important. Especially the first one." Posey found a pen from behind her ear and began filling in the date on the next available empty line. "The first rule of Wish Club," she was saying, "is that you do not talk about Wish Club."

Olivia nodded as Violet rolled her eyes.

"Wish Club?" Violet droned. "Unless Brad Pitt is hiding in that closet somewhere, I don't think a *Fight Club* reference is all that appropriate."

Olivia was close to laughing when she felt Posey's eyes, hard and severe, boring holes into the crown of her head.

"Okay." Olivia nodded. "Got it. Next?"

Posey snapped the pen into the binding of the open book. "The second rule of Wish Club," she went on, "is that you DO. NOT. TALK. About Wish Club."

She stared unblinking into Olivia's eyes, as Olivia began fiddling with her fingernails.

"Um . . ." She spoke tentatively. "Okay?"

"Seriously," Posey went on. "I know it's hard, but you can't tell a soul. Not about the dresses, not about the butterflies, definitely not about the wishes. Not even about me or this shop."

"Sounds like a pretty successful business model," Violet snorted. She was now wandering around the shop, glancing at a series of framed articles featuring photos of a much younger Posey and a large, gray-haired woman draped in a muumuu.

"I don't need the business," Posey said sternly.

Olivia could feel Violet taking a step back from the frames, as if she'd set off an alarm.

"All that matters to me is that I help people who need helping," Posey explained. "And if you go running to all of the Bay Area with this, I won't be able to do that."

Olivia nodded.

"It's important that your sister understands that one, too," Posey said.

Olivia looked back to where Violet was standing in front of one of the mannequins, inspecting its hard, angular face. Olivia threw her a look.

"Aye, aye," Violet said, saluting the frozen bust.

"I think we're good," Olivia reported back.

Posey indicated a line on the notebook and passed Olivia the pen.

"The rest of the rules are pretty straightforward," Posey continued, scratching a scabby bug bite near her wrist. "Every time I make you a dress, you get to make a wish. Three dresses, three wishes. You've already used one, so that leaves two."

"Why only three?" Olivia asked quickly, before flushing red. "Not that three's not enough. Just, you know, curious."

Posey shrugged, grabbed the edge of a low, wobbly table, and hoisted herself up to her feet. Olivia didn't get it; Posey looked and sounded like she was around her age, but the way she carried herself from place to place, her fragile bones and careful waddle, made her seem ancient.

"It's a magic number?" she offered, pulling her argyle sweater—itchy looking, and with a big hole at the collar—down over her nonexistent hips. "I really have no idea. Do you mind if we keep this moving? I have an alteration at ten."

Violet chortled from her perch by the window. "Shouldn't there be elves for that kind of thing?"

Olivia groaned. "Would you please shut it?"

Posey started, nearly dropping the crowded daybook she'd been consulting at her desk.

"Not you," Olivia assured her. "Sorry. Go on."

Posey looked up from her planner to quickly run through the rest of the rules:

Wishes will only be granted when the wisher is wearing a magical Mariposa dress.

No wishing for ridiculously unattainable and universal things, like world peace or an end to hunger and poverty.

No wishing the same thing twice.

No wishing for more wishes.

Olivia signed her name and Posey snapped the book shut.

"That's it," Posey announced. "Anything else is fair game."

Olivia crawled to her feet and joined Violet, already hovering at the door. "Wow," Olivia said uncertainly. "I don't even know what to—I mean, I've never really—"

"Don't mention it," Posey said, settling in behind her sewing machine. "Oh, there's one more rule. Whatever you wish, wish carefully, and make sure it comes from your heart. Those are the only wishes that count."

10

"At the end of the road, turn left." The persistent GPS narrator blinked from Violet's lap.

"There," Violet shouted in a mock-British accent, imitating the recording and pointing toward the on-ramp. "I believe he means right there."

It had been a full day of firsts for Olivia. Her first time seeing a ghost. Her first time *talking* to a ghost. Her first time believing in wishes and magical dresses . . .

And now, her first time driving across the Golden Gate Bridge.

When they'd gotten back to the house from Posey's shop, Violet had convinced Olivia that they absolutely *had to* spend the afternoon driving around the city and finding out exactly what Violet, in her reincarnated but bossy-as-ever form, could and could not do. Bridget was at work, and Mac was napping on the living room couch, CNN news tickers flashing against his sturdy, sleepy frame. The keys to the loaner BMW were on the counter. Technically, Olivia wasn't yet on the rental insurance, but Violet wasn't interested in technicalities.

They'd spent the afternoon getting lost in the peaks and valleys of North Beach, Russian Hill, and the Marina, window-shopping—where they'd learned that even though Violet was solid to Olivia's touch, she passed through everything else like ether. Much to Violet's dismay, this made shoplifting a basket of Kiehl's products or sipping a bowl of chai heartbreakingly impossible.

After a few rounds of their new favorite game, which involved Violet standing in the middle of the sidewalk as complete strangers walked directly *through* her body, Violet decided it was time for a road trip.

Enter Sir Hamish, as Violet had immediately christened the electronic device. She had programmed a secret destination into the boxy neon screen and was repeating affected commands as Olivia struggled to keep up.

"Where are we going?" Olivia asked, screeching to a stop at the crest of a hill.

"There it is!" Violet squealed, pointing through the windshield at the famous bridge, rising red and regal above the fog. "I can't believe we *live* here," she said, for the umpteenth time that day.

"I can't believe Mom *grew up* here," Olivia added. It still hadn't sunk in that all of the sights and sounds Olivia was experiencing for the first time every day had been the backdrop and sound track to her mother's youth.

Olivia followed Hamish and Violet's instructions and soon realized they weren't just admiring the bridge, they were crossing it.

"Man." Violet sighed, stretching out the window for a better look at the turquoise water, streaked with boats and dotted with little green islands. Olivia tried to sneak a peek but was anxiously gripping the steering wheel, trying not to think about the massive red suspension beams hanging high above or the choppy water far below.

Olivia finally exhaled as they bumped back over the grating and onto smooth pavement, the lush hills of the Marin Headlands ushering them through a mountain tunnel and into the quaint harbor town of Sausalito.

Bridget hardly ever talked about growing up in Sausalito, and the one time the Larsen family had visited the West Coast, when the girls were seven, they hadn't even seen her old house. Both of her parents—Grandma Sybil and Grandpa Joe—had already died by then, and the only somewhat nostalgic stop Bridget had made was to see her father's boat, a snazzy sporting yacht still docked in the marina.

"Mom inherited that boat, didn't she?" Violet pressed as they took a sharp turn down into the valley. "I thought we could go check it out."

"They're trying to sell it," Olivia protested, vaguely remembering her parents arguing about the upkeep and not having enough free time to enjoy it.

"Good luck," Violet dismissed her with a scoff. "I'm sure people are just lining up to buy luxury yachts in this stellar economy."

Olivia turned dramatically to face her sister, her eyebrows arched like horizontal question marks.

"I read things." Violet shrugged. "I've had a lot of time on my hands lately, okay?"

Part of Olivia wanted to know more. *A lot of time on your hands, where?* But another part, a bigger part, just wanted to enjoy the fact that she was sitting in a car next to her sister, on their way to another adventure, waiting for a stoplight to change.

The girls followed the winding cliffside road into town. The sun was just starting its long drop into the Pacific, and in the distance, T-shaped rows of clean white boats threw their reflections, shimmering and gold against the water.

They pulled into the Sausalito Yacht Harbor parking lot and Violet jumped out first. "There it is!" she shouted, pointing to a medium-size, sport fishing boat at the end of one row. Olivia immediately recognized the green canvas awning, and the gold lettering on one side of the wide, boxy hull. "*Sybil*." After they'd gone back to Willis, Violet had told all of their friends that she'd have a boat named after her one day, just like her dead grandmother in California.

"I can't believe it's still here," Olivia murmured, following Violet as she hopped over the margin of choppy water and landed heavily on the deck. Olivia ran her hands along the cool brass railings, stepping down into the cabin and peering inside the tinted, round windows.

"It looks like nobody's been in here for years," Olivia said, noting the sterile white sheets thrown over the silver-bottomed stools and heavy antique steering wheel. Like a flash, she remembered the tiny twin beds that were built into the wall in the cabin below. She and Violet had begged to sleep there, to stay the night on the boat by themselves. They didn't care if the boat left the harbor, they just wanted to play with all of the tiny things. Tiny pillows, tiny pots and pans, even a tiny toilet that flushed with a tiny, foot-shaped pedal.

"Remember when I thought I clogged the toilet and started to cry?" Olivia asked, pulling away and turning back to Violet.

All around her, the deck was empty.

"Violet?" she called out, the sharp quiver of her voice echoing into the ocean. Her eyes wildly scanned the flat, clean surface of the blue water, the deserted deck of the ship. *Was that it?* Olivia thought, her stomach dropping. Had Violet left? Was she all by herself again?

"Up here!" Violet sang.

Olivia felt blood rushing back up to her face and breathed a thick sigh of relief. She followed the sound of Violet's voice up the narrow flight of stairs that led to the upper level.

"Don't tell me you forgot about the roof deck!"

Olivia swung her legs over the railing and found Violet lying back against the pointed bow, knees bent, eyes trained on the deepening sky.

"We live in California," Violet announced, her voice slow and deliberate. "I used to tell everyone I was going to move here when I turned eighteen, remember?"

Olivia grabbed her sister's wrist and gave it a little squeeze. Violet's obsession with the *Sybil* had been only the first in a series of West Coast fantasies. She'd always said she was a California girl at heart, and had dreamed about living on their grandparents' boat and sailing it up and down the coast.

All this time Olivia had spent being miserable about the move, she'd forgotten it was the one thing Violet had wanted to do most. She had been living out her sister's dream and hadn't even realized it.

"I guess it's not so terrible here," Olivia allowed with a sad smile. A graceful sailboat glided across the bay, momentarily hiding, then revealing, bits and pieces of the flickering city lights.

Violet rolled her eyes. "It's no *Willis*, but you'll adjust."

Olivia laughed. "Everything's just so different," she said quietly. "At school, I mean."

"Come on." Violet nudged Olivia's shoulder with her own. "You just have to give it a chance."

Olivia nodded silently.

"Besides," Violet added, "we've got all *this* to play with."

She spread her arms wide, as if to wrap the city in a hug, and Olivia couldn't help but laugh. With Violet right there beside her, it was almost impossible to remember what life had been like before. It was as if she was suddenly seeing in color again, after months of living in black-and-white. Her old, gray life felt unimportant and far away.

As the sky faded from royal blue to inky gray, the sisters lay side by side, just like they'd done since they were small; Olivia connecting the dotted constellations, Violet holding out for shooting stars.

11

"Mmm," Violet moaned, holding her face over the bubbling layers of tomato sauce and fat round noodles. Olivia and her parents were about to sit huddled around the sloping kitchen table, eating a non-holiday meal together as a family for the first time in as long as Olivia could remember.

It hadn't actually been a planned thing. More like they'd all happened to be home and semi-near the kitchen around the time that Mac was pulling a casserole dish of steaming baked ziti out of the oven. Olivia had finished her homework and quickly set the table, catching herself before laying down a fourth place for Violet, who giggled at the faux pas from over Mac's shoulder at the stove.

"This is torture," Violet continued, slumping back against a row of lopsided cabinets next to the sink. Mac, the only Larsen who could pass for a cook, had a limited yet consistent repertoire of standby dishes, usually involving one pot, a preheated oven, and lots of melted cheese. Violet had always loved

Mac's pasta dishes best—especially during her biannual stints of vegetarianism—and baked ziti, tonight's entrée of choice, had been her all-time favorite. Sadly, the look-but-don't-touch rule of ghostly manners didn't allow for eating, either.

The front door opened and they listened for the sounds of Bridget's house keys, clinking in a dish on the entryway table. She'd been working at the office all afternoon, and Olivia watched as Violet's eyes jumped from the food to the kitchen door, flickering with soft anticipation.

"Something smells good," Bridget said as she entered the room, a cloud of gardenia perfume following in her wake. Probably because she had been the only one at work on a Sunday, she was wearing the casual version of her everyday suit: a champagne-colored cashmere sweater set with little pearl buttons, charcoal gray tailored pants, and black ostrich-skin flats. She gave Olivia a quick squeeze at the waist and dropped a little peck on Mac's cheek before opening the refrigerator door and taking out a glass bottle of V8.

The whole scene was so quintessentially *Mom*, and Olivia watched as Violet's eyes grew foggy. Olivia tried to imagine what it would be like, sitting there, sandwiched between her parents, not being able to touch them or talk to them. Feeling completely invisible.

Probably, she realized with a jolt, it wasn't so different from the way she'd been feeling lately herself.

Mac served up heaping plates of pasta and passed them to Olivia, who laid them on the table before settling in a seat next to her mother.

"Thanks, O," Bridget said as she tucked in her chair, taking her BlackBerry from her pocket and placing it next to her plate on the table. "How was the party last night? I didn't even hear you come in."

Olivia poured herself a glass of water from the multicolored ceramic pitcher on the table and took a big sip. "It was okay," she said. "I was home pretty early."

Mac ripped a big chunk of garlic bread from a steaming loaf wrapped in tinfoil and passed it across the table. "Did you have a good time?"

Olivia glanced quickly up at Violet, who was following the round of questions like a spectator at a tennis match.

"I guess." Olivia shrugged, hoping it was a better alternative to *Sure, until I humiliated myself, almost got sick in a cab, and made a wish on a floating butterfly. P.S. Violet's back.*

She felt her parents' eyes on the top of her head as she pushed piles of soppy noodles around on her plate. Bridget cleared her throat and took a sip of water before turning to Mac.

"How's the upstairs bathroom coming?" she asked. Olivia looked up from her plate as her father wiped the corners of his mouth with his napkin and shrugged.

"It's coming," he said with a quiet smile. "Just working on those cabinets in the basement. Another coat of paint and they should be good to go."

Bridget nodded and smiled before glancing quickly around the table and turning toward Olivia. "Could you pass the salt, hon?" she asked, gesturing to the crystal shaker next to Olivia's elbow.

Olivia reached slowly across the table, studying her parents with careful eyes. Were they actually having a calm, pleasant, *normal* family dinner?

89

Just then, Bridget's BlackBerry buzzed from its prominent position at the center of the table. Mac eyed the device warily.

"Hmm . . ." Bridget muttered, assessing the e-mail with angled brows. "It's Mike from the office. I asked him to take a look at the title for Grandpa Joe's boat and see what we'd have to do to get it on the market."

Olivia looked quickly up from the forkful of pasta she'd been pushing listlessly across her plate and caught Violet's eye. "You're really going to sell it?" she asked.

"We haven't decided yet," Mac said reassuringly, taking another bite.

"I don't see what there is to decide," Bridget said curtly, replacing the BlackBerry on the table and stabbing a tube of ziti with her fork.

Mac shot her a pointed look before getting up to refill his glass of water from the tap. Olivia snuck a peek at Violet, who was staring at the back of Mac's head. Probably noticing all the new gray hairs, Olivia thought, or the stiff, awkward way he moved around now. Like he was recovering from an injury, taking time to bounce back.

Only it wasn't an injury. And he wasn't recovering.

Olivia looked to Bridget, who was carefully chewing as if nothing was wrong. Her BlackBerry buzzed again and she quickly grabbed for it. Olivia lowered her eyes to her plate and pushed a noodle through a puddle of sauce.

Bridget made a few small sounds of acknowledgment before laying the device back down and returning to her pasta.

"Yikes," Violet muttered from her countertop perch. Olivia rolled her eyes in silent agreement.

Mac coughed abruptly as if a piece of food had gone down the wrong pipe, and reached for his water at the same time Bridget was helping herself to more salad. Their hands collided sloppily, sending Mac's glass toppling and water pouring onto the table.

"Damn it, Mac!" Bridget shouted, clutching her Black-Berry and backing violently away from the dripping table as if she'd been doused in kerosene.

"Well, I'm sorry," Mac grumbled. "But you shouldn't have that stupid thing at the table. We're trying to eat here."

Bridget dabbed at her pants with a dishcloth before carrying her plate to the sink. "Not anymore," she said coolly, wiping scraps of soggy food into the disposal with her fork.

Mac dropped his silverware onto his plate with a clank and pushed back from the table, throwing down his napkin and grumbling as he rose to his feet. He stomped across the kitchen and swung the basement door open, loudly descending the squeaking stairs. Moments later, the jumpy thud of a table saw vibrated up through the floorboards, shaking the legs of Olivia's chair like an aftershock.

Violet looked from Olivia to Bridget, who was still standing at the sink, quietly rinsing her plate.

Olivia sat frozen at the table, her ears throbbing, her fingers trembling in her lap, while her mother dried her hands with a towel.

"Do you mind running the dishwasher when you're finished?" Bridget asked, dropping a hand on Olivia's shoulder as she passed on her way upstairs.

Olivia brought her plate to the sink as Violet lowered herself down from the counter, pressing an ear against the basement door. Olivia pulled the heavy dishwasher door toward the floor and began to sloppily load the remaining plates and glasses.

"Well, that was fun," Olivia muttered under her breath, shoving a handful of silverware into the plastic divider. "Aren't you glad you came back?"

Olivia looked up to see Violet still pressed against the door, staring sadly at a spot on the floor by her feet.

Olivia wiped her hands on the tops of her jeans and turned a knob on the dishwasher as it jolted and whirred into action. She walked over to Violet, linking elbows and pulling her sister toward the stairs. "Because I sure am."

12

"Anybody who tells you to *just be yourself* was clearly a loser in high school."

Olivia was nibbling on a bagel by the library windows and counting tiles on the glossy checkerboard floor. After two bus rides' worth of trying to look normal with Violet chattering away beside her, Olivia had decided that her only hope was in the details. As long as she had something to focus her eyes on, she was golden. On the bus, it had been the fedora of the elderly man sitting in front of her—the silver hairs on the back of his neck had been trimmed into a neat, solid line.

And here in the hallway, tile-gazing did the trick while Olivia waited for homeroom bell, pretending not to be receiving the latest installment of Violet Larsen's *High-School Handbook*, the telepathic audio version.

"What does that even mean, anyway? *Be yourself.*" Violet was speaking rhetorically, gesturing like a frustrated philosopher. Olivia rolled her eyes and took a bite of cinnamon-raisin bagel, crumbs tumbling onto the lap of her honey-colored corduroys.

"I'm serious," Violet insisted. "Nobody has any idea who they are. Arguably *ever*, but certainly not in high school. Am I wrong?"

Olivia, starting to master the art of acknowledging Violet without looking like she belonged in the loony bin, shook her head no, in a way that could have been just as easily interpreted as a casual flipping of her hair.

"And who knows what makes some kids *cool* and some kids not," Violet continued, then paused. "Actually, I do. It's confidence. That's all there is to it. It really doesn't matter *who* you are, as long as you commit to being that person one hundred and fifty percent."

An overwhelmingly under-confident sophomore with shifty eyes and a slightly suspicious overcoat shuffled through the library doors. Violet gestured to him as evidence, just as the bell rang for homeroom.

Olivia wrapped up the rest of her bagel and shoved it into the outside pocket of her backpack, hopping down from the cushioned window bench and heading to class.

Violet skipped alongside her, continuing her foray into motivational speaking. "And it's a tricky thing," she went on, nodding as if agreeing with her own excellent point. "Because it seems like to be cool, or *popular*, at least, you have to be confident. But it's kind of tough to be confident when you're not already cool, right?"

Olivia snuck into homeroom, wishing Violet would save the question-and-answer portion of the seminar for a time when she wasn't slinking down the center aisle of a bustling classroom.

In the back corner, Calla, Graham, and other members of their crew convened at the floor-to-ceiling windows. They were sprawled out over any space that wasn't a chair, as if collectively allergic to the furniture. Graham leaned on a wooden ledge by the window, drumming his fingers on the glass, and Calla lounged on the floor, a strand of dark hair angled in her mouth, scribbling in a Moleskine notebook.

Olivia kept her head down and sat at a desk near the front, taking out her assignment notebook and needlessly confirming that she'd done all of her homework.

"But the good news," Violet said animatedly, hopping on the table and crossing her long legs over the list of checked-off assignments, "is that confidence can be faked."

Ravi, the lumbering physics teacher Olivia had for homeroom, started to call out roll. He had long, greasy hair, which he was forever tucking back behind one ear in a way that made him look simultaneously girly and like he needed a bath.

"Exhibit A: Listen to how people react to the sound of their own names." Violet nodded to the front of the room.

"Christian Baker," Ravi droned.

Christian, a small boy with an upturned nose and glasses too big for his face, mumbled an almost unintelligible response.

"*Not* confident," Violet judged disapprovingly.

Ravi ran through the list, Violet assessing each response for Olivia's benefit.

When he got to Calla, both Violet and Olivia held their breath.

"Calla Karalekas?" Ravi said, looking up with slightly more anticipation, it seemed to Olivia, than he had shown about anything else all morning.

"Morning, Ravi," Calla cooed. She waved one hand in the air, and Olivia saw that she was wearing red and black striped fingerless gloves.

Ravi looked quickly back to his book, marking Calla present with exaggerated effort. "Yes, uh, good morning," he stammered before moving on.

Violet gave Olivia a meaningful look. "Looks like Ravi could use a lesson or two," she remarked, giggling infectiously.

"Olivia Larsen?" Ravi continued down the list.

Olivia jumped at the sound of her name. The remnants of a probably-crazy-looking smile faded from her lips as she straightened abruptly, her head swimming with possible responses. *Here? Hi? Nice to see ya?*

"Present," Olivia said, too loudly and with a bit of a nervous tremor. It almost sounded like singing, and not in a good way. She listened hard for a chuckle from the back of the room, but there was only silence, charged and threatening to swallow her whole.

Violet cleared her throat and hopped down from the table. "Well," she said brightly. "The other good news is that there's always tomorrow."

🦋 🦋 🦋

It was finally lunchtime, and Violet was close to throwing in the towel.

For the most part, she had reported with irritation, Olivia wasn't even making any kind of effort to have fun. And when she did, it definitely wasn't the right kind.

First, there was the incident in studio art. Despite Violet's urging to sit at a table with some of the kids Olivia recognized from the party and homeroom—Austin, a pixie-haired blonde, and her boyfriend, the dreadlocked bass player Nemo, or Reno, or some other two-syllable word that wasn't actually a name—Olivia had chosen a seat by herself in an alcove by the materials closet.

The class was working on self-portraits, and while Austin and Tevo flipped through vintage photographs and album covers for inspiration, Olivia was stuck watching a gum-smacking goth girl work on an impressively scary piece of chain-link armor.

Remembering Violet's advice, Olivia turned to the gloomy girl and cleared her throat.

"How long do you think that will take?" Olivia asked with confidence. "Until your armor's finished, I mean."

The girl turned her languid eyes and downturned pouty lips in Olivia's direction. "A lifetime," she mournfully replied, before snapping another link in place.

Violet dropped her head dramatically on the table.

Next had been Eastern religious studies, which Violet had insisted they switch into, claiming that Olivia needed to be exposed to more interesting people and actually learn something, as opposed to re-memorizing the dates of the Hundred Years' War.

Violet had been right, for the most part, and so far the class had involved lively discussions about whose mother had converted to Buddhism on which trip to India and what Angelina Jolie's Tibetan tattoos *really* meant. Violet was so totally enraptured by the conversation about the exotic birthplaces and/or travel destinations of everyone in the class that she seemed to have forgotten her self-appointed role as Olivia's life coach.

Olivia absentmindedly doodled on the back of her binder, wondering what the Chinese symbol for "failure" was.

And then, at long last, lunch. Golden Gate was on a rotating schedule, with four different lunch periods, which meant that some mornings Olivia was forced to eat a tuna sandwich at some ungodly breakfast hour, and other days it was all she could do to keep her growling stomach from digesting itself way past noon.

Today she was somewhere in the middle, and so, it seemed, was everybody else: The courtyard was beyond packed as she made her way inconspicuously to a quiet corner by the pond.

As soon as she'd settled onto a rock and started to pull out the rest of her bagel, Violet dragged her up onto her feet and marched her back inside. "I have two words for you," she announced as they pushed their way through the glass doors and stepped onto the tree-lined street. "Open. Campus."

"I'm not hungry," Olivia muttered as Violet skipped down the block. She'd hoped that Violet's appearance would have signaled the return of her appetite, as well. But so far, no such luck.

"Fake it," was Violet's advice. "Or get a tea. People love their tea around here, huh?"

Olivia tore the sleeve of her sweater free from Violet's vise grip and pulled her sister into a sunken alley in the middle of the block.

"Face it," Olivia sighed. "I suck at this. It isn't me. Can't we just call it a day?"

Violet threw her hands in the air. "You're not even *trying*," she yelled. "It's like you don't even *want* to make friends."

Olivia shrugged and leaned back against the brick wall of the building behind her.

"Why do I have to?" she asked, quietly. "I mean, you're here now. Right?"

Olivia saw Violet's features soften out of the corner of her eyes, and then felt her sister's hand closing firmly around her shoulder. "Snap out of it," she commanded. "If not for you, at least for me. You're in the middle of the city, for God's sake. Act like it!"

Olivia looked into Violet's pleading eyes and grumbled, slumping toward the sidewalk and allowing her sister to pull her along.

The People's Republic, the popular coffee shop around the corner from school, was even more crowded than the courtyard, and Olivia figured that by the time she'd waited in the zigzagging line for a chai or a muffin, she'd already be late for next period. But Violet was on a mission. The girls stood patiently next to the glass counter, Olivia silently pondering the irony of vegan cream cheese, while Violet oohed and ahhed over the selection of flavored coffee drinks.

Once Olivia had successfully ordered a peppermint tea and an oatmeal cookie, she turned to find Violet already seated at a table in the center of the café, face-to-face with Calla Karalekas.

Violet waved her arms so wildly that Olivia was nervous she might somehow disrupt molecules and send an invisible tornado spinning across the room. Olivia felt her pulse drumming and tried to steady her ragged breath as she cut between tables toward Calla and her crew.

She carefully balanced her tea and cookie in the same hand,

using her free fingers to unwrap a lost strand of hair from around the tip of her nose. She took a final, leveling breath, her eyes meeting Violet's eager and encouraging stare. *Should I ask to sit?* Olivia anxiously wondered. *Or just sit. Probably just sitting without asking would seem more confident. Who asks to sit? It's a free country,* she insisted to herself in Violet's voice. She circled the table, planting herself beside Violet and lowering her drink to the table . . . at the exact moment that Calla spun around and stood up.

"Let's get out of here," Calla exclaimed hurriedly to her blond friend. "I forgot I told Soren I'd meet him at Amoeba. He's been trying to get me to buy the new MGMT for, like, weeks."

It wasn't a planned escape. Both Olivia and Violet could see that. Partly, it was just bad timing. But that didn't account for the fact that no matter what she did, Olivia seemed destined to remain, like her sister, hopelessly and irreversibly invisible.

13

"How's it coming in there?"

Olivia was sandwiched between piles of dresses, skinny jeans, and sky-high heels in an almost impossibly tiny dressing room, staring at her frazzled, half-dressed reflection in a three-way mirror. She struggled to remain decent at all times, as the door had no latch, and the chatty sales help—all of whom appeared to be identically twenty-two, rail-thin, and not at all shy about barging right in.

After a day of pushing Olivia to assert herself in class, strategically picking out places for her to sit at lunch, and counseling her on how to do everything from walk down the hall to demand (*not* ask for) permission to go to the bathroom, Violet had decided that the only thing left to overhaul was Olivia's tired and lackluster wardrobe.

"You want to know why nobody notices you?" Violet had asked during a dejected walk home from the bus. "It's because every single one of your sweaters is exactly the same shade of beige, and it matches the paint on the classroom walls. Half the time, *I* don't even see you."

And so, when Olivia returned home from school Monday afternoon, shocked to discover that her mother was working from home, Violet convinced her to do the unthinkable and ask Bridget to take her shopping.

Three hours, six boutiques, and two different covers of the same Rolling Stones song later, Olivia was pressed against the dressing room mirror, with eager, multi-pierced hipsters filing in and out, piling dress after vintage dress into her outstretched arms. At first, Violet had been there, too, assessing each item one by one, but even she had been overwhelmed by the cramped quarters and myriad outfits, and had vanished to peruse a selection of oversize sunglasses by the window.

"Olivia?" her mother called out again from the plush crimson armchair in the narrow hall, tapping her taupe Tod's loafer against the carpet and clicking through e-mails on her BlackBerry.

"She looks amazing," one salesgirl or another informed her. "Almost like a young Sophia Loren, don't you think?"

"Definitely," the other wholeheartedly agreed.

Olivia rolled her eyes and freed a belted, vestlike garment from a hanger, holding it out in front of her shoulders.

"A vest?" Olivia muttered to herself, slipping her slender arms through the open sleeves. "Who am I, Charlie Chaplin?"

"What's that?" her mother called out.

"Nothing," Olivia covered, choosing from a pile of skirts, many with pleats and almost all about six inches shorter than she would ever consider appropriate for public viewing. She was struggling to pull up a pair of thick knit stockings while standing on one foot when she lost her balance and tumbled backward into the door.

"Everything all right?" her mother tried again lightly.

Olivia sort of grunted as she shimmied the skirt back over her hips.

"Come out and show me."

Olivia looked at her reflection in the mirror. Her red hair was frizzy and her cheeks were flushed, and all she wanted to do was put on her favorite paper-thin zip-up sweater, even if it was the color of a dirty Band-Aid. She didn't care anymore if vests were all the rage—she felt ridiculous.

"Come on," she heard Violet calling. "You've been in there for twenty minutes—there has to be *something* you like."

Olivia sighed and pushed the door open, tugging at her sleeves and stepping out into the hall. She had been so closely watching for Violet's reaction that she almost didn't hear the small sounds Bridget was making in her chair, or the flutter of her fingertips as they searched for her mouth. She looked down and saw that her mother's eyes were clouding, the soft creases at the corners deepening into hard, tired ravines.

"Mom?" Olivia spoke quietly. "What's—"

Bridget shook her head silently from side to side as Violet stepped behind her, placing her hands lightly on the back of the chair.

"You look . . . I'm sorry, it's just, you look . . ."

Just like her, Olivia thought, silently finishing her mother's sentence. *Just like Violet.*

"She's right," Violet said softly. "You do."

Olivia chewed at the inside of her cheek, shifting her weight from one foot to the other. "I'm sorry, Mom."

She couldn't begin to say all the things she was sorry for. She was sorry her mom was upset. She was sorry that her very existence was a painful reminder of everything they'd lost. She was sorry she wasn't enough.

"No," her mother said through a little cough. "*I'm* sorry. I just realized—what time is it? I forgot I have to . . . I have to run back to the office. . . ."

Olivia watched with quiet alarm as Bridget gathered her purse and trenchcoat, opening her wallet and sliding out her MasterCard. "Here," she said, shoving the card and car keys into Olivia's palm. "I'll walk. Get anything you want, all right?" Without waiting for a response, her mother started hurriedly through the store and out onto the street.

Olivia closed herself back into the claustrophobic room. Her face burned and she felt sweat marks blooming under her arms. She imagined her mother speed-walking to her office building, sitting upright in the comfort of her high-backed, rolling leather chair, and burying herself in business.

The business of forgetting.

Olivia ripped the vest over her head and threw it to the floor. Suddenly, Violet's reflection was next to hers in the mirror, watching as Olivia hurried back into her own boring clothes.

"What are you doing?" Violet asked.

Olivia buttoned her oatmeal-colored corduroys and sat on the stool to zip up her boots. "I'm going home."

Violet knelt beside her sister, picking up the credit card from where Olivia had tossed it near the mirror. "Didn't you hear what she said?" she asked. "Carte blanche! Do you have any idea how many times I've dreamed about this?"

Olivia took the credit card and shoved it into the pocket of her fleece. "It's bad enough I look just like you," Olivia murmured. "I don't have to dress like you, too."

Violet rolled her eyes and blocked Olivia's path to the door. "Wait," she begged, grabbing her sister by the elbows. "Okay. Maybe the vest was a little much."

"You think?" Olivia asked dryly.

"But that doesn't mean we can't find something that's more . . . *you*," Violet insisted. "Just because you don't want to wear a kilt doesn't mean you have to dress like a piece of dry toast all the time, either. Right?"

Violet swung her sister around to face the mirror, and Olivia had no choice but to accept defeat. Her pants, her sweater, and her coat, were all exactly the same shade of tan. Even she could see that there was room for improvement.

Violet dug through a pile of sweaters on the floor and held one up, a gray and black striped tunic with a wide elastic belt. Olivia took it and pressed it against her torso.

"See?" Violet asked, her voice warm and soothing. "Baby steps."

14

Whether or not it had anything to do with the new teal tunic and pewter leggings, or the new slouchy faux-suede boots, Olivia's reign as Princess Invisible came to an end the following afternoon in AP English.

It was Olivia's first time in the class. She'd been accidentally scheduled into Remedial English 101, and it had taken her a day to convince her well-meaning but flaky guidance counselor, whose office was strung with Tibetan prayer flags and smelled like scented candles, that there had been a mistake.

After a couple of wrong turns that nearly landed her in the basement utilities closet, Olivia tiptoed in after class had already started, sliding behind a desk at the back of the room while Violet took up her usual perch by the window. Up front, Graham was holding a pristine and clearly unopened copy of *To the Lighthouse*, while a blond, preppy kid with a healthy dusting of youthful freckles straddled a seat backward at the front of the room.

"Virginia Woolf was a lesbian," Graham announced, waving his book for emphasis. "Didn't you guys see *The Hours*? She made out with her sister."

The class erupted into giggles and a lively discussion of Nicole Kidman's prosthetic nose, while the guy with the freckles dismounted his chair and flipped it around, settling himself against the teacher's desk.

"Thank you for that profound observation, Graham." Freckles spoke, and Olivia's eyes widened as she realized he was the teacher. She was busy wondering how this Dennis the Menace clone could be a day out of college, when he turned and narrowed his eyes in her direction. "Who's this?"

Sixteen heads swiveled around to face her.

"It seems we have a stranger among us. . . ." Freckles paced the length of the dry-erase board, picking imaginary pieces of lint from the waistband of his argyle sweater-vest. Olivia couldn't help but think he looked like an eager little boy borrowing his grandfather's clothes. The corners of her mouth started to twitch as she caught Violet's reflection in the glass, already puffing out her chest in a dead-on impersonation.

Olivia shook her head clear and shifted forward in her seat, sensing the fidgeting bodies around her and wondering where to start.

"Do. You. Have. A. Name?" Freckles articulated each word individually, as if speaking to a child or a house pet, an arrogant smirk spreading across his face.

"Olivia," she uttered, her brain locked, her face heating up.

"Just Olivia," Freckles repeated. "No last name. Like Madonna?"

The tips of her ears were on fire. Olivia couldn't believe that on her first chance to really hold her own—in new clothes, no less—she was being mocked by an underage imposter.

"Okay, *Madonna*," he went on. "Welcome to Advanced Placement English. I'm Mr. Whitley. I realize that a lot of teachers around here—in their overalls and their flowered skirts—prefer to be called by their first names. This is because they'd like you to see them as friends." Mr. Whitley paused dramatically in front of a row of desks, slowly rapping his knuckles against the polished wood. "I," he continued, drawing the word across many multi-toned syllables, "am not one of those teachers."

A quiet, irreverent chuckle came from the seat directly in front of Olivia's. A girl flipped her straight dark hair over one shoulder and Olivia immediately recognized the perfect profile, the dimpled chin, the almond-shaped eyes. Calla Karalekas.

Mr. Whitley shot a grave look in Calla's direction and Olivia sucked in a bit of air, certain things were about to heat up. But Calla simply lifted her thick, heavy lashes, staring the teacher down with what looked, from Olivia's partially obstructed perspective, to be an almost flirtatious smirk.

Mr. Whitley spun on his heels and resumed pacing.

"You're joining us a little late in the term," Mr. Whitley was saying to the tops of his chocolate-colored loafers, "so the learning curve might feel a bit steep. We're right in the middle of a unit on the Bloomsbury group, and today we're talking about one of Virginia Woolf's most significant novels, *To the Lighthouse*. I assume you got the reading list we sent out over the break?"

Olivia had a vague recollection of something coming in

the mail just before they'd moved, but those last few days had been enveloped in such a gauzy haze of chaos and denial that she wasn't sure what had happened to the envelope en route.

"Oh, um, I think so," she quietly stuttered. "I mean, no, I think I—"

Mr. Whitley had already turned his back to the class, pen poised at the board. "It's not a trick question, Madonna," he barked, scribbling a list of dates in shiny red ink. "Perhaps you could borrow a copy over the weekend. You'll find you have a great deal of catching up to do."

From the corner of the room, Graham enthusiastically waved his book in her direction. Olivia kept her eyes trained on the back of Mr. Whitley's bobbing head, the anxious drumming of her pulse quickening into an angry roar.

Suddenly, Violet was kneeling at her feet, eyes wild and glistening. "Oh, no," she muttered. "You can't let him talk to you like that. A teacher like this will *ruin* you until you put him in his place."

Olivia looked down at her sister, who was nodding enthusiastically and gesturing toward the front of the room.

"You've read that book a thousand times!" Violet encouraged. "Don't tell me you've forgotten your precious Homework Room?"

Olivia's cheeks flushed, remembering the intense feminist phase she'd gone through in the middle of freshman year. After reading one of Woolf's most famous essays, *A Room of One's Own*, Olivia had decided that in order to properly do her homework, she would need a room of *her* own, co-opting a section of the mudroom at the back of the house. It was true. She knew most of Woolf's novels by heart, even the really complicated ones that had taken her months to decode. *To the Lighthouse* was not one of her favorites, but she certainly knew enough to have an opinion.

"Now," Whitley continued. "Who can tell me what exactly Woolf was trying to accomplish by—"

"I've already read it."

Olivia leaned forward in her seat, the sharp points of her elbows resting lightly on the desk. The words came from somewhere so deep inside of her, they tasted funny.

Mr. Whitley froze, his arm raised midscrawl. Slowly, he turned his head. "I'm sorry?"

Bodies shifted as, once again, the entire class turned to look in her direction. Olivia's nervous gaze darted from one eager face to the next, before locking with the pair of piercing dark eyes in front of her. Calla's perfectly sculpted eyebrows were knit together in anticipation.

Olivia cleared her throat. "*To the Lighthouse*," she managed, eyes darting up and down from Violet to the class. "I was just saying, I mean . . . I've read it."

Olivia looked down, her eyes wide and pleading with Violet for help.

"Excellent," Mr. Whitley said, his voice dull and flat. "Then I'm sure you won't mind sharing your observations with the rest of the class."

Olivia swallowed. "Like, now?"

Mr. Whitley nodded. "Like, yeah," he mocked.

Olivia cleared her throat and steadied her hands on either side of the desk. Violet was still crouching beside her, and rested a hand on her back.

"You can do this," Violet said. "It's just like back home.

You'll feel better once you start putting yourself out there, I promise."

Olivia uncrossed her ankles and looked up, taking a deep breath before speaking.

"Honestly," she said, drawing the word out to buy time, "I think the novel is self-indulgent." Olivia cringed, holding her breath. She watched the shock travel down from Freckles's eyes, tightening his smile into a pursed frown.

"Care to elaborate?" he asked.

Violet hopped up and down with glee, as Olivia settled an inch or two deeper into her chair. A familiar calm settled into her bones as she surveyed the class around her. Violet was right. She was back in her element, and she felt better already.

"I mean, clearly," she continued, "the book was little more than an attempt by Woolf to reconcile her feelings of inadequacy and guilt over the debt she owed her Elizabethan predecessors, from whom she struggled to separate herself to varying degrees of success for the remainder of her career."

Olivia inhaled the thick silence around her, her ears ringing and her face hot. Violet leaned in to whisper in her ear.

Olivia felt the corners of her mouth turning up as she leaned farther back into her seat. "Plus," she continued, repeating her sister's prompt, "she was a lesbian."

It took Mr. Whitley three minutes of knuckle-rapping and the empty threat of detention to finally get the class to stop laughing.

🦋 🦋 🦋

"Hey, Madonna!"

Olivia was halfway across the street when she realized

111

two things. One, for the first time in her life, she had a nickname. And two, Calla Karalekas was shouting it from under the branches of an evergreen tree, at the corner of Page and Masonic.

Olivia dodged an oncoming cab and hustled to the corner, where Calla was waiting with two other girls. One was Graham's onstage girlfriend, the petite Asian lap-snuggler from the courtyard, and the other was a Nordic-looking giantess, with a broad, shiny forehead and icy blue eyes.

"Madonna, this is Lark," Calla announced, gesturing to the sporty blonde, who waved the tops of her fingers and smiled. "And this," Calla continued, linking arms with the petite girl to her left, "is Eve."

Eve's shoulder-length black hair was pin-straight and styled in hard angles at her chin. She offered her hand for Olivia to shake, and Olivia noticed that even her little birdlike fingers had tiny, perfect nails.

"Madonna kicked ass in Shitley's class today," Calla announced. "He went into his Little Napoleon routine and she barely even flinched."

Olivia tried not to let on that her memory of the experience was slightly different, as Violet nudged the back of her elbow.

"See?" she whispered, slapping her own forehead with one open palm. "Man, I could have had a future in this."

"So what did he want?" Calla asked, her dark eyes warm and curious. There was something about the way she held herself that put Olivia instantly at ease, and reminded her of Violet's confidence pep talk, but in a totally-without-trying kind of way.

"Who?" Olivia asked. A breeze had picked up, and the green and white Golden Gate school flag was flapping noisily overhead.

"Whitley!" She laughed. "I hope he wasn't too hard on you after class."

"Oh," Olivia replied coolly. "No, nothing like that. He just told me about the partner projects."

Olivia had done her best impression of nonchalance when Whitley had asked her to hang back after class, even though she'd been certain he was going to expel her there and then. Instead, he'd simply given her a handout detailing the project that was due in a few weeks, a scene-adaptation from *To the Lighthouse*.

Which was quickly becoming Olivia's least favorite book.

"Oh, good," Calla exclaimed. Her thick, dark brown hair fell in one perfect wave over her shoulder and had that fresh-from-the-hairdresser look. "I thought for sure he was going to nail you with extra work or something. He lives for that shit."

Olivia felt a twinge of guilt. Never in her life had she even contradicted a teacher in public. She felt Violet proudly beaming at her side, and was wondering if maybe this wasn't the most brilliant start to her new academic career, when Calla reached abruptly into her bag and retrieved a shiny, goldenrod envelope.

"Anyway, I have something for you," she said, placing the envelope in Olivia's palm. "It's for this iWIN fundraiser my mom is hosting at the Academy of Sciences this weekend. Come."

"IWIN?" Olivia repeated, taking the envelope and holding it as if it were a small bird that might fly away.

"International Women in Need," Calla explained. "It's my mother's pet project. I'm junior chair. It should be fun. You know, speeches, cocktails, drunken debauchery. . . ." Calla gave Olivia's hand a quick squeeze before releasing it and skipping off to meet the other girls huddled around a waiting town car.

Olivia felt the envelope turning damp between her sweaty fingertips and looked down to see one word, written in sharp, precise script:

Madonna.

15

"Hey, neighbor."

Olivia and Violet were walking toward the Muni stop the next morning, Olivia's eyes trained on the parallel cable-car tracks, per the tested *I'm not hearing voices* routine. She didn't see Miles until she'd almost walked up and over the tops of his fungus loafers.

"Oh." Olivia stopped short. "Hey, Miles."

Ever since their mothers' office reception, where they'd discovered that they lived a mere two blocks apart, Miles, Bowie, and Olivia had found themselves on similar commutes to and from school. At first, it had seemed a coincidence, and Olivia was happy for the (real-life) company. But Miles's timing quickly became alarmingly precise, and lately it seemed that he was always there alone, waiting at the bus stop whenever Olivia arrived.

"Missed you on the ride home from school yesterday," Miles said lightly. Over his shoulder, Violet's face was locked in a sort of half grimace that Olivia couldn't read.

"Yeah," Olivia said, as the J Church Muni car squealed to a stop at the curb. "I got held up talking to a friend." It felt a little premature to be calling Calla her friend, but Olivia figured it was easier than explaining the whole Madonna incident to Miles. Plus, something told her that he wouldn't exactly approve.

"No problem." Miles shrugged, as if Olivia had apologized without meaning to. Olivia found a seat in the middle of the trolley and Miles planted himself standing beside her. Olivia turned to look out the window, hoping to avoid the uncomfortable reality of sitting face-to-face with his crotch.

"Hey, I've been thinking," Miles boomed from over her head, hugging the metal railing close to his chest. "You don't, I mean, you haven't picked a, uh, partner yet. For Whitley's project, I mean. Have you?"

Olivia's memory stalled and she searched for Violet, who was perched on a plastic red seat across the aisle. Miles was *in* her English class? She hadn't even noticed him. Violet was vigorously shaking her head from side to side, and out of habit, Olivia did the same.

"Awesome," Miles replied, and Violet hopped across the aisle, tugging on Olivia's sleeve.

"No!" Violet whispered. "I meant, 'no,' as in, *don't do it*!"

Olivia looked down at her hands folded in her lap and took a deep breath. "Oh," she said, then quickly looked back up to Miles. "I mean, I thought Mr. Whitley was assigning us groups?"

Miles hoisted the strap of his black messenger bag up higher on his shoulder as the bus pulled to a stop in front of school. "Nope," he said happily, making his way to the front.

"And this is perfect, because I was planning on working with Jake, but I think he's trying to get with Leah, you know, that girl with the tongue ring? So he probably already asked her."

Violet gripped her head in her hands, and Olivia winced, following Miles down the steps and onto the sidewalk.

"I mean, not that the only reason you'd ask a girl to be your partner was if you wanted to *get with* her," Miles backtracked, waving his hands in front of him as if declining a second helping of dessert. "What does 'get with' mean, anyway? That's so lame. I don't even say that, really, I was just, I mean, I was thinking, because we're neighbors, and everything . . ."

"Oh, no," Violet interrupted. Olivia assumed she was reacting to Miles's sudden attack of verbal diarrhea, when a voice sang out from behind her.

"Madonna."

Olivia whipped around to find Calla, perched on one of the benches on either side of the stone walkway leading up to Golden Gate's glass doors. She was draped in an open, wide-sleeved ivory cardigan, a mammoth canvas tote covered in pastel scrawls of French graffiti cradled in her lap. On the bench to Calla's left was Eve, her button nose scrunched as she navigated the screen of her iPhone, and standing to her right was Lark, with one sturdy hip angled forward, tapping one toe of her black-and-tan vintage Pumas against the cement.

"I was hoping to run into you today," Calla said, standing and reaching a hand through the bamboo handles of her bag to lightly touch Olivia's wrist. "Do you have a second?"

Olivia felt Violet not-breathing behind her and Miles's watchful eyes on the back of her head. "Um, I guess," Olivia stuttered. "I mean, I—"

Violet jabbed her fist into the small of Olivia's back.

"Sure," Olivia squeaked. "What's up?"

"I was just thinking about the fundraiser on Friday," Calla said. "Do you think you'll be able to come?"

Although Olivia had hardly thought about anything *not* fundraiser-related since Calla had given her the invitation yesterday, it had been mostly in an abstract, disbelieving kind of way. RSVPing hadn't exactly crossed her mind.

"Easy," Violet cautioned. "Say yes, but not like it's a given."

"Oh," Olivia said, shifting her bag—which was much heavier and less practical than her old backpack—from one shoulder to the other. "I mean, sure. Yeah, I think I can make it."

Lark and Eve exchanged curious glances behind Calla's back, but Calla smiled widely and exhaled, lifting her dimpled chin to the clear blue sky. "Great." Calla sighed. "Because I have a kind of big favor to ask."

"A favor?" Olivia repeated, taking a step onto the grass as a carpool of giggling freshman girls piled out of a Lexus SUV and scrambled onto the path.

Calla nodded, twirling her thick black hair at the nape of her neck. "I have nothing to wear," she said plainly. "I'm so sick of everything in my closet, and I haven't been able to stop thinking about that amazing dress you wore to Graham's party."

Olivia drew a bit of air into her lungs. Not only had Calla noticed her at the party, she'd noticed what she was wearing. And she'd *liked it*. Olivia smiled, trying not to notice Violet doing what appeared to be some form of spastic victory dance over a row of yellow tulips.

"Do you remember where you got it?" Calla asked. Eve

pocketed her iPhone and Lark crossed her arms, tapping the outsides of her elbows with long, shiny nails. All eyes were on Olivia.

"Uh-oh," Violet said, freezing midlunge.

Olivia tucked her thumbs into her fists, anxiously digging her nails into the soft, fleshy mounds of her palms.

"Say *something*." Violet panicked, jumping into the middle of the cobblestone path.

"Oh," Olivia managed. "I'm not, I mean, I don't exactly know where—"

"Because I was thinking maybe you could take me sometime," Calla said, inching a few steps toward the double doors. Lark quickly followed and Eve stood to do the same. "I have a peer theater meeting after school today, but I'm free tomorrow, if you are."

Violet was back at Olivia's side, hanging on her shoulder with both hands. "You have no choice," she said. "She's asking you to take her shopping. That's girl for *be my friend*. If you say no, you're missing a very big opportunity, and who knows when the next one will be."

Olivia tucked her hair behind one ear, pulling at the corner of her lower lip with her teeth as she followed the girls inside.

"That is," Violet continued dramatically, "if there is a next one."

Calla held the door open for Olivia as Lark and Eve stood impatiently on the other side.

"Sure," Olivia said, and felt Violet start breathing again as they stepped into the lobby. "Sounds fun."

Calla held out her hands on both sides of her hips, palms up. "Thank you," she exhaled. "You're a lifesaver."

She tossed Olivia a wink before spinning on her heels and linking her arm into the crook of Lark's elbow. Eve waved and the threesome started through the lobby, passing Bess at the reception desk and disappearing down the hall.

"So," a small voice started behind her. "What do you think?"

Olivia had completely forgotten about Miles, who had apparently been hanging by her side the whole time, his brown eyes eager and blinking.

"We don't have that much time until the adaptations are due," he said, hooking his thumbs in the pockets of his baggy cargo pants. "We could get to work at my house after school today, if you want."

Olivia's head was swimming, and half of her had already waltzed down the arched corridor after Calla, so the sound of her own voice echoing against the polished lobby floors came as a surprise.

"Sure," it said, like a dreamy, broken record. "Sounds fun."

16

"My mom's a freak for Zimbabwe."

Olivia sat on a couch in the middle of Miles and Bowie's living room. The apartment, a high-ceilinged duplex by the park, was decorated in dark reds and oranges and crowded with a dizzying collection of African art. It had taken Olivia's eyes a few moments to focus on any one thing, as handcrafted sculptures and small, ambiguously functional pieces of furniture seemed to be stuffed into every square inch of the space.

"She does these documentaries about women in third-world countries," Bowie explained, helping herself to a handful of cashews from a wooden bowl carved in the shape of a lily pad. "She says if she's not being threatened or shot at, she's not filming in the right place."

The couch was skeletal, more like the bare frame of a futon, and covered in a yellow tapestry with a giant red sun at its center. Olivia sat at one end and Miles leaned over a square arm at the other, pulling out a three-ring binder from his bag. Violet had decided that school projects were a punishment only the living should have to endure, and had opted instead to eavesdrop on a bickering couple at the coffee shop on the corner.

"So I was in the shower this morning and I had an idea," Miles said, immediately flushing purple from the neck up. Olivia slipped her feet out of her new boots and tucked them beneath her on the sofa, trying not to picture Miles in the shower.

"I mean, I was thinking," he continued after nervously clearing his throat. "It seems like, in the book, the Ramsays are just totally stuck in the past. And Lily, the main character, she wants to move forward. And it's kind of like today, how some people are just in total denial about the threat of global warming, which is really, you know, real, and—"

"You can't be serious," Bowie spat from her perch on an angular and armless wooden chair. "Miles, it's fiction. Not everything has to be about saving the environment."

"See?" Miles said, pointing an accusatory finger in Bowie's direction. "That's exactly what I'm talking about. Until people are willing to accept that this is *happening* . . ."

Olivia let their bickering wash into background static as she gazed around the room. An unfinished claw-foot coffee table stretched out in front of the couch, and a handful of framed family photos were displayed from end to end: Miles and his mother, looking elegant and holding up a heavy glass award; Bowie and her mother baking in the kitchen, frosting stuck to their fingers and hair; Miles, Bowie, and Bowie's mom, goofing around on a movie set, Bowie mugging for the camera while Miles diligently maneuvered sound equipment, a giant microphone poised overhead.

"Olivia?" Miles called from across the couch. "Hello?"

Olivia jumped and looked up. "What happened?" she asked, her voice startled and panicked.

Bowie laughed. "I was just praying that you had a better idea," she pleaded. "You know, maybe one that wouldn't put people in a coma."

"Shut up." Miles snapped his binder closed. "You're not even in our class. What are you doing here, anyway?"

"I live here," Bowie answered sweetly, a salted cashew balanced precariously between her top and bottom teeth.

Olivia looked from Bowie to Miles, who was nibbling at his thumbnail and furrowing his brow. She glanced back to the framed photos on the table and suddenly had an idea. "What if we made a movie?" she asked.

Miles looked up from his binder and leaned forward on his knees. "A movie?" he asked. "You mean, like, filming a scene from the book?"

Bowie smiled, clapping her hands free of cashew dust. "That's more like it," she said, as sounds of the front door creaking open and footsteps clacking across the hall wafted up from downstairs. Bowie hopped to her feet.

"And *that* is my cue," she whispered, running for the hallway and ducking her head back inside. "If Caroline asks, I'm in my room studying. As I have been all afternoon."

Olivia looked to Miles, who rolled his big brown eyes. "She's on probation," he explained. "Caroline's her mother. God forbid she call her *mom*."

Olivia smiled, remembering the days of covering for Violet. At the time, it had been a chore, always having to come up with some excuse for where her sister was, or why she would

123

be late. Now it was just another fuzzy memory from a life that belonged to somebody else.

"So," Miles said, turning back to his notes. "Are you serious about this movie idea?"

Olivia shrugged, picking at a loose thread at the hem of her new dark denim, high-waisted jeans. "I like to write," she offered quietly. She still hadn't cracked any of her old journals, but lately she'd been missing the way it felt, curling up with a crisp lined notebook and a glossy ballpoint pen. "I could come up with some kind of a script, and you could film it. It wouldn't be so bad."

"Film what?" Bowie's mom called out from the kitchen, dropping two canvas bags full of groceries on the low center island. "Hi, Olivia."

Olivia smiled and started to stand, following Miles into the kitchen.

"We're working on a project for school," Miles explained. "Do you think we could borrow a camera?"

Caroline flipped her dark-rimmed glasses up over her short, choppy hair, pinned back from her face with what looked like a hundred tiny bobby pins, and began unloading colorful piles of vegetables onto the kitchen table. "You know the rules," she said, inspecting the stems on a fat bunch of asparagus. "Use whatever you want, just as long as I get a producer's credit."

Caroline winked at Olivia and passed her the asparagus. "Do you mind trimming these?" she asked, reaching for a heavy wooden cutting board and a knife. "They had the most amazing morels at the farmer's market today, and there's this asparagus bread pudding recipe I've been dying to try."

Olivia took the asparagus and the knife, holding them away from her like artifacts from a lost civilization. Noting her hesitation, Miles gently took the knife, showing her how to slice off the coarse, white ends in precise, diagonal cuts.

The front door creaked open again and a voice called out from downstairs.

"Hello?" Phoebe Greer draped her tailored suit jacket over a six-foot-tall sculpture of a grazing giraffe and started up the spiral stairs.

Olivia glanced up through the long kitchen windows at the slope of the park below. The sun was still shining through the leafy cover of trees, mottling the concrete paths with geometric patterns of light. She could count on one hand the number of times her mother had come home from the office before dark, and here were not one, but *two* moms, together in the kitchen at 5 p.m.

"Hi, love," Caroline called out in greeting, squeezing past Olivia to lower a mesh carton of juicy red strawberries down onto a shelf in the fridge. "How was your day?"

"A total drag," Bowie droned melodramatically, jumping out from her room at the end of the hall.

Bowie kissed each woman European style on both cheeks, while Olivia and Miles squished against the table to make room. The kitchen area was not exceptionally spacious, and all five of them were squeezed in there together, lounging between the sink, a bare round dining table, and the hall.

Olivia glanced up from the cutting board, remembering back to what passed for a family dinner in her house. Her parents still seemed to be giving each other the silent treatment after Sunday night's debacle.

"Hi, Olivia," Phoebe said, laying a hand on her shoulder. "You're staying for dinner, I hope?"

Olivia watched as Caroline flitted from the sink to the stove, readying ingredients and searching through cupboards for bowls. She imagined the four of them sitting down at the table, passing plates, happily crowded and talking over one another to be heard. Her heart ached at the idea of being a part of something so . . . alive.

But then she thought of Violet, waiting for her at the edge of the park. And she thought of her father, eating takeout from plastic containers, standing up in the kitchen, or sitting alone in front of the flickering TV.

"I would love to," Olivia said softly. "But I should probably get home. My parents will be wondering where I am. We always have dinner together."

The lie felt heavy and awkward coming out of her mouth, but nobody seemed to notice. And for a moment, Olivia felt like it could have been true.

As she said her good-byes and let herself out onto the street, her shadow stretching long and dark across the sidewalk, she let the idea linger, as if taking it out for a test drive. She *could* be a girl, like any other girl, walking home to dinner on the table, or parents who talked to her and each other. She *could* be a girl with a life that was whole, the way her life had been before.

She *could* be normal, she thought. But, as she rounded the corner to her street, she saw her building, the dangling, crooked shingles, and the heaps of debris outside waiting for a trip to the dump. And she saw Violet, the invisible ghost of her once-dead sister, crouched at the corner of her stoop. And that was when she remembered:

This was her life, and there wasn't anything normal about it.

17

*O*livia turned up the volume on her iPod and was settling into a comfortable jog, her feet thudding against the smooth pavement around Lake Merced, when she realized she was being quietly gained on. It was the first day of a cross-country unit in gym class, and it took her a few moments to identify the grungy old New Balances sneaking up alongside her as belonging to a certain green-eyed Adonis.

Olivia had been avoiding Soren to the best of her ability since Graham's party, which hadn't been hard, as their only class together was gym. The class had met once earlier in the week, where Olivia had been horrified to learn that the physical education curriculum at Golden Gate included a unit on yoga, taught by a pigtailed instructor named Morningstar. Olivia had quickly determined that there were certain ways her body was not meant to bend, and so the introduction of twice-weekly jogging field trips around the lake couldn't have come at a better time.

Olivia wasn't even halfway through her first lap around the

lake when she realized that Soren was hovering beside her, his feet landing on the pavement in short, choppy strokes.

"Sorry," Olivia stammered, looking up and noting an expectant sparkle in his emerald eyes. "Did you say something?"

"Oh, I was just giving you the answers to life's biggest riddles," he said. "Too bad you were listening to your iPod."

Olivia smiled and slowed her pace to match his lazy, shuffling stride.

"Anything good?" he asked, gesturing to the silver mini she was gripping in her palm.

She racked her brain for the hippest and most obscure indie band she could remember from Violet's quickly shifting groupie allegiances, silently cursing her sister's resolute commitment to steering clear of gym class (and, for that matter, any type of rigorous physical activity). And what was that band Bowie had mentioned at the party? The Lion Kings?

Ultimately, Olivia settled on the truth. "Beethoven," she offered uneasily. "'The Moonlight Sonata'."

If Soren was surprised, he did a good job of hiding it. He pushed his lower lip forward, nodding, and Olivia wasn't sure if it was a gesture of approval or disgust, but it was too late to turn back now.

"Classical music keeps me calm while I run," she explained. Olivia had been something of an accidental track star at Willis, and even held a record for the mile. Running was always something that came naturally to her, but she didn't care much for competing. On the bus before meets, the team captains—a pair of senior girls with matching shorts and taut, hairless limbs—would lead raucous cheers to pump up the team. Olivia would watch their mouths move in silence, their fists punching the air like they were ridiculous, angry puppets, while a soothing string quartet played on her headphones. That was one chapter of her old life she was happy to leave behind. But she did miss running, the freedom she felt as she flew around the track.

Soren, on the other hand, seemed to be more of a Sunday stroller.

"Beethoven, huh? I'll have to try that sometime." He smiled, looking off toward the water, where a family of tourists in orange life vests was posing for a picture and nearly capsizing their rented rowboat in the process. "I usually just count the number of botched photo ops on the lake."

He ducked his head in a bit closer, his elbow accidentally brushing hers and spiking the little hairs on her forearm to attention. "In case you haven't noticed," he stage-whispered, "I'm not much of a runner."

Olivia grinned, shrugging. "I thought you were just enjoying the scenery," she joked, lifting her eyes to meet his. His face was open, his lips slightly parted and approaching a smile, his teeth overcrowded and imperfect in a way that softened the rest of his chiseled features. He seemed more comfortable here than he had been at the party, and there was something about the way he held her gaze that made her feel instantly at ease.

"Not bad, huh?" Soren gestured with the clean line of his jaw at the sprawling green on either side, against a backdrop of painted rooftops and giant sky.

"Definitely beats yoga," Olivia agreed.

Soren considered her skeptically from beneath his thick

lashes. From this angle, Olivia decided that he was almost too pretty.

"Oh, come on," he said, kicking a fallen branch out of his way with the side of his muddy sneaker. "You were a natural."

Olivia's heart tightened, little red splotches spreading at the base of her throat. He had noticed her in yoga? Her feet automatically hit the pavement in heavier, shorter strides, pulling a foot or two in front of him as they followed the path under a canopy of tangled cherry blossoms, the hanging pink petals blurring in her vision overhead.

"So how are you liking the city so far?" he called out from behind her. His voice shook a little bit, like he was trying to keep from talking too loud but was afraid she wouldn't hear him.

Olivia slowed until he'd caught up again, looking down at her maroon-and-silver Nikes as they matched his sluggish pace, step for step. She'd never thought about it before, but running with somebody else felt a little bit like dancing.

"It's great," she said. "I mean, I haven't really done much of the tourist stuff yet."

Olivia half expected him to laugh, or tell her she wasn't missing much. There was something about being the new girl in a city so fabled that was a little embarrassing. It seemed much cooler to be the jaded traveler than the wide-eyed transplant.

But instead, Soren turned to her, his eyes quick and serious. "You have to do it all," he said with genuine concern. "I mean, there's some stuff you can skip. Fisherman's Wharf is always crazy crowded and kind of lame, but it's still worth seeing. And then there's Golden Gate Park, Coit Tower, the Presidio, the farmer's market at the Ferry Building. . . ."

Olivia felt her shoulders relaxing as he talked. Usually, talking to guys made her feel like she was on trial. But Soren was different. He kind of reminded her of a little kid.

"I have a question," she started, feeling suddenly braver. "I mean, I can pretty much guess, but I've technically never been, so I was just wondering . . . what exactly is a farmer's market?"

The only market Olivia had ever been to was of the *super* variety, and she'd pretty much assumed that farmers only existed in paintings and history books. Ever since Bowie's mom had returned with overflowing bags of vegetables that looked freshly picked, Olivia had been curious about where they came from.

"You've never been to a farmer's market?" Soren asked. His voice was light and free of judgment, like he was simply excited for her to finally find out. "There are a bunch of them around the city," he explained as they rounded a corner of the shimmering lake. "But Saturday at the Ferry Building is the best. Farmers from all over the area bring whatever's in season, and there are tons of amazing samples. Skip breakfast and you can make a whole meal out of just tasting things. . . ."

Olivia smiled and listened, watching Soren as he animatedly gestured with his hands. They were coming up around the final bend, and Olivia felt a shade of disappointment creep up around her heart. Soon they'd be back at school. Maybe he'd wave or smile in the hall, but she knew they wouldn't get another chance like this to really talk.

But she kept smiling and nodding as Soren went on about

the various vendors and their farming techniques. She realized that along with the subtle disappointment, another, more foreign sensation rumbled inside of her, a physical feeling she had almost forgotten how to recognize.

She was hungry.

18

Olivia hustled through the crowded lobby after school with Violet hopping up and down beside her. The girls' volleyball team, led by Lark, the team's captain, was parading en masse out of the locker room and down the hall. Violet was snaking in between them, craning her neck for a better look.

"I knew we should've left class early," Violet worried. "What if we already missed her?"

Violet had been prepping Olivia all afternoon for her shopping trip with Calla, and Olivia had done her best to pay attention. But she'd left gym class that morning in a hazy fog, mentally replaying and analyzing excerpts from her lakeside conversation with Soren. Needless to say, the idea of spending time with his girlfriend was a little bit of a downer.

"There she is," Violet screeched, pointing through the glass to one of the dark wooden benches outside. Calla looked lovely as ever in a faded scarlet tunic with golden sarilike embellishments at the collar, stretchy indigo jeans, and a bright yellow circle scarf slung around her neck.

She was chattering into her iPhone, and Olivia stood quietly off to the side so as not to interrupt. "No problem," she said sweetly into the phone, indicating with a smile and one finger that she'd be just a minute.

Olivia glanced across the street to where Eve and Graham were attempting to double-mount a rusty orange beach cruiser.

"Sorry," Calla said to Olivia, tucking her phone into the inside pocket of her extra-large tote. "I'd asked my dad's driver to take us around today, but it's so nice out I thought maybe we could walk instead. Do you mind?"

"Sure," Olivia agreed. "I mean, no. I don't mind."

Calla smiled and folded her patched army coat into her bag. Olivia suddenly felt like a snowman in her heavy winter peacoat, and was wondering how casually she might be able to slip out of it, as Calla waved to Eve across a line of carpool traffic.

"Hey, guys," Calla called. Graham was now standing on the pedals as Eve attempted to balance between the cruiser-style handlebars. "What, no helmets?" She laughed.

"We're only going to Amoeba," Eve called back. "I thought you had a lit mag meeting today."

"Change of plans," Calla said, linking arms with Olivia. "We're going shopping."

They turned onto Haight Street and had hardly walked a block when Olivia noticed that just about every person they passed—from the clusters of runaway teens to old men push-ing grocery carts, to camera-toting tourists at spinning postcard racks—stopped to watch Calla as she passed. A few of the more brazen onlookers whistled or called out, and if Calla noticed, she didn't let on.

"I didn't even ask you where we're going," Calla said as they waited at a crosswalk, her smile easy and infectious. "I hope it's somewhere nearby."

Olivia felt her pulse quickening, Posey's warning about telling anybody about the shop echoing in her ears. As if summoned, Violet hustled up beside her, grabbing Olivia by her other arm.

"Don't worry, O," Violet said. "You're not giving anything away. And besides, you saw how slow things were at Posey's. You'd be doing her a favor."

Olivia clenched her teeth, doubting Violet's logic but forcing herself to at least pretend to believe it.

"It's near Dolores Park," Olivia told her.

"Okay." Calla shrugged happily. "A bit of a hike, but I'm up for it if you are."

Olivia nodded and smiled. Her legs were sore from the two miles she'd run that morning with Soren in gym, but somehow she didn't think this was appropriate information to share.

"Oh, I bet I know," Calla guessed. "Is it that little boutique with the handmade baby onesies? I swear, everything in there smells like candy. I'm, like, instantly starving, the second I walk in."

"Um, no," Olivia stuttered, realizing it would probably be better to prepare Calla ahead of time for Posey's shop. "It's actually not much of a store. More like a . . . custom-design studio."

Olivia held her breath, expecting Calla to stop short or turn around, or at least pry for more details. But she kept walking, untangling her flowing dark hair from under the thick strap of her tote, and smiling over her shoulder at Olivia. "I love it already."

🦋 🦋 🦋

"Butterfly," Calla announced as they turned a corner at the park.

Violet whipped her head around, locking eyes with Olivia.

"What . . . where?" Olivia asked carefully, watching as Calla took a few steps backward and out into the street. Calla pointed up at the shabby awning, which appeared even older and grimier, caught in the unforgiving glare of the late-afternoon sun. For the first time, Olivia noticed a row of chipped, crooked letters, painted on the underside of the faded fabric. Either Posey's grandmother had been going for a mysterious, windblown advertising effect, or the awning had been hung upside down.

"*Mariposa*," Calla read. "It means *butterfly* in Spanish."

Olivia shared a quick, charged glance with Violet before clearing her throat.

"Let me guess," Calla said, squinting with a sly smile. "You take French."

She didn't wait for an answer, skipping across the curb and peering curiously through the darkened window.

Olivia forced a choppy laugh and followed Calla inside, her stomach turning anxious flips.

"Hello?" Olivia called out to the seemingly empty shop, as soon as the chimes had stopped tinkling overhead.

"Wow." Calla sighed, glancing around at the mannequins,

which were even creepier than Olivia had remembered. "It's like a museum."

Olivia peered around a corner, to where a narrow spiral staircase led to a door in the ceiling.

"Posey?" Olivia called upstairs, listening for footsteps.

Calla crossed the room to where an embroidered wedding gown was draped in plastic over one arm of the ratty old couch. "So how does this work?" she asked Olivia. "You just tell her what you want and she makes it for you?"

Violet squatted on the arm of a rocking chair. "Yeah," she muttered. "Or she makes you something else, which may or may not have the ability to bring people back from the dead."

Olivia shot Violet a hidden glare before turning to Calla. "Maybe we should come back," Olivia said delicately. "I think she usually does these things by appointment."

"You're kidding," Calla said, her hazel eyes darkening with disappointment. "That's too bad. I had such a good feeling about this. And my feelings are so rarely wrong, you see. . . ."

Calla smiled and Violet cocked her head up toward the staircase, urging Olivia to investigate.

"Let me see if she's upstairs," Olivia said uncertainly, before gripping the loose railings and gingerly climbing up.

She rapped gently on the ceiling and pushed the hatch open. A warm gust of air whooshed past her ears as she hoisted herself up, lifting the top half of her body into what appeared to be a cluttered kitchen.

"Hello?" she called out. "Posey? It's Olivia. I have a friend with me and—"

Hurried footsteps approached the stairs and Olivia glimpsed a pair of old leather clogs shuffling around a corner. Feeling suddenly like an intruder, Olivia let the door fall shut and scurried back down the stairs.

"She's coming," she announced to Calla, who was casually flipping through a book of sewing patterns. "I think."

Calla shrugged, as if to say she was in no rush, and turned a page.

The heavy door creaked open and Olivia looked up to see Posey leveraging her miniature frame down the spiral stairs.

"Oh, hi," Olivia called up. "Sorry. I just wanted to let you know we were here."

Posey nodded and, without saying a word, moved silently and awkwardly toward the desk. "Full house today, huh?" Posey said, lowering herself into the cracked leather armchair tucked behind the desk. "I take it you want another dress."

Violet looked quickly to Olivia as Olivia's eyes grew round. She hadn't even thought about the dress she'd need for herself.

"Oh," she said quickly. "Well, yeah. But also, my friend Calla—"

Olivia opened her arm to include Calla, who had already scurried to her side.

"Hi," Calla said, extending a warm hand. "I saw what you did for Olivia last weekend. The black gabardine, right? I am completely obsessed and have seriously been daydreaming about something like it ever since."

Posey glanced at Calla's outstretched fingers as if they were an alien life-form she wasn't quite sure how to process, before turning her attention back to a pile of loose receipts.

"I hope we're not interrupting," Calla said with genuine alarm.

Posey, in turn, said nothing.

Olivia looked to where Violet was crouching on the rickety desk, her jaw swinging open and her arms flailing in disgust.

"No," Olivia stepped in, suddenly feeling protective and eager to make Calla feel comfortable. "Posey's just surprised to see me back so soon, I bet. Right?"

Posey looked up and met Olivia's desperate stare. "Never saw it coming," she replied, her voice dripping with dry irony.

Olivia felt Calla's shoulders relaxing as she wandered from one mannequin to another.

"Well, how about if I tell you what I was hoping for, and you can tell *me* if I'm totally out of my mind," Calla joked, laying a hand on the shoulder of a long-sleeved crimson sheath.

"Please don't touch that," Posey asked, settling into her chair. "And yes. You are."

"Holy PMS," Violet gasped.

Olivia watched as a tiny vein in Posey's neck throbbed.

"Well," Calla said, slowly lowering her hand to her side. "Maybe this is a bad time. I guess I should come back when I can give you more notice."

Calla strolled back toward the door before turning and smiling warmly at Posey. "It was nice meeting you," she said. "You do beautiful work."

Posey bowed her head. "Thank you," she muttered, and Olivia finally exhaled.

Calla pressed through the door, turning back to Olivia. "Coming?" she asked.

Olivia nodded. "Just a sec," she said, nodding back to Posey. Calla smiled politely and stepped through to the street.

Olivia leaned across the desk toward Posey. "I'm really sorry," she said. "I don't know what I was thinking."

Posey shrugged, refusing to make meaningful eye contact as she stuffed a pile of receipts into a manila envelope.

"Do you still want your dress or not?" she asked.

Olivia felt like leaping across the room and hugging her, but managed to restrain herself to a simple "Yes, please."

Outside, Calla was ruffling through her bag for a purple Nalgene water bottle.

"I'm so sorry," Olivia gushed. "I had no idea she'd react that way."

Calla took a sip and waved the apology away. "Don't even worry about it," she insisted. "Creative people are always moody. You don't get to pick and choose clients if you don't have talent."

Olivia nodded as Calla threaded her slender, tanned arms through the sleeves of her green army coat. The wind had started to pick up and the sun was hiding behind a low layer of clouds.

"I guess I should do the usual shopping rounds," Calla sighed. "I can't believe how long I've waited to deal with this. It's been, like, nonstop planning, helping my mom get everything together."

Olivia nodded with what she hoped was a sympathetic smile, hugging her arms to her waist, keeping warm against the chill.

"Oh, well." Calla smiled, checking the clunky, leather-strapped men's watch she wore around one slender wrist.

"Oh, my God! My mom is going to lose it. I'm supposed to meet her at the caterer's in ten minutes. Apparently there was some kind of shellfish crisis. . . ."

Violet made a face and Olivia laughed. Luckily, Calla did too.

"See you tomorrow?" Calla asked.

Olivia nodded. "Sure," she said, hefting her book tote higher up her arm and bringing her loose, wavy ponytail down over one shoulder.

Calla turned on her worn gold gladiator flats and waved as she crossed the street. "Wish me luck!" she called back to Olivia. "Oh, and thanks again for trying."

"Anytime," Olivia answered, and realized that she'd meant it.

19

Olivia and Violet sat in the back of a musty-smelling cab, bottlenecked at the entrance to Golden Gate Park. The wide avenues of the city dead-ended into a lush, dense forest, and in the distance Olivia could just make out the winding paths snaking in and out of exotic trees and plants.

"Enough," Violet said as Olivia glanced anxiously from her watch to the window for the seventeenth time since they'd left the house. "Nobody gets to these things on time, anyway."

Olivia nodded and began absentmindedly picking at the hem of her dress, which Posey had left in a familiar folded bag at the top of the Larsens' stoop late the night before.

After the disastrous encounter at the shop with Calla, Olivia worried that Posey might not come through this time, or worse, lock her into wearing something heinous. But one glimpse inside the dusty garment bag had laid all of Olivia's fears quietly to rest.

The dress couldn't have been more different from the first gown Posey had made, although the effect was the same. For starters, it was short, much shorter than anything Olivia had ever worn before. And it was strapless. But the silver bodice was constructed from layers of bunched tulle and was busy enough to make Olivia feel like she wasn't fully exposed, while still managing to be both sexy and understated.

"Damn," Violet had said when Olivia first tried it on. "What that girl lacks in personality she certainly makes up for in style."

Now, as Violet spotted Olivia anxiously tugging at the bottom of the clinging skirt, she swatted her sister's hand away. "Cut that out," she said. "The fastest way to ruin a great outfit is to fidget."

Olivia folded her hands in her lap, successfully keeping them still for all of three seconds before she began anxiously picking at her fingernails.

"Relax!" Violet commanded. "What can we do to calm you down?"

Olivia shrugged and turned her attention back toward the window, where what looked like a sea of blurring brake lights stretched out ahead of them, red and pulsing as far as the eye could see.

"Maybe we should get out here and walk," Olivia said, leaning forward through the glass divider as Violet held out an arm and forced her sister back into her seat. She had seen a sign for the Academy of Sciences a few yards back, and figured they couldn't be far.

"I have a better idea," Violet said slyly. "Let's talk about what you're going to wish for tonight."

Olivia sighed heavily, settling back into the upholstered seat. She closed her eyes, just as the traffic started to move, picking up into a steady slide against the dark, wet pavement.

"You have something amazing here," Violet continued. "I've been trying to stay quiet because I know you're not exactly the wishing type. But think about it. Anything you want to happen can happen. You just have to decide what that is."

Olivia squeezed her eyes tightly shut, searching the deepest crevices of her brain for inspiration.

Anything, she thought. *I can have anything.*

But still, her mind drew a big fat blank.

Before she'd known she could wish for things, she probably wouldn't have had so much trouble at least coming up with ideas. And before Violet had come back, the only thing that she'd ever dreamed about was one more day with her sister. But now that Violet was here, right here beside her again, wishing for anything else seemed frivolous and fake. She had her sister back. What more could she want?

Olivia opened her eyes, just as a great lawn and pillared, domed structure came into view.

"Here you go," the grumpy driver barked from the front seat as the cab slowed to a stop at the bottom of a long, wide staircase.

"Saved by the taxi," Violet groaned as Olivia reached into her purse for her wallet.

She stepped out onto the damp grass and straightened the ruffled layers of her skirt, looking up at the modern building and sleek revolving doors. "How do I look?" Olivia asked quietly, turning back to her sister.

Violet smiled, already skipping up the stairs toward the door. "Like me," she said. "Only better."

W W W

"Is this thing even on?" Calla was standing on a square, raised platform, tapping a microphone against the palm of her hand and conferring with a scruffy-faced guy in a pin-striped suit, earlier introduced as iWIN's cultural ambassador.

The Academy of Sciences, Olivia had decided, was basically a science museum on steroids. A glass-walled cafeteria enclosed in the middle of the atrium had been set up as a posh bar and buffet, and looking in from the other side gave the scene a sort of exhibition effect, as if the partygoers themselves, sipping champagne from flutes or nibbling on organic munchies, were part of a real-life diorama.

On either side of the building were two enormous bio-domes, one an enclosed, living rain forest, with hanging vines and flowering plants pressed up against the glass, and the other a high-tech planetarium. Neither exhibit was open for the reception, but just being sandwiched between them made Olivia feel cultured and important.

"She even makes public speaking look fun," Violet marveled from where she was sitting cross-legged on a table doubling as exhibition space. Olivia glanced at her smiling sister and felt a hard lump in her throat. Most of the time, it was easy to forget that Violet wasn't actually there. But during moments like this, when the contrast against real life was so stark—the rest of the room in their elegant black-tie and Violet looking like she'd stepped off the beach in her ratty denim shorts, bare knees, and long, pale arms—it was too much to think about.

"Thanks everybody so much for coming," Calla shouted into the now-working microphone to a round of warm applause. "I know my mom told you a little bit about the work we've been doing and how important your contributions are, and I just wanted to remind you that volunteering doesn't have to be, you know, building houses or going all the way to Africa. . . ."

The crowd laughed agreeably and Olivia looked around the room.

"In fact," Calla went on, "some friends and I have been planning a project of our own at Golden Gate Prep, and you don't have to look any further than your closet to help!"

Olivia heard Violet whistle and turned around. "Oh, hello there," Violet cooed flirtatiously, waggling her eyebrows until Olivia followed her gaze. Standing by himself, just a few feet away from her and leaning over an EarthBox display, was Soren. His straw-colored hair was neatly combed, his face freshly shaven, and he looked endearingly uncomfortable in penguin shoes and a pressed steel gray suit. He glanced up and their eyes met for a moment before Olivia turned quickly back to face the stage.

"We've decided to start our very own thrift store," Calla announced to the crowd, but Olivia was hardly paying attention. The fuzzy shape of Soren was getting closer in her periphery, and Olivia's breath tangled in her lungs.

"All proceeds will go to charities like this one," Calla went on. "We'll be taking donations starting next week, and we're planning a really exciting fundraiser. . . ."

Calla's voice faded out as Olivia turned to find Soren, now planted directly at her side. His hands were in his pockets and one of his elbows was so close to her arm, she could almost feel the cool fabric of his coat against her skin.

"I put in a request for Beethoven," Soren said, gesturing to a high school jazz trio in the corner of the room, quietly stumbling through African beats. "They said it wasn't in their repertoire."

Olivia smiled and held her shoulders back, straightening the clean, strapless line of her dress. "Amateurs," she joked.

Soren's fake-serious frown gave way to a goofy smile, the sides of his cheeks turning red. He gestured back to the exhibit behind them and cleared his throat.

"Did you read about the living roof?" he asked, taking a few steps back toward the display. Olivia followed and pretended to study a series of photographs detailing the Academy's innovative rooftop garden. "It's pretty awesome," Soren continued, pointing at a pair of blue jeans hanging from a line on clothespins. "The whole building is insulated with denim instead of fiberglass."

Olivia nodded, the way somebody who appreciated fiberglass might nod, but couldn't stop noticing the adorable way that Soren kept tugging at his starched shirt collar, or accidentally dipping the sleeve of his open coat into the decorative mounds of dirt.

"There you are." A crisp voice suddenly broke in from over Olivia's shoulder. Olivia hadn't even realized that Calla had left the stage, and suddenly there she was, holding a pair of champagne flutes and offering one to Olivia. "I was hoping you guys would get to meet tonight."

Calla moved to Soren's side, linking her arm inside the crook of his elbow. Her gown was pale green, to pick up the emerald flecks in her hazel eyes, and made from sleek, slippery satin. On anyone else it would have looked like lingerie, but somehow, draped across her honey-colored skin, the dress looked sophisticated and elegant.

"Sorry, babe. I could only steal two," Calla said to Soren's profile, holding up her drink. Soren shrugged and glanced uncomfortably at the polished bamboo floor. "Have you tried one of these yet?" Calla asked Olivia.

"Um, no," Olivia managed, trying to focus less on the frantic flutter in her stomach and more on her drink, which was light pink in color and gently carbonated. "What's in it?"

Calla shrugged. "It's like a Bellini, but stronger," she said, taking a small sip and smiling.

Olivia nodded, going for a look that said, *Yes, Bellini, of course. My favorite!* when actually all the name conjured was a scrolling list of Italian film directors and executed Fascists.

Soren freed his arm from Calla's grasp and pulled back his sleeve, as if searching for a watch that wasn't there. "My parents want to introduce me to some musician guy they said was going to be here." He gestured vaguely toward the buffet. "I should go find them." He started across the room, briefly turning to Olivia as he passed. "It was nice meeting you," he said, his voice oddly formal and precise.

Olivia nodded and smiled. "Me, too," she said. "I mean . . . yeah."

Olivia's heart skipped as she prayed that Calla hadn't noticed her blubbering fumble. But Calla was already following Soren away from the exhibition table, turning to smile at Olivia, and rolling her eyes as she passed. Olivia watched the couple walk away, her heart twisting and her eyes glazing over as they disappeared into the well-dressed crowd.

"You're drooling." Violet laughed suddenly from over her shoulder.

Olivia abruptly turned her back to the room, pretending to be absorbed in an exhibit at a table in the corner, this one about solar ovens and sustainable yurts. "What are you talking about?"

Violet perched on the table and tossed her sister a knowing grin. "Perhaps you've forgotten the time last fall when you decided you were obsessed with a certain tennis-playing senior," she recalled. "And I guessed it before you'd even been to a single match?"

Olivia shrugged. "I don't know what you're talking about," she said steadily under her breath, but she could hear the stubborn smile in her own voice.

Violet crossed her arms and tapped her long fingers slowly against her elbows.

"Even if I *was* . . . interested . . . in somebody here," Olivia said quietly, "which I am absolutely not . . . it's not like it would matter. He has a girlfriend. What's the point?"

"What's the *point*?" Violet repeated, her voice becoming gravelly and almost harsh. "You know, life doesn't have to be something you watch happen to everybody else. You say you want things to change, but nothing's going to change until you change it."

Olivia looked quizzically at her sister. "I don't know what you want me to do," she whispered, glancing around her periphery for partygoers nearby. This was exactly what she *didn't* want to happen tonight: Not only had she found herself, as usual, standing all alone in the corner, but even worse, she was standing in the corner, arguing with a ghost.

Violet rooted herself firmly on the table and stared into her sister's eyes. "What I want you to do is to admit that you really *want* something for once," Violet said. "In a perfect world, it would be *you* with the guy."

Violet tossed her hair toward the rear of the room, where Calla was leading Soren through the back door and into a lantern-strewn sculpture garden.

"And not just any guy. *That* guy," Violet whispered. "Come on. Live a little," she teased.

Olivia smiled sadly and rolled her eyes. "I wish you were right," she said softly, her eyes blurring over. "But you know it's not that easy."

Violet linked her arm into Olivia's and pulled her in for a long, suffocating hug.

"I don't know . . ." Violet said, her voice low and plotting. "With a little help from me, it just might be."

20

"**F**armers are hot."

Olivia and Violet were standing at the outskirts of a white sea of tents, trying to stay out of the way of bargain-hunting shoppers on a mission for the freshest produce Northern California had to offer.

The night before, as Olivia changed into her pajamas after the gala, Violet had insisted that they do some more sightseeing the next morning. Olivia had told her about the places Soren had mentioned on their run, laying casual emphasis on the Ferry Building market and secretly hoping Soren would be there.

"Seriously." Violet was staring googly-eyed at a rugged-looking guy in overalls, refilling baskets of avocados from heavy crates in the back of a truck. "Why didn't I know this before?"

Olivia smiled and shuffled slowly through the stalls, eyeing careful piles of plump oranges and wooden boxes of loose leafy greens with names she'd never heard of, like rainbow chard. She was helping herself to a tasting sample of hand-churned, herb-rolled cheeses when she heard a voice over her shoulder.

"I thought it was you."

She recognized Soren's skateboard first. Next, his belt. It looked like it must have belonged to his grandfather—the leather was worn and the silver buckle so tarnished that it was almost black.

"Hey." She smiled, balling up the napkin she'd been given by the apron-wearing dairy girl behind the table.

Soren reached across to help himself to a piece of bread and cheese.

"This is so weird," he said, shaking his head with a bemused little smile.

She looked away as he popped the crostini into his mouth. There was nothing more awkward than watching a guy you liked chew up close.

"What's weird?" she asked, trying to sound casual. *Farmer's market, rainbow chard, randomly running into each other in the dairy tent?* "Cheese?"

Soren smiled, searching for little crumbs at the corners of his lips with the back of one hand. "No," he said, squeezing out of the way of a couple bickering in rapid-fire Chinese. "I just had a feeling I might see you here."

Olivia felt a pull at the sleeve of the open white linen shirt Violet had insisted she wear over a denim wrap-dress and thick gray tights. Olivia thought the look was way too floppy and disheveled, but she was gradually realizing that her own fashion instincts were probably better off ignored.

Olivia shook her arm carefully loose and tried to do something with her hair, something that looked casual and sexy and carefree, but most likely came off as some sort of tic.

"So what do you think?" Soren asked, bending down to lift his skateboard and tucking it under one arm. "Your very first farmer's market, huh?"

"It's awesome," Olivia gushed. "I never knew there were so many different kinds of cheese."

Violet might have tried not to laugh, but she failed. "Okay," she managed, catching her breath as Olivia's neck bloomed a thousand shades of red. "Let's step away from the dairy."

Luckily, Soren had a similar idea and turned toward the opposite end of one row.

"Have you hit up any of the prepared-food stands yet?" Once they had wedged their way through the crowd and back out onto the open sidewalk, he dropped his skateboard to the ground and started pushing it along slowly with one foot.

Olivia shook her head beside him. "No, we just—" She hiccupped. "I mean, I just got here a few minutes ago. I had trouble figuring out which bus to take."

Which was a total lie, but it was something to say.

"Yeah, public transportation can be a disaster around here," he allowed. "But you made it, so that's cool."

Olivia felt a heavy moment hanging between them, Soren pushing off on one navy blue Converse sneaker and rolling along. Olivia kept her eyes on the cracks of the sidewalk ahead.

"This used to be a really great skate spot," he said, pointing to a section of the pier with waist-high cement structures and a shallow flight of stairs. "See how the ledges are all waxed up?" He pointed to an iron railing, covered in a maze of discolored stripes and scratches.

Olivia nodded. "How come you can't skate here anymore?"

Soren shrugged, hopping up on a lower step, his board following like it was glued to the soles of his shoes, and gliding back down to the curb. "We got kicked out, like everywhere else."

Olivia expected his face to be hard or bitter, but that perma-smile was still solidly in place. "Doesn't that make you mad?" she asked. She didn't know what it was, but something about his glass-half-full attitude felt almost like a challenge.

Soren stepped hard on one end of his board, grabbing the other end with an open palm. "Nah." He laughed. "I kind of get it. It's always crowded down here, full of tourists. I wouldn't want a bunch of skate rats buzzing around and messing up my home movies, either."

Violet, who had been lagging behind, shook her head in disbelief. "Really?" she said, standing next to Soren with her hands on her hips. "I mean, are you seriously this adorable?"

Olivia bit her lip, pulling back a smile as Soren gestured to a crowded pier at the end of the row of tents. "You've been to the pier already, right?" he asked. Olivia stared at him blankly, and his green eyes grew wide. "Seriously? You haven't seen the sea lions?"

Olivia smiled shyly and shook her head. "I told you," she said. "I'm new."

Soren rolled his eyes and took a few steps toward the fountain at the beginning of the long wooden dock. "All right, new girl," he teased. "If you're going to be a tourist, you might as well do it right."

Olivia hung back, scuffing the tops of her metallic flats against the curb.

"Aren't you coming?" he called back, pausing when he realized she hadn't moved.

Olivia stalled. Should she say she had somewhere else to be? What if somebody saw them?

Violet turned to Olivia, her head tilted sideways, just a hint of impatience brewing in her smiling blue eyes.

"Sea lions?" Violet repeated. "Come on. What's cuter than that?" And with one swift motion, she shoved her sister into the crowd.

🦋 🦋 🦋

"Is this your car?"

After a full hour of gawking at groups of slippery sea lions rolling around the dock, and tasting everything at the market from braised tempeh to rice paper patties, Soren had convinced Olivia to go for a ride. They had left the bustling strip of the Embarcadero (and Violet, who had opted to continue her farmer-prowl) and walked up a narrow side street, until Soren stopped in front of an electric blue Toyota Prius.

"Welcome to the space egg," he gestured, unlocking her door and pulling it open for her to crouch inside. The front and back bumpers were plastered with recycling logos and all of the other earth-loving sentiments a person would expect to find advertised on a hybrid vehicle.

"It was my sister's," he admitted as he squeezed in behind the wheel, looking ridiculously lanky in the cramped, curved space. "She went to NYU last year and didn't need a car. Just another hand-me-down."

Olivia smiled as he pulled out into traffic, expertly navigating a sharp turn and steering them straight up a gravity-defying hill.

"Not that I'm complaining," he clarified. "It does get really good mileage."

Olivia clasped and unclasped her fingers in her lap, suddenly hyperaware of the fact that she was enclosed in such a small space with a boy, let alone a boy who had the potential to melt her into the folds of the fabric upholstery with one sideways look.

"Did I just say that out loud?" he asked, shaking his head. "'Really good mileage'?"

Olivia laughed and felt her shoulders relax, like a marionette suddenly snipped free of its strings.

"I'm sorry," Soren said. "I don't know what's wrong with me. I feel like I can't stop talking, and every time I open my mouth the most ridiculous things are coming out of it. Does that ever happen to you?"

Olivia laughed, a real, Violet-type laugh that she didn't have time to censor. "Um, yeah," she managed. "All the time."

Soren turned quickly to look at her, a tamer version of his usual goofy grin twitching at the corners of his lips.

"Cool." He sighed, then inhaled and exhaled slowly, as if he had forced a pause on himself and was dealing with the consequences. His non-driving knee was jumping furiously against the inside of the door, and he would occasionally tap it with one hand, as if weren't a part of his body he was able to otherwise control.

Olivia glanced at Soren curiously from the corner of her eye. He cleared his throat as he pulled the car over to the side of a narrow street, high in the hills above downtown.

"What's this?" she asked, peeking through the rounded window. They were parked in front of what looked like somebody's front stoop.

"You'll see," Soren said, unlocking the doors and stepping out onto the street.

The closer Olivia got to the bottom of the steps, the more of them she could see, hundreds of tiny little stairs built into the hillside, disappearing high above the rooftops where the trees met the sky. This was definitely more than just somebody's front stoop.

"I thought we might want to walk off some of that rice paper," Soren suggested, taking the first steps two at a time.

Olivia followed suit, and soon found herself surrounded by hanging wildflowers creeping out of cozy backyards. Chatty birds called out, as if beckoning the slowly departing late-afternoon sun to stay just a while longer. It was as if they'd left the busy city and suddenly entered a tropical paradise.

"There's a documentary about these birds," Soren said, pointing to what looked like a chubby parrot, perched on a branch overhead. "There's a dude in one of these houses who feeds them. He gives them names and everything, like Romeo and Juliet or Brad and Angelina. I guess they mate for life, like penguins."

Olivia smiled and tried to respond, but with every step up, steady breathing was becoming more and more of a challenge. Despite his sluggish laps at the lake, Soren proved to be completely comfortable as they trudged up the endless hill of stairs.

"Here we are," he announced as they approached a clearing. Olivia craned her neck up toward the sky and saw that they were at the base of an enormous stone tower.

"Coit Tower," Soren explained. "It's famous. There's a museum inside, from the Depression, and you can go up to the top. But that's not why we're here."

Soren circled her wrist with one strong hand and pulled her up the last remaining steps. Trying to concentrate on her footing and *not* on the fact that they were holding hands (or wrists, but *still*), Olivia followed him to a low brick wall bordering the tower's semicircular grounds.

"This," he said, gesturing his arms wide in a panoramic swipe around him, "is why we're here."

Olivia turned and felt her rib cage swell.

It was the most spectacular view of the city and bay she had seen yet. A deep purple haze lit up the fog and fell dramatically over the Bay Bridge and the little islands just off the coast. The lights of downtown were just starting to twinkle, and the headlights of cars winding up and down Lombard Street looked like ornaments on the zigzagging low branches of a Christmas tree.

"Oh, my God," she gasped, as Soren swung one leg and then the other over the wall, gesturing for her to take a seat. "It's beautiful."

Soren nodded as she settled in beside him, feeling the warmth of his body against hers. Out of the corner of one eye she could see his profile, the clean line of his jaw and soft slope of his nose, the delicate blinking of his long, dark lashes.

The sounds of the city below them blended together like a sort of urban weather, and they sat so quietly and for so long that Olivia found herself wondering if either of them was ever going to speak again.

"Did you have fun at the gala last night?" Soren finally

asked, stuffing his fists into the pockets of his brown leather bomber jacket. Like the belt, the coat looked like it had a story to tell, with worn, buttery patches at the elbows and a missing button on one sleeve.

"Yeah," Olivia said, swallowing a mouthful of air to steady her nerves. The whole afternoon had felt like it was happening in some alternate universe, where it was just the two of them in their own private world. Remembering the party brought Olivia back to reality, where she was just the new girl in town, and Soren was . . . Soren.

She looked up at him and realized that he was staring at the inside soles of his shoes, his eyes lost and far away.

"What about you?" she asked softly. "Did you have a good time?"

Soren shrugged, scrunching his nose. "Not really," he admitted. "I mean, I guess the party itself was okay, but . . ." He flattened his palms onto his knees, rubbing them up and down against the fabric of his light-washed jeans. It reminded Olivia of one of those toy cars you have to wheel back and forth a bunch of times before it takes off across the floor. He was gaining speed.

"But what?" she prompted.

"Calla and I broke up," he said. His voice came out in a burst of sound, breathy and full. His hands stopped moving and his shoulders fell, and for a minute Olivia was nervous that he was going to do something terrible . . . like cry.

Olivia's insides were flopping around like a barrel of half-dead fish. She couldn't even begin to untangle the mixed emotions she was feeling. She should be happy, right? But how could she be happy when he looked so sad?

"I'm so sorry," she said, and was surprised by how genuine it sounded. She really *was* sorry. Sorry he was upset, which he certainly seemed to be. Sorry Calla was upset, if she was.

"Did you . . ." The question forced its way out before she could take it back completely. "I mean, was it, like . . . a mutual thing?" Olivia flinched, as if a question so moronic might actually come back and punch her in the face.

But Soren just shrugged. "Not really," he said. "I mean, as much as it could be. Nothing's ever mutual, I don't think. But I knew it had to end. I think she did, too."

"Yeah." Olivia nodded, as if she had any idea. As if she'd ever been in anything that could pass for a relationship, let alone been responsible for ending one.

Soren took a deep breath and folded his hands together, pushing them away from his body and cracking his knuckles all at once. The sound was jarring, but somehow had the effect of starting over, clearing the slate.

"Anyway," he huffed, finally turning to face her. His eyes were less cloudy and his face smooth and calm. "I don't exactly know why, but I felt like telling you. I guess I thought you should know." He took a deep breath and smiled before turning back to the water. Olivia did the same, the quiet of the early evening settling in between them as they waited for the sinking sun.

Later, when she was falling asleep, Olivia would remember that smile, and the way it made her feel tingly and warm. It wasn't a smile that said a whole lot. It wasn't suggestive, or romantic, even. It was just that it was trusting, and easy, and real.

21

"About face!" Violet commanded, hopping up from where she'd been lounging against the bottom of the Larsens' front stoop.

After Soren had driven her halfway home, Olivia had decided to take advantage of the warming weather and walk the (mostly uphill) twenty blocks back to her house. Her legs were trembling and all she wanted was to take a shower and hop into bed, but Violet, as usual, had other plans.

"My feet . . ." Olivia groaned as Violet pulled her toward the car, pressing the keys into the palm of her hand.

"I don't want to hear it," Violet insisted as Olivia unlocked the front door. "You have some serious beans to spill."

Olivia slouched forward, flattening her cheek against the steering wheel, and turned toward her sister. "Can't I spill them on the couch?"

Violet rolled her eyes and pulled her hair back into a loose bun. "Sure," she said flatly. "If you feel like screaming."

Olivia raised an eyebrow and Violet took a deep, preparatory breath.

"Dad accidentally put a hole in the wall of Mom's office. Mom has a big deposition in the morning," she began, squinting to remember the details. "Dad is 'lazy' and 'disrespectful'; Mom is a 'workaholic' who 'loves to complain . . .'"

Olivia grunted and turned the key in the ignition. "Grandpa's boat?" she asked.

Violet nodded silently and Olivia pulled out into the street.

It took a lot of restraint, but Olivia refused to share any juicy gossip about her afternoon with Soren until the sisters were squarely settled on the deck of the sparkling yacht, spread out on a blanket and staring up at the fading night sky.

Violet leaned on her side and propped herself up with one arm. "Tell me everything."

Olivia inhaled a lungful of sea air and covered her face with her hands, the giddy smile she'd managed to repress forcing its way out through the web of her fingers.

"Oh, no," Violet gasped. "It's bad, isn't it?"

Olivia lowered her hands and looked into her sister's eyes, darting around like little blue lasers, searching Olivia's face for more.

"What happened?" Violet squealed. "It's bad enough I'm stuck in family court while you're out on the world's most romantic date—"

"It wasn't a date," Olivia said firmly.

Violet huffed and flipped her hand over in the air. "Whatever," she said. "It was datelike."

Olivia blushed and sat up, pulling the edge of the fuzzy fleece blanket up and over her legs.

"It was weird," Olivia said, after a while of being quiet. "There were a couple of times when it was kind of awkward. Where it really felt like we were two strangers hanging out. But most of the time, he was just so easy to talk to." Violet nodded and turned her chin back toward the purple night sky. "It was like I knew everything he was about to say, before he said it, you know?"

Violet made a little humming sound and smiled. "Like what?" she asked, crossing her bare ankles and wiggling her toes. Olivia glanced down at the bubble-gum polish on her sister's feet, and for a moment was transported back to last summer on Martha's Vineyard. They were sitting on the back deck, painting each other's nails. Violet had borrowed her mother's collection of OPI colors and was choosing between Sweet 16 and Daddy's Girl. Olivia, who rarely paid any attention to her nails, other than to bite them, decided that they should both pick Sweet 16, in honor of their upcoming birthdays.

The birthday that only one of them would celebrate.

"Hello?" Violet pressed, sitting back up. "Where did you go?"

Olivia shook her head and smiled sadly. "Sorry," she said. "I'm here."

Violet gave her a funny look before leaning back on her elbows, her light eyes reflecting the twinkling yellow lights of downtown across the bay. "So what did he say?"

Olivia nibbled at the inside corner of her mouth. "Well . . ." She hesitated. "He told me he broke up with Calla."

"He what?" Violet shot up, her hair whipping around her

face like water. "When? And *how* did you not lead with this information?"

Olivia looked down at her fingers in her lap. Her own nails were stubby and streaked with little chalky lines. Her mind clouded as she remembered the way Soren's shoulders had slumped when he'd told her the news. She'd known Violet would be excited, but she couldn't help feeling that it was all so complicated. It probably wasn't the best idea to get involved with someone so soon after a breakup.

"I don't know." Olivia sighed, squinting at the water, lapping in dark little waves against the angled beams of the wooden dock. "I don't know how I feel about it yet."

Violet leaned forward, taking one of Olivia's knees in each of her open palms. "What's to know?" she asked with a laugh. "The guy you like but couldn't *have* because he had a girlfriend . . . doesn't!"

Olivia wrangled her legs free of Violet's grip and pulled herself up to her feet. She pressed her hips against the cool brass railing and swayed forward, the gusty breeze picking up a light spray off the water and stinging the freckled tops of her cheekbones. Violet was quickly there, too, straddling the banister, her bare feet swinging and knocking back against the hull.

"You're worried about Calla, aren't you?" Violet guessed. Her voice wasn't as edgy as Olivia expected. It was soft and almost understanding.

Olivia nodded. "It just sucks," she said, hearing herself whining but too upset to care. "Why does the first guy I feel this way about have to be the boyfriend of basically the only girl I've talked to at school?"

"Ex-boyfriend," Violet corrected.

"Yeah, of, like, fifteen minutes," Olivia deadpanned. She stretched her arms out and leaned back, gripping the railing with such force that her knuckles blanched and looked ready to pop out of her skin. "I just don't want to let myself get too excited."

Olivia tilted her neck back and looked up at the sky. There were a few dull stars peeking through layers of gossamer clouds, but not enough to allow her to make out the pointed shapes of constellations.

"What did you promise me?" Violet asked, laying a hand on her sister's shoulder. "Remember? At the gala? You said you were going to let yourself want things." Violet looked out at the water, giving her sister's shoulder a little squeeze.

"But what if it doesn't work out?" Olivia asked, following Violet's gaze out across the horseshoe bay. A waiter at a waterfront restaurant was pulling down umbrellas and bringing plastic chairs inside, closing up for the night. Violet took a deep breath and smiled, and Olivia thought she noticed a mischievous little dance in the corners of her sister's eyes.

"Trust me," Violet said, rocking gently against Olivia's side. "It will."

Olivia felt her pulse starting to steady and the sharp pounding at her temples recede into a background ache. "You really think so?" she asked quietly.

"I really do."

Olivia felt the tight knots in her neck and shoulders starting to loosen, a smile brightening her lips. The queasy feeling she'd had squirming in her belly all evening was starting to settle. Her whole body was relaxing, as if her sister had drawn the tension right out of her, one limb at a time.

22

All it took was a full day of pretending that nothing was going on between her and Soren for Olivia to realize that "getting excited" wasn't going to be much of a challenge. Every time she so much as caught a glimpse of him at school, through the window of the language lab door, or doing tricks on his skateboard in the courtyard at lunch, her stomach twisted into a giant pretzel.

Determined to orchestrate at least one accidental-on-purpose hallway encounter, Violet had tracked Soren's schedule and planted Olivia in the upstairs student lounge just before the last bell of the day. This way, Violet reasoned, Olivia could position herself for a casual crossing-of-paths while innocently working on homework, the prop of her math notebook open in her lap.

"I'm so glad I found you." A soft voice suddenly spoke from behind Olivia's shoulder. Olivia looked up from a scramble of calculus equations just as Calla collapsed into the nubby couch on the other side of the glass table.

"Hey, Calla," Olivia said, willing her pulse to stop drumming in her ears. Violet spun around from where she'd been perched on the top of the stairs, her eyes wide with concern. This wasn't exactly the accidental encounter they'd had in mind. "What's up?"

At first glance, Calla seemed okay. Her dark wavy hair was clean and shiny, and she looked perfectly put together in skinny jeans, a soft white V-neck, and a tangle of long brass chains. The only thing suspicious about her appearance were the oversize black sunglasses she was wearing inside.

"Are you busy this afternoon?" Calla asked, rummaging around in her bag for her water bottle and unscrewing the round top. Olivia's eyes jumped back to Violet, who appeared too stunned to be of much service, and then back to Calla, who was swallowing a big sip of water and sighing like she'd been parched in a desert for months. "I could really use your help with this fundraiser we're putting together for the thrift store. We have our first committee meeting after school today, and it would be great to have you on board."

Olivia caught a flurry of movement and looked up to see Violet shaking her head deliberately and crossing her hands over each other back and forth.

"Oh," Olivia stuttered. "That sounds great, but, unfortunately, I—"

"The thing is," Calla whispered as she leaned across the table, a tumble of hair falling over her shoulder, "Lark and Eve are supposed to be helping out, and I know they're trying. It's just . . . well, usually I'd do everything myself, but I had kind of a . . . crazy weekend. . . ."

What did *crazy* mean, exactly? Crazy busy? Or crazy sad?

Olivia felt a sharp tightening in her stomach as she imagined Calla after the gala, telling her friends what had happened. Explaining that it was over with Soren.

Calla shook her head gently, the scent of vanilla shampoo floating in the air between them. Then, with slow, careful motions, she lifted both hands to the sides of her face and pulled her sunglasses down onto her lap. She brought her eyes up to meet Olivia's, and Olivia could see that they were pink and swollen, like bugs had been biting around them all night.

All signs were pointing to crazy sad.

"Please," Calla said evenly. "Say you can make it."

Olivia didn't really have a choice. Even Violet could see that. Her sister tossed her a helpless shrug, shaking her head as she looked down at the beige and white–squared carpet.

"Of course." Olivia closed her notebook and tucked it into her soft leather tote. "I'd love to help."

Calla rocked back in the couch and smiled, before pulling herself up to her feet. "Thank you *so* much."

Calla started down the spiral stairs toward the lobby, and Olivia followed close behind. Heavy footsteps passed by her head and she turned to see the door to the ceramics studio swinging open, a familiar pair of blue Converse shell-toes stepping out into the hall.

"Don't look back," Violet warned as they passed through the lobby. Olivia felt her cheeks splotching red and hoped Calla wouldn't notice. They turned a corner and swung through a pair of French doors into the faculty lounge.

Lark, Eve, Graham, and a half-dozen other kids were already scattered around the circular room. Graham and Eve were lounging on the floor, their legs intertwined as

168

they leaned back against a gurgling watercooler. Lark had claimed a high-backed chair at the head of an oval mahogany table. Her thick blond hair was pulled back into a swinging ponytail, with a static-electric halo clinging to her head. She stood up as Calla entered the room, indicating the open seat by her side.

"Hey, Cal," Lark said, capping her pen and placing it on the top of her spiral notebook. "I was about to get started without you."

Calla circled the table and hoisted herself up onto the sill of a bay window overlooking the courtyard. She swung her legs over the back of the empty chair as Lark settled back into her seat.

Olivia was starting toward the table when Violet put a hand on her shoulder.

"How about the couch?" she suggested, motioning to a checkered love seat in the corner, wedged underneath an oil painting of a country farmhouse. Olivia quietly sank into one of the soft square cushions. "Just try to lie low," Violet advised, crouching on the floor beside her. "You'll be fine."

Calla removed a small oval case from her tote. "First of all, thanks so much for coming today." She exchanged her dark shades for turquoise-rimmed, rectangular eyeglasses, slipping them carefully onto her face. Naturally, they made her look even more effortlessly glamorous and hip, and Olivia actually found herself hoping that her own 20/20 vision would some-day deteriorate.

"I know this is a really busy time for everyone," Calla said, quietly taking in the room. "And it means a lot that you're taking the time to be here."

"Really." Lark beamed, rapping her pen against the spiral binding of her notebook. "It's great to see so many new faces. I mean, remember when it was just me and you and Kiko at that Burmese place on Clement? I never would have imagined—"

"So as you know, we're hosting a fundraising event for the thrift shop," Calla cut in, gazing out over the top of Lark's head. "The goal is to raise enough money to open at Golden Gate before the summer. My cousins started one at their school in Manhattan, and it's a great way to generate a steady flow of income for a cause."

Violet yawned dramatically from the floor and Olivia shot her a silencing glare.

"Lark's handing out some information we put together last week," Calla explained. "We've decided, since we're already getting so many donations, that the best way to get people excited would be to showcase some of the pieces in a fashion show."

Olivia noticed Violet's spine straighten and her eyes light up. All anybody had to say was *fashion* and suddenly her sister was all ears.

"So," Calla said, flopping her hands against her lap. "Any thoughts about locations?"

"How about a vineyard in Napa?" Eve quickly suggested, her dark almond eyes blinking as she nestled into her perennial position on Graham's lanky lap. "We could do a wine tasting before the show."

There were a few bored snickers from the back of the room, and Graham gallantly came to his lady's defense. "It could be cool," he said, stretching out his long legs. He was wearing faded black skinny jeans and lime green Nike high-tops with paint-splattered soles, which Olivia decided were one part trendy and one part toddler. "What better way to get people to write fat checks than by getting them wasted first?"

The crowd rumbled with giggles and nods of approval.

"Maybe," a heavy baritone interjected from the other side of the room. Olivia turned to see a petite boy with a blond crew cut and an upturned nose leaning on his elbows at the table. "But how about Sonoma instead of Napa?"

Olivia had seen him before in the halls. He looked a little bit like some baby-faced child actor she couldn't quite place, but his voice was like sandpaper.

"Napa is like the Disney World of wine country. It's played out," he boomed. "Sonoma is the new Napa."

There was another swell of laughter across the room and Lark spun violently around in her seat.

"Seriously, Logan?" she spat. "You've never even been to Napa. I read that issue of *Sunset* in Mom's bathroom, too. Do you want to quote the rest of it for us?"

Graham keeled forward, laughing so hard that he nearly knocked Eve onto the floor. Olivia smiled as she registered the sibling rivalry. Now that she thought about it, Lark and Logan did have the same golden hair and too-perfect skin.

"All right," Calla said loudly, quieting the giggling crowd. "I like the drunken check-writing theory, but I don't know if we have time to plan something so involved. The event is less than a month away, and we haven't even booked a space. We're going to have to get creative here."

"Graham's dad is on the board at the Palace of Fine Arts," Eve offered, turning her heart-shaped face up to Graham's and beaming proudly.

"That could work." Calla nodded eagerly. "Graham, since you've got the hookup, do you and Eve want to work on location?"

"No problem," Eve said sweetly, tucking a section of her slick, layered hair behind one tiny ear.

"Great. Did you get that, Lark?" Calla tapped her finger on Lark's notebook and looked around the room. "What else? Oh, I know." Calla stood with her back to the table glancing down at the tops of her mango-colored painted toes, her long dark tresses falling over her shoulders and covering both sides of her face. She took a deep breath and looked up.

"So, I thought I was going to be able to handle overseeing everything on my own," she began. "But it turns out my mom needs me for some more iWIN stuff, plus I'm busy with peer theater meetings and the meditation workshops. . . ."

"Oh, is that all?" Violet added. "What about the paper bag police? Doesn't somebody have to stand outside the supermarket and hand out reusable totes?"

Olivia tossed her sister another stern glance.

"So it looks like I'm going to need a little help after all," Calla said, quickly laying a hand on Lark's shoulder. "And Lark is in the middle of volleyball season . . . so what I'm looking for is a volunteer for cochair." She looked out at the room, lifting her chin high over Lark's head and eagerly scanning the crowd.

"Ouch," Violet hissed. "Write *that* down, Lark."

172

Olivia swiveled swiftly around in her chair and hissed at Violet.

"Quiet!" Olivia grunted without thinking. As soon as the word had left her lips, Olivia felt twenty pairs of eyes on the back of her neck. Violet's features were locked in a pre-panic grimace as she glanced carefully around the room.

"Madonna?" Olivia turned to see Calla hopping down from the window and starting toward her on the couch. "Was that you?"

Olivia swallowed and glanced up at the table. A guy she recognized from her religion class, with greasy long hair and a black plug in one ear, had his head on his elbows and appeared to be sleeping.

"Um," Olivia stalled. She hadn't even wanted to come to the meeting in the first place, and now she had accidentally volunteered to cochair the entire event? "Well, I don't know. . . ."

"Perfect," Calla said, standing over her by the couch. "Don't worry—it's not like there's tons to do, and I think it'll be fun to work together. Don't you?"

Violet stood next to Calla, her eyes frantically darting back and forth. "Uh, no?" Violet prompted her sister. "Not so much fun as *totally inconvenient*. Olivia, this is not a good idea."

But Calla was already heaving a sigh of relief. "Thank you *so much*," she said to Olivia with a warm smile before heading back to the front of the room.

Violet collapsed dramatically on the couch beside her sister. "*Whyyyyy* did you do that?" she moaned.

Olivia chewed at the inside of her lip. What was she supposed to do?

173

Calla settled back against the window, swinging her legs against the wall like a little girl. "Madonna Is My Copilot," she joked. "Not a bad bumper sticker, huh?"

Violet scoffed and dropped her head in her hands. "So much for lying low."

23

"Watch your step," Olivia warned Miles as they stood at the front door to her house. Her key was wedged in the lock and she was trying not to touch any of the fresh red paint, drying in streaks on the frame. Her dad had decided to keep all of the original primary colors and was in the process of touching them up. Olivia thought it gave the house a circus-tent feel, but she had to admit that the outside entrance was getting a little less disgusting every day.

Inside was a different story.

Miles followed her into the hall, carefully sidestepping the legs of a broken ladder on the floor. He had a bulky black camera bag slung over one shoulder and was clutching it to his side, the way a supermodel might protect her teacup Chihuahua.

"Wow," he said, craning his head up toward the spiderweb cracks in the ceiling.

Olivia dropped her bag to the floor and plopped her keys into the dish on the front table. She was already regretting her decision to suggest her yard as a place to film part of their scene for Whitley's class. But as soon as Miles had said they needed to find a spot for the garden scene, somewhere lush and overgrown, Mrs. Havisham style, she'd known her neglected backyard would be the perfect place.

Still, if she hadn't run into him waiting for the bus after school, she probably would have forgotten that today was the day they had arranged to shoot it. She'd spent most of the day imagining a secret afternoon rendezvous with Soren, maybe at an out-of-the-way coffee shop, or another hidden hike. But she'd hardly even seen him in the halls all day. She was starting to wonder if maybe she'd read too much into the time they'd spent together. He hadn't even asked for her number or anything. Maybe he just wanted somebody to talk to.

Olivia sighed, seeing the demolition zone that was her home as if for the first time, through Miles's untrained eyes. "Sorry. I should've told you to bring a hard hat or something."

Miles laughed and rested his hand on the inside of the open door frame leading to the downstairs den. "No," he said, "this place is amazing. Look at the detail. It must be all the original molding, right?"

Olivia shrugged, kneeling down to rifle through her bag. Molding? Wasn't that a bad thing? The house was old and nothing worked. "I think I left the script in my desk upstairs," Olivia muttered and turned toward the rickety spiral steps.

Miles leaned over to examine the fireplace, also nonworking and currently doubling as Mac's toolbox.

"The backyard is through the kitchen," Olivia said, pointing over his shoulder to the big picture window on the far wall. "I'll be right down."

She skipped up to the third floor and into her room. She half expected to find Violet waiting for her, but quickly remembered that her sister had taken the afternoon off, deciding that homework, much like gym class, was not suitable for ghostly entertainment. There was an Andy Warhol exhibit at the de Young and she'd been talking about sneaking into it ever since they'd seen the poster on the side of a city bus.

Olivia opened the rollback top of her antique desk—the one piece of furniture she'd been allowed to pick out for herself—and flipped through loose papers and photographs. This was where she'd stuffed everything that she didn't have a place for yet—old journals, half-finished homework, pictures she hadn't yet framed.

She had finally located her yellow English composition notebook when her gaze shifted, landing on the curling edge of a photograph, sticking out from underneath an unopened package of Post-its. She pulled the picture out and held it in one hand, pressing back the bent corner with her thumb.

It had been taken two summers ago on the Vineyard, on one of the first sticky-hot days of the season. They'd all decided to go out on Mac's motorboat, a cranky old whaler he'd had since before the girls were born, and were puttering around in the bay. Violet had figured out how to set the timer on Bridget's digital camera and wedged it up and over the steering wheel, catching the four of them squinting into the sunlight, tanned and carefree.

It was the one photograph Olivia had of her whole family where everyone was smiling.

"That looks like fun."

Olivia jumped and turned to find Miles standing at the foot of her bed. "You scared me."

He reached for the photograph and sat down on the edge of her comforter. Olivia felt her fingers trembling and her cheeks getting hot. She'd couldn't tell if it was because there was a boy in her room on her bed, or because that boy on her bed was Miles, or because that boy on her bed was Miles *and* he was looking at a picture of her family with Violet . . . but whatever it was, it was wrong. All wrong.

"Man." He shook his head as Olivia tried not to hyperventilate. "You and your sister. Wow. I mean, usually there are little differences with twins, but you guys are, like, totally identical."

Olivia glanced out the window. He was right. Even to people who had known them for years, it was a challenge to tell the twins apart on film. They'd always worn their long, red-blond curls to the exact same wispy, midback length. Their blue-gray eyes caught the same shimmering light in the same hidden corners, and neither had any defining facial markings—though Violet had experimented with a nose ring for a few weeks (until Bridget had threatened to relieve her of that portion of her face completely).

"And your parents look really cool," Miles said. "It must be nice to be so close."

Olivia looked sharply at Miles and exhaled through her nose. *Close?*

"We're not," she said. It came out harsher than she'd intended, so she tried to soften it up. "I mean, not anymore. My mom's never home, and my dad's always busy with the house."

Miles nodded, handing the photo back to Olivia. "Oh," he

said. "I just assumed, I mean, the other night when you left, you said you guys always had dinner together."

Olivia tossed the photograph back on her desk and hurried toward the hall. "We should probably start filming while the light is still good," she said, waiting for Miles at the door. She'd been caught in her stupid, pointless lie, and all she wanted to do was run away, even if it was only as far as outside.

"Hey," Miles said gently. He was still sitting on the corner of her bed and gave no sign of standing up. "After you told me about, you know, about your sister . . . I didn't really know what to say. I've been meaning to ask you about it again, but I don't know how. I mean, I don't want to make you think about something you'd rather forget, you know?"

Olivia looked down at the little bows on the tops of her quilted flats. It seemed weird to have her shoes on in her room, but she'd forgotten to take them off downstairs. She was kind of glad to still be wearing them, as if they were armor she'd feel naked without.

"Not that you want to forget her. Your sister, I mean. But I guess I just wanted to say that I'm here, you know?" Miles looked up at her and smiled, in a way that looked like it hurt. It wasn't that he didn't mean what he was saying; it just looked like such an *ordeal*. As if smiling was stretching the muscles in his face in a way they weren't used to moving. "I mean," he went on, tightly gripping the engraved bedpost with one hand, as if for support, "if you ever want to talk, or anything . . ." He trailed off. His eyes hopped round from the floor to the window to the door, like he was stuck in a maze and couldn't find a way out.

Olivia realized he was just as uncomfortable as she was,

and something in her softened. "Thanks, Miles," she said, and meant it.

Miles nodded deliberately, like an executive checking off an item on a to-do list at a meeting. He rose to his feet, squeezing past her through the doorway and starting down the stairs.

It was nice of him to try.

※ ※ ※

"How's my favorite movie star?"

Olivia was sitting up in bed, her marine biology homework open in her lap, when Violet finally returned from her afternoon of culture.

"Was it an Oscar-worthy performance?" Violet joked from the open window, one long leg dangling out onto the balcony, the other swinging against the inside wall. "What was your motivation?"

Olivia smiled and shook her head. Since Miles had gone home, she'd been trying to focus on homework, but hadn't been able to stop thinking about Soren. Tortoises and beluga whales were not exactly the most engaging of distractions, and she was glad to have Violet back.

"We were just doing a scene of Lily painting," Olivia explained, resting her pen in the open crease of her textbook. "She wants to be an artist but she's really self-conscious. She's working on this one painting for, like, the whole book, and she can't bring herself to put on the finishing touches. It's like she's afraid to finish and move on."

Violet nodded, hopping down from the window ledge and picking up the family photo Olivia had left behind on the desk. "What's this?" Violet asked.

Olivia looked up and felt her heart sink. She had meant to put the photograph back at the bottom of the pile before Violet saw it. She still felt guilty about being so curt in her room with Miles, but she didn't exactly want to bring this subject up with Violet. There was something about talking about not talking about your dead sister, with your dead sister—it was a little too meta. "Oh," Olivia said quietly. "I found that today."

Violet nodded and sat down at the desk, carefully examining the photograph, running her hands over its glossy surface. "Wow." She sighed. "I can't believe how happy we all look here."

"I know," Olivia said. Violet's shoulders slumped forward, and Olivia knew her sister was upset, but she had no idea what else to say. It seemed unfair to try to comfort her, when they both knew it was true. They *had* been happy. They *had* been a family. Until . . .

The high-pitched jingle of the house phone rang out from the silver cordless on Olivia's bedside table.

"Get it!" Violet urged as the phone rang again.

Olivia checked the caller ID and gulped loudly. "It's Soren," she managed.

"Answer it!" Violet yelled again.

Olivia hesitated as the phone kept ringing.

"Olivia Riley Larsen, if you don't answer that phone this instant . . ." Violet seethed.

Olivia smiled and reached for the phone, taking it in her lap.

Olivia: Hello?
Soren: Hey. It's Soren.
(Pause. Long period of mouth-breathing.)

Soren: Oh, uh, sorry. Is Olivia there?

Olivia: This is Olivia. *(Attempted casual breeziness.)*

Soren: Cool. Hey. It's Soren. *(Pause.)* Sorry, I guess I said that already.

Olivia: That's okay. What's up?

Soren: Not much. I was just watching this movie on TV, this documentary thing about bass fishing. And it reminded me to call you.

Olivia: Bass fishing?

Violet: Easy with the sweet talk, buddy.

Soren: Yeah, or maybe tuna. I don't really know. Anyway, it reminded me because it's a documentary, and there's this other documentary playing at the Little Roxie on Saturday. I thought maybe we could go.

Olivia: *(Heart exploding, but BREEZY. CASUAL.)* Oh. This Saturday? *(Pause. On purpose.)* Sure, that sounds fun.

Soren: Yeah? Cool. All right. Well, cool. I said cool already, too, huh?

Olivia: Yup.

Soren: Okay. Well. See you in school tomorrow?

Olivia: See ya.

Soren: Okay. I'm hanging up now.

Olivia: Me, too.

Soren: Cool.

Olivia: Cool.

Soren: Bye.

Olivia slowly moved the phone down from her ear and held it carefully in her lap, as if it were a rare blue egg that she was trying to keep intact.

Violet hopped back up on the windowsill.

"Well," she said slowly, crossing her arms and leaning back against the glass. "Aside from the train wreck at the end there, I thought that was pretty okay."

Violet winked at Olivia, and Olivia tucked the phone back into its cradle. She turned back to her open textbook and picked up her pen, as if nothing odd or unusual had occurred. As if Soren called and asked her out every day.

Who knew, she even allowed herself to think, her eyes blurring over the shiny sidebar image of a snapping turtle. Maybe someday he would.

24

*A*fter almost a week of accidental elbow-brushes in the hallway, heavy-lidded looks waiting for coffee at the Depot, and hidden smiles across the courtyard, Olivia was starting to wonder if maybe Saturday was purposely taking forever to arrive, just to piss her off. What was Saturday's problem? Didn't Saturday realize that it needed to hustle up and get here already so she could hang out with Soren again alone?

But, as she walked the few blocks from her house to the theater, where they'd arranged to meet at noon, Olivia found herself delivering silent pep talks to her feet, just to keep them moving in the right direction. How could it possibly be Saturday already? She hadn't had nearly enough time to prepare.

Violet, who had been horrified by the early hour of the date—"Who goes to a movie at noon?"—had dressed Olivia in a pretty embroidered peasant blouse, tight jeans, and her quilted ballet flats, and then decided to stay home to give her sister some privacy.

Olivia had actually been relieved when Soren said he had band rehearsal Saturday night and suggested they catch a matinee. It felt less scary meeting him while the sun was still up, like it could almost pass for something she didn't have to get totally worked up about.

Which was not to say that her stomach wasn't still jumping around like a hopscotching acrobat as she turned off of Guerrero, the enormous neon letters of the Roxie marquee looming like a spaceship overhead.

Soren was the only person standing outside, leaning against a poster for a French film, which appeared to star a midget and his pet iguana. He had tiny white headphones plugged into his iPhone and was nodding to a silent beat when Olivia shuffled up beside him.

"Hey," she said timidly, and when he didn't turn, she laid her hand lightly on the shoulder of his coat. It was a warm day, sunny and dry, but in the shade Olivia felt a chill and was already kicking herself for leaving her own jacket at home.

Soren jumped and unstrung the ear buds from around his neck.

"Hey!" He smiled. His coat was open and underneath he was wearing a snap-button, red and white checked shirt, and dark jeans that fell perfectly somewhere between hipster-skinny and slacker-slouch. His hair was still wet from the shower and when he turned toward her she could smell his shampoo—earthy but sweet.

"I already got us tickets," Soren said, holding up two paper rectangles and gesturing for her to follow him inside.

The lobby was empty and Olivia glanced around at vintage posters and schedules for upcoming festivals. Standing in line for popcorn and a bottle of Clementine Izze natural soda, Soren explained that the Little Roxie was a smaller screening room built adjacent to the original full-size theater, for smaller-run independent movies and obscure documentaries.

The screening room was tiny and felt a little bit like somebody's half-finished basement, with ratty furniture and what looked like a really big projection TV. Aside from a pair of elderly ladies in the front row, it was completely empty, but Soren looked around dramatically, making a show out of finding the perfect seat. Olivia smiled as he led her over to a small, denim-covered couch in the back corner, which looked like it would smell like cologne and old cigars. Thankfully, it didn't.

"I've been trying to see this one for a while," Soren said eagerly, shooting his eyes toward the dark screen. He pulled at the fabric of his jeans, settling back against the lumpy sofa. Olivia sat carefully beside him, holding her breath as the side of her hip bumped up against his leg.

"What is it?" Olivia asked, realizing with a wave of embarrassment that she hadn't even bothered to ask what they were seeing.

"It's about these . . ." Soren started but quickly censored himself when one of the old ladies in the front row spun around to face them. "Shhh . . ." the woman hushed, a beaded loop attached to the ends of her eyeglasses catching at the top of her frizzy gray bun. Soren glanced pointedly around at the still brightly lit theater and rows of empty seats between them, before turning to Olivia with one eyebrow perched high, the other angled down toward his nose. Olivia tried not to laugh.

"I haven't been to the movies in forever," she whispered, their heads huddling closer together. She was suddenly unspeakably grateful that she had heeded Violet's advice to chew a piece of gum on her walk over, discreetly dropping it in a trash can outside.

"Really?" Soren whispered back. "I go all the time. Sometimes I hide in the back and stay all day."

"Violet and I used to do that all the time," Olivia said, too loudly for the ladies up front, who swiveled around again to shoot them a second warning glare. Olivia bit her lip, realizing what she'd said.

"Violet?" Soren asked, smiling. "Was she a friend back home?"

Olivia's stomach tightened into a hard little knot. It wasn't that she didn't trust him, or feel comfortable saying the words. But there was something about the picture she had of herself when she was with him. It was like she was totally free and clean, untouched by any of the things she was always trying to forget. And she wasn't ready to taint that picture. Not yet.

"Yeah," Olivia said quietly. "She was."

Soren nodded, pushing his hair out of his eyes and tapping his knees with the flat part of his hands. "I can't imagine moving," he said, the flickering images of a preview for an animated feature reflecting in his clear green eyes. "I'd miss it here so much. That must've been hard."

Olivia shrugged. She still wasn't sure what was worse: the fact that she sometimes missed home, or the fact that most of the time she didn't.

"Mostly I just miss the stars," she said, and as soon as the words left her mouth she realized how true they were. Nothing she'd found in San Francisco had come close to capturing the feeling she'd had at home in Willis, or on the Vineyard, lying on the roof with Violet. It was grounding, a feeling of forever . . . the idea that no matter what happened, they'd always have each other, and they'd always have the stars.

"Yeah, it's tough here, with the fog and all of the lights," Soren admitted. "But sometimes I think it's better this way. It's like, when you finally do get to see them, you appreciate how special they are. You know?"

Their eyes met and Olivia smiled as darkness fell and the screen lit up before them. Hyperaware now of how close their bodies were pushed together, she felt her heart pounding in her chest. These weren't traditional movie seats, and there was no bulky armrest to keep them apart. There was a dip in the cushions that guided their shoulders in toward each other, and their knees knocked awkwardly as they slouched deeper into the musty fabric.

The film, which turned out to be about the Iditarod, a competition for sled-pulling huskies in Alaska, had barely gotten under way when Soren wedged his hand under Olivia's, their fingers carefully intertwining one by one.

Olivia remembered back to the only other time she'd held a boy's hand in the dark. It had been at a Halloween party the year before, when a bunch of Violet's friends had gotten together to watch scary movies in Jackie Ryerson's home theater. Shep had convinced one of his football buddies, Jay, to sit next to Olivia, mostly so he could have Violet to himself in the back. About halfway through the opening credits Jay had sloppily reached for her hand. His palm was fleshy and moist and his thick knuckles gripped the sides of her fingers like a vise. She'd sat quietly for as long as she could, eventually excusing herself to the bathroom during a particularly gory killing spree, nervous that Jay might lose himself in the moment and actually crush all of the bones in her hands, like so many empty cans of Natty Ice.

This wasn't anything like that. As soon as Soren wrapped her hand in his own, his long thumb overlapping hers, the creases of bone and skin interlocking like soft pieces of a puzzle, Olivia could tell. It was a perfect fit.

❧ ❧ ❧

"This place has the best burritos in all of Northern California," Soren said as they waited to cross the street. Their eyes had still been adjusting to the stark white glare of the afternoon sun when Soren mentioned he had some time to kill before rehearsal. "It looks like a hole-in-the-wall," he continued, gesturing down the block to where a short line had formed on the sidewalk. "But it's always packed. And worth the wait."

They stopped at the end of the line in front of an art gallery next door, the warm smell of baked tortillas and fresh-squeezed lime juice wafting onto the street. Olivia peered through the window and saw that Soren was right. It didn't look like much; just a cramped little takeout joint with tile floors and a linoleum countertop, behind which a handful of men in white aprons and dark mustaches scurried around, piling ingredients high on soft tacos in their hands.

Olivia rubbed the sides of her arms to keep warm. The air conditioner in the theater had been on full blast, which had given her an extra excuse to cuddle close to Soren. But now that they were outside, it was taking her a while to thaw out. "Are you cold?" Soren asked, already peeling his arms free from the sleeves of his worn leather coat. Before she had a chance to respond, he was draping it gallantly over her shoulders, just like he would have done in the parallel movie version of her life. Could it be possible that this was one scene she wouldn't have to rewrite?

As happy, burrito-toting customers left the cozy café, Soren and Olivia shuffled slowly forward, edging nearer and nearer to the door. Olivia was admiring the red skirt of a short girl with dark, choppy hair, edging her way outside and reaching back to grab the hand of her lanky, orange-haired companion. . . . What was that on her skirt? A hedgehog?

Eve and Graham!

Olivia swung around to gauge Soren's reaction, but he was busy admiring the neighboring gallery's window display.

"Check out these sculptures," he said, oblivious to the impending confrontation. Thinking fast, Olivia slid out from under the weight of his coat and tossed it quickly in a heap at his feet. There was a stocky row of newspaper boxes at the corner, and she had just enough time to duck behind them before she was spotted at Soren's side. "They're like birds with human heads or— What the?"

Olivia watched with her face half-hidden as Soren bent down to pick up his coat from the ground, catching her eye on his way back up. She quieted his questioning glare with a single finger to her lips, and gestured up to where Graham and Eve were now standing, directly overhead.

"Hey there, butterfingers." Graham laughed. Olivia could hear the sounds of hands slapping five and Soren clearing his throat.

"Hey," he said, a slight tremble in his voice that Olivia prayed only she had noticed. "What are you guys doing here?"

Olivia cringed.

"Uh, eating?" Graham laughed.

Eve, pointedly, did not.

"Hi, Eve," Soren said, regaining his composure and leaning over to inspect Eve's folded burrito. "What did you go for?"

Olivia watched Soren's feet shuffle around uncomfortably against the pavement, and imagined the cold stare that Eve was most likely leveling in his direction. After all, he *had* just dumped her best friend.

"Soyrizo," she said flatly. "Like always."

"It's the bomb," Graham agreed. "I swear, if this place wasn't here, I'd probably never make it to rehearsal. It's the perfect pre-jam snack."

Soren and Graham laughed and Olivia held her breath, waiting as they said their good-byes and watching Eve's red skirt disappear around the corner. When she was certain the coast was clear, Olivia stood to her feet, the backs of her knees numb from crouching so long.

"That was interesting," Soren said when she reappeared at his side. He was wearing his coat again, his hands shoved deep in the pockets.

"Sorry," she said quietly. "I panicked."

Soren shrugged as they inched forward in line. He wouldn't look at her, his light hair falling over his eyes as he studied a narrow strip of grass where the brick wall met the sidewalk.

"I just figured, you know, with Calla and everything," Olivia stuttered, tugging at the elastic waistband of her peasant shirt. "It's such a small school, and I'm still just the new girl—"

"I know," Soren said softly. "I just hate sneaking around."

191

Olivia nodded and hugged her arms to her chest. "Me, too," she said. "And I don't want to do it forever. But I kind of got roped into cochairing this fashion show thing with Calla now. I guess I was just hoping we could, you know, keep things quiet until that was done?"

Soren nodded and kicked at the grass with the top of his sneaker. "Yeah," he said quietly. "I guess you're right."

He didn't look mad, and she knew he understood, but there was an uneasiness in his voice that made her heart quiver. She should have been happy that he wanted people to know about them hanging out, but it just reminded her of how sticky and complicated the whole situation was.

They inched forward and finally made it through the open door.

"Do you know what you want?" Soren asked.

The lump in Olivia's throat made it difficult for her to imagine eating anything, but she glanced up at the chalkboard menu, reading through the various options. Soyrizo had been helpfully defined as a type of spicy vegan sausage. Also available: tempeh scramble, grilled tofu, and bean-lover's delight.

What ever happened to good old chicken burritos?

Suddenly feeling hot and claustrophobic, Olivia tapped her foot nervously against the tiled floor. "Um," she stumbled. "I'm not really sure."

Maybe this was all a mistake. Maybe she'd never fit in. She couldn't even make sense of a takeout menu at a Mexican restaurant. Would she ever feel like she really belonged?

Soren looked at her out of the corner of his eye and stepped up to the counter, where an older man with leathery skin was impatiently tapping the counter with his pen.

"Hey, can I get two burritos with everything, please?" Soren asked, reaching in his back pocket for his wallet. "One chicken, one beef."

After handing over some bills, Soren spun quickly on his heels and took Olivia's elbow in is palm. His eyes were sharp with concern.

"Wait a minute," he said, in one quick breath. "You're not veggie, are you?"

Olivia smiled and shook her head. Maybe she could belong after all.

25

"hat is *The Great Wall of China*?' Are you kidding me? Somebody get this guy an encyclopedia."

It was Friday night and Olivia was curled up on the living room couch watching TV. Her dad was angled back on the leather recliner beside her, dipping pretzel sticks into a container of fat-free cream cheese, alternately berating *Jeopardy!* contestants and laughing at Alex Trebek's crooked toupee. Normally, Olivia might have been embarrassed to spend a Friday night hanging at home with her dad, but after a week of fashion-show planning, chasing Violet around the city, and staying up late to whisper on the phone with Soren, she was so flat-out exhausted it was about all the excitement she could handle.

Violet was stretched out with Olivia on the couch, her head resting between Olivia's L.L.Bean-slippered feet, only inches from Mac's hand and the remote. It was one of only a couple of times that they had been so close, and every so often Olivia would catch Violet glancing over at Mac, as if to make sure he was still there.

"Come on," Mac groaned, waving a hand at the screen. "Where do they find these people? The official language of Brazil is *Portuguese.*"

Olivia looked up from the copy of *Vogue* Bridget had brought back from the salon and shared a quick look with Violet. Watching *Jeopardy!* had once been a school-night ritual. Mac would make sure dinner was in the oven by seven before sitting down in the living room with the girls to wait for Bridget to get home from work. He had very little tolerance for wrong answers, which was not to say that he had many of the right answers himself. Usually, he'd wait for Alex to correct a bashful guest, and then passionately underscore the correction.

"You tell him, Alex," was a Mac favorite.

Violet rolled her eyes and nudged the small of Olivia's back with her bare foot. The blue squares on the screen went blank and the telltale jingle faded into a commercial for organic dog food.

Mac took a loud chomp of a pretzel and looked over at Olivia. She'd gotten used to him sneaking glances in her direction at every commercial break, taking shallow breaths, raising an eyebrow as if about to say something, and then stuffing food in his face instead.

This time, he held the open bag out in her direction.

"Hungry?" he asked.

Olivia wasn't, actually, but she pulled herself over to the other side of the couch, leaning over Violet's lap to reach into the bag for a handful of salty sticks. Mac offered her the cream cheese to dip in, but Olivia politely declined.

"You're crazy," Violet muttered, longingly eyeing the snack. Cream cheese and pretzels had been a Mac-and-Violet tradition.

"I don't blame you," Mac said, holding up the blue and silver container. "This fat-free stuff your mom makes me buy tastes like chalk. If everybody's so worked up about being healthy, why can't somebody make healthy food that actually tastes like food?"

Olivia thought about telling Mac about the farmer's market but decided against it. He'd pretend to be interested, but she knew he'd never be able to handle the crowds and massive selection. He was a by-the-book kind of guy, and had already memorized the aisles of the nearest Safeway, bragging about how he could get in and out of the market in twenty minutes flat.

"Here we go," Mac said, as the theme song returned and Double Jeopardy began. Olivia was considering helping herself to more pretzels when the sound of her mother's kitten heels clopping down the stairs interrupted them. Both Mac and Olivia reflexively straightened in their seats, as if watching TV was only acceptable from an upright position. Even Violet brought both feet to the floor.

Bridget stood in the doorway to the kitchen, looking shiny and sleek in a black pantsuit. A mandarin orange sweater snuck out from under the lapel of her coat, a splash of color picked up by the little orange bows on her black patent leather heels.

"Is that what you're wearing?" Bridget said, assessing Mac in his flannel pajama bottoms and Boston Celtics T-shirt.

Mac, held rapt by a Daily Double clue, grunted with his eyes still trained on the screen.

"Huh?" he asked. "I thought I was sitting this one out."

Bridget crossed her arms and stood behind his chair, her eyes blinking and darting from the screen to the top of his head.

"Sitting it out?" she repeated. Her voice was almost completely void of emotion, and the lack of anger was what scared Olivia most. "What am I supposed to tell Frank?"

Frank, Olivia had gathered from snippets of her mother's tired complaints, was one of the partners at the firm, and had invited Bridget and Mac to his newly renovated town house in Noe Valley for dinner.

Mac leaned toward the screen, holding his breath until the contestant, a cat-lady type with librarian bifocals, managed to eke out the correct answer at the last minute.

"Wow," he muttered, shaking his head when the wager, a measly two hundred dollars, was revealed. "Too bad you didn't bet like a man." He slowly rolled the top of the bag of pretzels, the plastic crinkling for what felt like a solid hour, before kicking the footrest back into the cushioned seat and heaving himself up to his feet. "Give me a minute," was all he said as he started up the stairs toward their room.

Olivia kept her eyes on the television, feigning interest in a glowing celebrity endorsement for acne cream. She could feel her mother's eyes on the side of her face but couldn't bring herself to look up.

"Do you have any plans tonight?" Bridget finally asked. Every question her mother asked was delivered in a way that left no ambiguity as to which answer she preferred. Usually, Olivia sensed that answer intuitively and quickly offered it up, eager for her mother's approval. But tonight, it was the exact opposite. Olivia knew Bridget desperately wanted her to move on, to make friends, to start fresh in a new city, with a fantastic new life. And in a way, she was. But why should her mother get the satisfaction of knowing anything about it?

"You're looking at it," Olivia said, lying back against the couch and propping her feet up on Violet's legs.

A tight smile grew on Bridget's lips and she tapped the back of the armchair with her long, buffed nails. "Tell your father I'll be waiting in the car, all right?" she said. "We shouldn't be home too late."

Bridget paused a moment, as if she wanted to say something else, before turning on her heels and clip-clopping down the hall and out the heavy front door.

Olivia rolled her eyes, grabbing for the bag and tearing it back open. But when she looked up, Violet was frowning.

"Poor Mom," Violet said, stretching out on the couch.

Olivia nearly choked on a pretzel and turned to her sister with narrow eyes. "What?" she whispered. "Poor *Mom*? Can you imagine being dragged around to every one of her stupid events? Thank God I only had to go to that *one*."

Violet pointed her toes and shrugged. "Dad's being a baby," she said flatly. "He knows she doesn't have a choice. It's part of her job, showing up at these things. All he has to do is go and eat free food. He just likes to be difficult."

Olivia stared at her sister, jaw frozen midbite. In the old days, Violet had never stuck up for their mom. She and Mac had been a team; frankly, it had always made Olivia a little bit jealous the way they got along. Sure, Olivia and Bridget had more in common, and talked more about things like school, colleges, clubs . . . but they didn't "get" each other the way

Violet and Mac had. And now, all of a sudden, she was turning on him?

Mac bounded down the stairs, looking boyishly handsome in a baby blue golf shirt and loose-fitting corduroy pants.

"Mom's in the car," Olivia called to him as he passed through to the kitchen.

"Thanks," Mac called back, opening and closing the refrigerator door. "There's leftovers in here if you get hungry later."

Olivia perched up on the couch to wave as her dad hustled down the hall. "Thanks, Dad," she said. "Have fun."

She watched him disappear down the stairs through the window before turning back to her sister. Violet had been watching him, too, and Olivia saw now that her eyes were wet at the corners, the tip of her nose turning red.

And that was when she got it.

Maybe it was easier this way. Maybe it didn't hurt as much to see the flaws as it did to remember the good.

"Hey," Olivia said, wobbling her sister's shin with one hand. "Are you okay?"

Violet sniffed quickly and shook her head, her wild hair bouncing over her shoulders. "I'd be a lot better if you got out of those sweatpants and invited Soren over."

Olivia rolled her eyes and smiled. "I told you," she said. "I'm too tired to do anything tonight."

Violet stood and motioned for her sister to get off the couch. "That was before you had the house to yourself," she said, pointing toward the stairs. "This is a whole new ball game. And we gotta get you suited up."

26

*I*nviting a boy over when her parents weren't home probably wouldn't have been Olivia's *top* choice for the world's most comfortable second date.

But Violet was convinced it wouldn't be such a big deal, and to prove it, she gave the following three reasons:

1. Technically, it was the third date. Even though the first time they'd hung out at the farmer's market had been an "accident," they'd spent an awful lot of time alone. And while they were getting all technical with the date defining, shouldn't all of those gym-class runs and late-night phone calls count for something, too?

2. They weren't really going to be alone, since Violet would (half) be there, too.

3 Really? Did she really need a third reason? Had she forgotten how freakishly cute and·practically perfect he was in every way?

If she had forgotten, it didn't take much more than Soren showing up at her door, armed with a pint of Ben & Jerry's Coffee Heath Bar Crunch and the entire Wes Anderson catalogue on DVD, to jog her memory.

They were halfway through *Bottle Rocket* when Olivia decided she was starving. Also, she had basically zero idea what was going on in the movie, since every time Soren shifted on the couch to tug at the bottom of his jeans, or cleared his throat or, you know, breathed, her heart swelled up to the size of a watermelon at the thought that maybe this would be it. Maybe this would be the second when she would finally get kissed.

She wasn't really sure what came over her. It wasn't like she was especially experienced in the kissing department, unless she counted the time she'd met Micah Greenberg behind the athletics shed for some choreographed pecking and teeth-gnashing. Which, usually, she didn't.

During the Roxie dog-umentary, she had been perfectly content with holding Soren's hand, and probably wouldn't have known what to do if things had progressed beyond that. And in the quick little rendezvous they'd had over the last week, at the lake after gym, or in the alley near school, she'd been too paralyzed with fear that Calla or someone would turn the corner at any time to even entertain the possibility of making out. Even when Violet had brought up the idea of inviting Soren over to an empty house, Olivia's first thought had naturally been: *But what will my excuse be when he leans in for a kiss?*

So she was a little confused by the fact that every time he looked in her direction, the overriding sensation tingling through her veins and making it nigh impossible to focus on anything else wasn't exactly *fear,* so much as mind-scrambling, heart-blasting, pulse-quickening *anticipation.*

Olivia fumbled around on the coffee table for the DVD remote and quickly found the pause button. "Are you hungry?" she asked, hopping over the back of the couch and rounding the corner island that separated the living room from the kitchen.

Soren pushed a handful of honey-colored hair back from his forehead and shrugged. "I'm always hungry," he said, his crooked smile twitching into place as he palmed the tops of his knees. He was wearing the same dark jeans Olivia loved, and a light gray waffle shirt with a thick red stripe at the bottoms of the sleeves. It wasn't supertight, but she could definitely make out the narrow lines of muscles beneath the fabric when he stretched his arms out all the way.

Olivia found a pile of delivery menus in a drawer by the sink and hopped back onto the couch, tucking her knees beneath her. Violet had talked her into wearing the pale yellow, sweatshirt-material American Apparel skirt they'd bought the week before, paired with a gauzy button-down with tiny purple flowers and short, frilly sleeves. Violet insisted that the outfit said "casual" and "feminine," but Olivia was now regretting the skirt decision, since she was constantly pulling the garment down over her knees, terrified that it might ride up whenever she shifted positions.

"What do you feel like?" she asked him, automatically organizing the menus by cuisine.

Violet, who was settled into the overstuffed armchair across the room, dramatically cleared her throat.

Olivia looked up to find Soren staring at her from across the couch.

"What?" she asked, checking to see if anything was amiss. It was her skirt again, wasn't it?

"I'd say he's hungry for something else," Violet stage-whispered, and Olivia cringed. She was already regretting allowing Violet to stick around, and wondered if her sister would ever give the running commentary a rest.

"Nothing," Soren said, quickly shifting his gaze to the menus. "Sorry, I was just—I actually ate at home."

Olivia looked quickly to Violet, who shrugged.

"Oh," Olivia said, dropping the menus into her lap. "Okay, well, we don't have to order anything. . . ."

"No, you should," Soren encouraged. "I could probably eat something. My parents made me try these satay things they're learning to make in their Indonesian cooking class."

"Cooking class?" Olivia asked.

Soren rolled his eyes. "Yeah, that's Wednesday night's activity," he said dryly. "They sign up for every papermaking workshop and Farsi language class in the Bay Area."

Olivia tucked her finger underneath the elastic of one short sleeve, tugging it down toward her elbow. "What do you your parents do?" she asked. It seemed weird that she didn't already know this. It also seemed weird, she realized with a jolt, that Soren had parents. He seemed to exist completely independently of anybody else . . . friends, family, anyone. It was like Soren was part of his own little universe, and she still couldn't believe she'd been invited inside.

"They're graphic designers," he said. "They have a business designing logos for websites and things."

Olivia nodded, wondering when somebody was going

to answer this question in a way that made sense. In Willis, everybody's dad was in finance, and everybody's mom stayed home, or maybe sold real estate on the weekends. Mac and Bridget had been the exception. In San Francisco, Olivia hadn't met a single person whose parents did anything . . . normal. They were all ambassadors or filmmakers or web designers or puppeteers. Olivia had never known these things were actual jobs.

"They used to be artists," Soren continued, pushing up the faded sleeves of his shirt. "I mean, they still are, I guess. My mom paints and my dad does these weird wire sculpture things. They have a studio in the backyard."

Olivia smiled. "They must really get along," she said, trying to imagine her parents taking classes together or working together in the same space. It was such a foreign concept she couldn't even envision what it would mean. Would they eat lunch together, too?

"They're like one person," Soren said. "They even kind of look alike. It's ridiculous." He sank back into the leather couch. "They're pretty lucky, though," he conceded. "If I had one wish in the world, it would be to be able to do all the things I love, all the time. I guess that's why my parents started their business. All they ever want to do is make things and hang out at home. And that's basically all they do."

Olivia imagined a life of hanging out with Soren at home and making things. It didn't matter that she didn't know how to use a glue stick, let alone paint or play an instrument or ride a skateboard. She'd learn.

"What about you?" he asked, tapping the top of her knee with the side of one finger, a sly smile turning up the corners of his mouth. "If you could have anything, *anything at all . . .* what would you wish for?"

Olivia's eyes grew wide and found Violet across the room, frozen and staring back at her sister, her eyes round as saucers. "Hmm," Olivia pretended to consider. "I don't know. Pizza?"

Soren smiled, propping one elbow up on the back of the sofa and tilting his head closer to hers.

"I'm serious," he said. "Haven't you ever thought about it?"

His words settled in the air between them. Olivia felt her smile fading and lowered her chin, a cool tumble of still-damp hair tripping over her shoulder and covering one side of her face.

Right then, if she had been wearing a magical dress, she would have wished for words. Words to be able to tell him that not only had she *thought* about it, but she'd already made a wish, a pretty big wish, and the result of that wish was sitting across the room from them, watching their every move.

Or maybe words to tell him that she still had two wishes left, and despite all of Violet's suggestions, and all of the early-morning hours when she should have still been sleeping spent searching the farthest reaches of her brain for inspiration, she couldn't even think of anything to wish for.

She looked up and saw that Soren had inched just slightly closer, so that his chin was centimeters from her face. He reached forward, tucked the strand of escaping curls back behind her ear, and Olivia felt a shock travel up her spine, a swirling tingle at the base of her neck.

There it was. Her answer. If she could do anything, right there, right then, it would be to kiss this boy, sitting across from her, apparently waiting to be kissed.

And so she did, leaning forward just enough to press her lips softly against his. His mouth was open a little and he tasted like warm toothpaste, his cheek smooth and cool against her chin.

They were kissing! And suddenly she was full of wishes. She wished this moment would last for the rest of her life. She wished she could jump up and down (without having to stop kissing). But mostly, she wished Violet would leave the room.

As if on cue, she heard Violet pulling herself out of the chair. Olivia opened one eye and peered out over Soren's shoulder, to where Violet was standing at the door.

"Good answer," Violet said, tossing her sister a knowing wink as she hurried up the stairs.

27

Olivia stood in her matching turquoise Gap Body bra and boy-shorts in front of the open closet door. Soren had left late the night before, barely missing her parents coming home, and Olivia had hurried to bed and pretended to be fast asleep, cradling her marine biology textbook, a wistful smile permanently fixed on her face.

In the flurry of events she'd forgotten to set her alarm, and had woken up with hardly enough time to shower before she was supposed to be at Calla's house. The fashion show was less than two weeks away, and they still hadn't decided on the entertainment. Today's plan was to sift through the DJ samples they'd collected and finally book somebody for the show.

"What do you wear to audition DJs?" Olivia asked, arms crossed over her narrow, naked waist as she perused her hanging clothes for inspiration.

"I refuse to be of any assistance until you've given up the goods," Violet sulked as she stared out the window. She had been trying all night and morning long to get details of Olivia's "alone time" with Soren, to very little avail.

"I told you," Olivia said sternly. "I don't kiss and tell."

"Well, I *know* you kissed," Violet scoffed. "It's what happened after the kissing that I'm worried about."

Olivia whipped a sweater across the room at her sister. "What kind of girl do you think I am?" she laughed, feigning modesty.

Violet groaned and hopped down from the window ledge. "That's what I was afraid of," she said, peering over Olivia's shoulder into the closet.

"Here," Violet said, reaching for a high-waisted jersey dress with a loud geometric print.

"Too festive," Olivia vetoed, opting for an oversize, scoop-necked pearl-colored sweater, dark skinny jeans, and her beloved charcoal boots instead.

Violet shrugged and lowered herself to the floor, scrunching up against the edge of the bed. "So what's on the agenda for us today?" she asked.

Olivia climbed into her jeans and pulled them up over her hips.

"I'm not really sure," she answered vaguely, tugging the fuzzy sweater down over her head. "I think just listening to a bunch of cheesy wedding DJs. I'd stay home if I could."

Olivia chewed the inside of her bottom lip and held her breath. She felt awful asking Violet not to come along, but it was getting increasingly difficult to keep all of her stories straight *without* having to pointedly ignore a chatty ghost while doing it. After all, it was publicly arguing with Violet that had gotten Olivia into this copilot mess in the first place.

"That was subtle," Violet said, staring out the window. Olivia lifted her makeup bag from the top of her dresser and fumbled around for her Kiehl's grapefruit moisturizer. She squeezed a dollop of thick cream into her palm. "It's not that I don't want you there," she hedged. "It's just—"

"I get it," Violet said, pulling herself to her feet and stalking back to the window. "But are you sure it's a good idea to spend so much time with Calla? Now that things with Soren are so . . ." She trailed off.

Olivia froze, her hand cupping the bottom of one dry elbow. "You told me to go for Soren—"

"I know, I know," Violet admitted. "But that was before you started hanging out with Calla every day."

"I do not hang out with her every day," Olivia argued. "But what am I supposed to do? Quit the committee? Stop seeing Soren?"

"I don't have *all* the answers, O. I'm just trying to help," Violet said, sulking against the window and pressing one side of her freckled face against the glass. She hugged her legs to her chest, her pale arms looking like fragile twigs wrapped around her bony, scraped knees.

Olivia looked at her sister and was slowly reminded of the little girl she used to watch climbing the craggy oak tree in their backyard. Violet would always manage to climb just a little too high, getting stuck in the tallest branches while Olivia barked orders from the ground. *Come down,* she'd insist, stomping a foot, arms crossed. *You'll get hurt.*

Olivia quietly screwed the cap on the tube of moisturizer and placed it back on her dresser. She sat down on the bed, stepping out of her boots and lining them against the wall.

"What are you doing?" Violet asked. "Aren't you already late?"

Olivia shrugged as she slid back on the bed, crossing her legs and leaning against the headboard. "I think Calla can handle choosing a sound track without me," Olivia said quietly. "And besides, I'd rather hang out with you."

Violet suddenly laughed. "Oh, no," she said from the window. "Not the pity hangout."

"It's not pity," Olivia insisted. "I'd just rather be here."

Violet looked at her sister long and hard before joining her on the bed.

"Well, guess what?" she asked lightly. "I'd rather have the afternoon off. What do you think about that?"

Olivia squinted at her sister carefully. "Are you sure?"

"Sure I'm sure," Violet said. "You can't hang out with a ghost all day. And really, you have no choice. You have to go. You're a cochair, that's what cochairs do: co-go."

Violet pointed to Olivia's boots that were slumping against the wall.

"Are you sure you don't want to come?" Olivia asked.

Violet scoffed. "And be stuck inside, listening to bad party techno all afternoon?" she asked. "I think I'll pass."

Olivia smiled gratefully at her sister and pushed off the bed. As she reached out to tuck the closet door closed, her eyes caught her own reflection in the hanging mirror. Her hair was falling in loose, copper curls down past her shoulders, her skin looked creamy and fresh, and for once, she didn't hate the confetti freckles across the bridge of her nose.

"You look beautiful," Violet said softly from the bed. And for the first time, Olivia believed her.

"Is this a human or a robot?" Eve asked from the middle of Calla's canopied king-size bed. Eve, Lark, and Calla were all huddled on top of the sea-foam down comforter, weeding through a stack of CDs and discarding ones with weird names or questionable cover art.

"Maybe both?" Calla suggested, raising an eyebrow and smiling as she saw Olivia at the door. "You made it!"

"Sorry I'm late," Olivia said, settling into a studded plush armchair by the window. She was worried that she'd left the lower half of her jaw at the bottom of the massive marble staircase she'd just climbed from the grand foyer below. Calla's room was on the third floor of a stately, pillared Victorian that seemed to occupy much of a full block in Pacific Heights.

"No problem," Calla said, scooping up a pile of pens from a cup on her bedside table and passing them out to the group.

It was strange to see her in her natural habitat. Every article of clothing was neatly tucked into a glass-windowed, knob-footed armoire; the pillows rose from the headboard as if they had been freshly fluffed; and the ivory rug was plush and without a single stain or marking. It looked more like a room you'd pay to see from behind a velvet rope than one you'd have a sleepover in. Even *Calla* seemed a little out of place.

"Okay," Calla began, separating the CDs into smaller piles. "Remember, we're looking for something cool but not intimidating. We know our parents, and we know they like to think they're still as hip as we are, but secretly they're just hoping for a lot of Bob Dylan and Joni Mitchell."

"I love Bob Dylan," Eve pouted.

"Yeah, well, so does everybody," Calla teased, "but nobody wants to listen to him whining while they're trying to get drunk." She stood and crossed the room to where Olivia was sitting. "And, as Graham so eloquently pointed out, the drunker people get," she went on, "the bigger the checks they'll be writing for the thrift shop, right?"

Olivia nodded as Calla handed over a grouping of discs and promotional materials.

"Madonna, you're too far away," she said flatly as she settled back on the bed. "Come on the bed with us. We don't bite." Calla's hair was wet and looked heavy as she piled it on top of her head and smiled. She stretched the long, slender line of her neck from side to side, reminding Olivia of an exotic bird or sleek jungle cat.

"Lark might," Eve added, and she and Calla erupted into a fit of caustic laughter. Lark flipped her pen at Eve's knee as Olivia slowly made her way over to the showroom-style bed, settling gingerly into one corner.

"Progress." Calla smiled, turning to her bedside table, where a Bose alarm clock and CD player stood proudly at the center of a semicircle of framed photos.

Olivia squinted to better see the people in the pictures as Eve bent forward to pick one up.

"What is this?" Eve asked dryly. Her dark eyes narrowed, the corners of her pouty lips turned down.

As she brought the picture into her lap, Olivia could see that it was a black-and-white shot of Calla and Soren, sitting against one of the stone benches in the courtyard at school. Calla was leaning into Soren's lap, and Soren's chin was resting in the nook of her shoulder. She was midlaugh, her skin smooth and flawless, her eyes sparkling. His smile was quieter, but undeniably happy—the calm smile of somebody comfortably, assuredly in love.

Olivia's fingers tingled and the back of her neck grew hot.

"Oh, no," Lark said, grabbing the frame and opening the top drawer of the nightstand. "This *cannot* be on display."

Calla intercepted the frame and replaced it next to the speakers. "What's the big deal?" she said defensively. "Just because we're taking a break doesn't mean we're not still friends. I don't have to pretend he's dead or anything."

Lark stared pointedly at Eve for a long moment, her arms crossed against her chest. "Well?" Lark asked coolly. "Are you going to tell her?"

Eve pulled the sleeves of her polka-dot wrap shirt down over her thumbs and fidgeted with the fraying seams.

"Tell me what?" Calla asked, her eyes darting from one girl to the other.

Olivia's heart dropped to the bottom of her stomach. Had Eve seen her that day on the street? Was she going to give her up now, in front of everyone?

"What's going on, guys?" Calla asked, soft and slow and in a way that made it clear she didn't really want to know the answer.

"Nothing," Eve muttered, glaring at Lark before turning to lay a comforting hand on Calla's knee. "It's just, well, Graham said that Soren told him something at band practice last weekend, and I've been trying to decide if I should tell you or not, because I didn't know if you were—"

"He's seeing someone else!" Lark interrupted, exploding

like a popped balloon. She exhaled heavily and turned to Calla. "I'm really sorry, Cal. But I thought you should know."

Calla's eyes hadn't moved from the pile of CDs in her lap. For a long, loooooong moment, nobody said anything, and Olivia uncomfortably shifted her weight from one arm to the other. Was that all Graham had said?

"Well," Calla said, stacking the CD cases so that the edges lined up. She looked up at the three of them and smiled, a tiny, heartbreaking, helpless smile that made Olivia want to bury her face in one of the super-fluffy pillows and smother herself to death.

"What you need is a distraction," Eve said abruptly, climbing up to her knees. "Maybe it *is* just a break with Soren, but you can't just sit here moping while he's running around having fun."

"Who's moping?" Calla asked, but even Olivia wasn't completely fooled by her bravado.

"Oh, my God!" Lark shrieked, lunging off the bed and reaching for her iPhone in the outside pocket of her leather hobo satchel. "I completely forgot. Remember my cousin Farley, the poet?"

"The one who used to write sonnets and give dramatic readings at your holiday parties?" Eve asked, rolling her almond-shaped eyes.

"Yes," Lark said impatiently, "but that was during his angsty high school phase. He goes to Berkeley now, and we ran into him at that coffee shop out there—remember, Calla?"

"Sure." Calla nodded, busily rifling through the CDs and removing one at random from its case. "He was pretty cute, right?"

Lark scoffed. "I mean, he's my cousin," she said, with a thin layer of fake disgust. "But yes. He is ridiculous. Like, in that quiet, scholarly-but-not-geeky-smart-and-still-totally-hilarious kind of way. Plus, he does crew, so his body is insane."

"How do you know?" Eve asked suspiciously. "Does he do his readings shirtless these days?"

Lark threw a pillow at her and Eve pretended to fall backward off the bed. "Anyway," Lark went on, "he's asked about you maybe seventeen times since that day you met, and let's just say he was *very* interested to learn about your breakup."

"Break," Calla corrected, popping a disc into the stereo and closing the lid. "Not breakup."

Eve and Lark shared a quick, charged look. Olivia realized it had been a while since she'd filled her own lungs, and searched Calla's hardened face with desperate eyes.

Calla pressed a button and a sudden burst of halting, loud electronic music blared from the speakers. She quickly stabbed at the stereo's center console and an abrupt silence fell around them.

Calla raised her dark, full brows and turned to Lark, exhaling a thin stream of air.

"Well?" she asked, a wry smile settling into the corners of her lips. "Did you give him my number or what?"

Lark and Eve smiled, and Olivia felt a shift in the room, as if a window had opened and the air had changed.

"Consider it done," Lark said. "Maybe I could even convince him to come up to the beach house next weekend."

Calla shrugged as Eve passed her another CD and snapped open the case. "Yeah," she agreed vaguely. "Maybe." She stuck a finger in the hole of the plastic disc and held it over the stereo before turning abruptly to face Olivia at the foot of the bed. "Madonna, I almost forgot. Next weekend a bunch of us are going to help Lark open her house at Stinson Beach. You should totally come."

Olivia felt her stomach squirming and tried to plaster on a smile as Eve jumped in to continue.

"We do it every year," she said, tucking back a section of her layered black hair with a silver bobby pin. "It's such a blast."

Olivia nodded and swallowed. She felt like a thousand tiny hands were pulling her in different directions.

"My parents aren't coming up until Saturday," Lark said. "So Friday night we'll have the place all to ourselves."

"Just us, though, right?" Calla asked, her voice high and a little anxious. "Last year it turned into this huge thing— everybody came up. But this year I just want it to be our closest friends."

Our. Closest. Friends? Olivia's breath caught in the back of her throat, and she imagined her heart freezing, all of the blood flowing backward in her veins and drawing the color from her cheeks. Olivia imagined them all hanging out by a bonfire and staying up late, sleeping on the beach and waking up with sand in their hair. . . .

But she knew it was impossible. First of all, Violet would never go for it. She'd say it was too dangerous, and she'd be right. What if there were more of those fizzy pink drinks— what were they called? Fellinis? What if Olivia had one too many and said something stupid about Soren? And besides, after what had happened with Violet that morning, Olivia was feeling a little bit guilty about all the time she'd been spending away from home. She'd been given the gift of her sister back.

Shouldn't they spend as much time together as they possibly could?

"What do you think?" Calla asked again, her finger hovering over the play button. "Can you come?"

Olivia took a deep breath, shifting positions on the bed so that her long legs dangled over the carpet. "I don't know. I think I'm supposed to go away with my parents next weekend. I'll have to check."

"Okay." Calla shrugged, turning back to the stereo and adjusting the volume. A Bollywood remix of "YMCA" blasted through the speakers and everybody recoiled.

"Next!" Calla shouted over the offensive music. The girls laughed, and Olivia exhaled, grateful for the interruption.

28

"**I** think you make a perfect Lily."

It was Monday afternoon and Olivia was sitting across from Miles at a cramped sushi place a few blocks from school, with square, metallic tables tucked between red-cushioned booths and low-backed chairs. Her yellow composition notebook was open to an empty page, where she was supposed to be jotting down notes for their scene project, due in Whitley's class the following week.

Instead she was doodling her name, and transforming the perforated holes on the lined pages into little oblong hearts.

"Hello?" Miles laughed. "What are you writing over there?"

Olivia hurried to cover the page with her hand and looked up. Miles was staring at her expectantly, a small bowl of edamame untouched between them.

"Sorry," she said. "What was that?"

Miles rolled his eyes playfully and reached for a soybean pod. "I was just saying," he said, sucking the beans between his teeth and discarding the wrinkled shell on a plate. "I snuck a look at the footage we shot in your yard, and you look—I mean, it looks great."

"Oh, good," Olivia said, her voice distant. She hadn't seen Soren since Friday night at her house, and he hadn't called all weekend long. She'd been replaying the night over and over in her head, trying to figure out what could have gone wrong.

"So what did you get up to this weekend?" Miles asked, and Olivia felt her pulse throbbing in her ears. What did he mean, *get up to*? Had somebody found out Soren had been at her house? Was that why he hadn't called?

Miles accidentally knocked the strap of his vinyl messenger bag off the back of his chair. He fumbled around with his feet, wedging the bag back under the table and scooting his chair a few inches in.

Olivia bit down on the bean pod in her mouth and pulled the hard little beans out of the fuzzy skin through her teeth. "I'm cochairing this fashion show fundraiser for the thrift store with Calla," Olivia said happily. "I was pretty much busy all weekend with that. . . ." She trailed off as she realized that Miles wasn't really listening. "What about you?" she asked, sitting back in her seat.

Miles shrugged. "Not much. I was hoping we could take a drive down to Santa Cruz and shoot some footage of this lighthouse down there," he said, pushing a pile of empty soybean shells around on his plate with a fork. "I tried calling your house, but your dad said you were out."

Olivia looked up, momentarily surprised that her dad hadn't at least left her a note, before remembering that he'd hardly come up from his shop in the basement all weekend long.

"What about this weekend?" Olivia asked. "Could we do the drive then?"

Miles looked up as a petite waitress in a gold leaf kimono arrived at their table, bearing a bamboo tray of neatly cut hand rolls. Olivia was admiring the tiny carrot shavings arranged in an igloo sculpture at the corner of the plate, when something outside the window caught her eye. She looked up to see Soren crossing the street, waving at her discreetly from behind an expired parking meter.

Olivia glanced back at Miles, who was breaking apart his chopsticks and rubbing them together, sanding down the splintered wood. Soren was standing directly on the other side of the glass behind him, and Olivia tried to sneak a smile over Miles's shoulder.

"I guess this weekend would work," Miles said, while Soren took out his phone and pointed at it sideways, mouthing the word *broken* a few times, until Olivia understood and nodded. Miles looked up and she quickly brought a hand to her neck, pretending to be stretching out a kink.

"Cool," she said, waving the tips of her fingers to Soren, who was now doing a mimed performance of dialing on an old-school rotary phone, explaining that he'd call her later from his house. Olivia imagined how absurd he must look to people on the street, and had to cover her mouth with her hand to keep from laughing.

Miles looked up, catching her before her smile had completely disappeared. He followed her gaze back over his shoulder, just as Soren was tucking his phone into the pocket of his coat and stepping out into traffic. Unfortunately, the light had just changed, and Soren had to hop back up on the curb, nearly avoiding a scary collision with an oncoming trolley.

"Are you . . . ?" Miles started, looking back to Olivia across the table. "I mean, are you and Soren . . . ?"

Olivia tucked a spicy tuna roll in between the open ends of her chopsticks, hoping the wasabi would help explain away any redness in her cheeks.

"No," she said quietly. "We're just friends."

But as she looked up for the soy sauce, she saw that something in Miles's posture had changed. He had stopped chewing, and his eyes were big and blank, like he was busy processing something he couldn't quite believe.

Olivia cleared her throat. "Could you pass the ginger?"

Miles swallowed his bite and pushed the tiny glass bowl of pink ginger across the table. "Sure," he said, taking the red cloth napkin from his lap and wiping it across his mouth.

"Thanks," Olivia said, the pounding of her pulse in her ears fading to a distant patter. "So. Let's talk lighthouses."

29

"What about that one?" Violet asked, pointing up at the dense night sky.

It was after sunset, and the girls were stretched out against the sloping bow of Grandpa Joe's yacht, naming constellations as they flickered into view behind sweeps of clouds and thick hanging fog. Olivia had decided that the likelihood of ever spotting a shooting star in this city was slim to none, and Violet was gamely attempting to prove her wrong.

"No," Olivia said, tucking the old fleece blanket they'd found under one of the built-in benches around the tops of her bare feet. "That's a plane. It's red."

Violet peered closer at the sky, her arms crossed around her knees, the straps of her green camisole down around her elbows.

"Really?" she asked. "Maybe it's a planet. Isn't Mars red?"

The blinking light in question broke through a patch of clouds and began its descent toward the airport on the other side of the jagged city skyline.

"Unless Mars is coming in for a landing," Olivia said with a laugh, "I'm pretty sure it's a plane."

Violet shrugged and stretched her long legs out over the blanket, leaning back onto her elbows. "What time is it?" she asked with a yawn.

Olivia reached into the back pocket of her jeans for her phone. Nine twenty-two. It was a little late to be out on a school night, but her parents weren't exactly keeping tabs on her every move these days. In fact, they were the reason Olivia had suggested a late-night escape to the boat in the first place.

Olivia had been in her room, quietly working on a paper for her Eastern religion class and listening to the CD Soren had burned for her of his favorite bands (which ranged, incidentally, from the Kinks to the Pixies, making a number of stops at other plural nouns along the way), when the evening's yell-a-thon had begun. This time, it seemed to revolve around Mac's lack of motivation, and whether or not any actual progress had been made on the house. The "plan" had been for Mac to do some quick, necessary improvements on the house, enough to make it livable, and then find steady work as a contractor, like he'd had in Willis.

Mac played the "failing economy" card, and Violet, listening at an open crack in Olivia's bedroom door, rolled her eyes. Olivia's heart hurt at the idea of her dad struggling to find work, even if there was work to be found. She knew what it was like to feel stuck.

It wasn't until Bridget brought up the boat that Olivia decided she couldn't take any more. The broker Bridget had hired had found buyers, filthy rich newlyweds from Marin, and they would be taking the boat for a test trip down the California coast. If all went well, the boat would be theirs. When Mac protested, Bridget had even more ammunition: "Maybe if you were working, we wouldn't need to sell it!"

Olivia and Violet couldn't imagine not having their refuge in the Sausalito harbor, and decided to take advantage of every minute they had left.

"Do you think it's safe to go back?" Olivia asked, dreading the thought of returning home to more slamming doors. She'd been so caught up with everything going on in her own life, ping-ponging between Soren and Calla, and having Violet back, she'd hardly even noticed that her parents had become practically unrecognizable from the people they'd been before. They'd always been different, but they used to complement each other. Bridget kept everything in order, while Mac gave her something to tidy up. Now their communication styles oscillated between two polar extremes: red-faced screaming fits and harsh, pointed silence.

"I don't know," Violet said softly. "I'm worried about them."

Olivia kept her eyes on the blurry night sky but felt the sides of her neck getting hot. "Me, too," she whispered.

Her eyes stung as she turned her face toward the salty ocean breeze. She listened to the lull of the waves, her chest rising and falling with each steady breath. All of a sudden, happy, playful voices approached from the end of the dock. Olivia turned to see two shadows walking toward the boat.

"Oh, no," she whispered as a couple appeared in the floodlights, tottering down the wobbly plank in fancy shoes and pointing directly at . . . her. "Should we hide?"

Violet turned and then gestured to a small crack between a built-in bench and the shiny white wall of the upper cabin. "Squeeze in there," Violet directed.

"What about you?" Olivia asked, crawling beneath the edge of the hull and folding herself into the cramped, narrow space.

Violet, wedged on the bench on top of her, flopped her head down to stare Olivia in the eyes. "I think I'll manage," she said dryly, and Olivia smiled.

Right. The ghost thing. How convenient.

Olivia held her breath as the voices grew louder and closer. The man sounded vaguely British, or maybe Australian, and the woman was definitely after-dinner tipsy.

"I just wanted to look at it again," the woman slurred. "I can't wait for this weekend. I've always dreamed of sailing down the coast." She giggled as the man pulled her closer to him.

"And I've always dreamed of making your dreams come true," he said.

Olivia had to swallow hard to keep from gagging.

"Come on," the man said, as the dock creaked beneath them. "Let's get you to bed."

The sounds of footsteps faded back down the dock toward the parking lot, and Violet's upside-down head appeared in front of Olivia.

"All clear," she whispered, as Olivia stretched her legs and shimmied out of the space.

"Disgusting," Olivia muttered, swatting at her jeans and leaning over the dock to see the couple climbing into a stocky black convertible. "I can't believe we're losing our boat to people like that."

Violet was standing at the railing, looking down at the gentle waves lapping against the swaying dock. "They're just excited. I would be, too, if I was about to go on my dream trip."

Olivia stood next to Violet, sneaking glances at her sister's profile, washed in the pale reflection of the moon-drenched bay. Sometimes Olivia forgot that her sister was always seeing things from the outside, as somebody who used to be a part of things and was now just an observer. It must be terrible to know you'd never do all of the things you'd dreamed of doing.

Violet took a deep, thoughtful breath before turning to her sister. "Anyway," she said, waving the wistful moment out of the air with a swipe of her hand. "What's up this weekend? Anything fun?"

Olivia leaned back on her heels, balancing against the cool metal railing. "Not really," she said. "Calla's going away, so I won't have any cochairing to do."

"She's going away the week before the fashion show?" Violet asked, her voice deep and drenched in mock horror.

Olivia smiled and shrugged. "Yup," she said. "I guess it's an annual thing. Everybody goes up to Lark's beach house to open it up for the season. There's a party on Friday night. Calla invited me, but I don't really feel like going." Olivia swallowed hard, expecting a *What did I tell you?* speech about getting too close to Calla. But Violet said nothing, just nibbled gently at the corner of her lip and considered Olivia through half-squinting eyes. "Besides," Olivia went on, "it's supposed to be nice out this weekend. I was thinking we could check out Angel Island. I heard there are some really pretty hikes."

Violet nodded slowly, her eyes wandering off to one side of Olivia's head.

"Violet? What's wrong?" Olivia asked, turning around to follow her sister's vacant stare.

"I think you should go this weekend." Violet stared into the distance a moment longer before looking back at Olivia with a soft, sad smile. "You're going to need friends, after—"

Olivia's heart jammed up against her ribs. "After what?" she asked. "What are you talking about?"

Violet shook her head. "Nothing," she said, swinging her hips to nudge Olivia's side. "But as long as you have something to do, maybe I could stow away with the love-birds. . . ."

Olivia considered her sister out of the corner of her eye. "You're going to go with them?" Her hair was flapping wildly in the wind and she struggled to keep it out of her face.

Violet shrugged, lowering herself to a rounded blue bench built in against the bow. "Why not?" she asked, tucking her bare knees up to her chest and leaning her head back against the railing. "It's not like they're going to notice an invisible third wheel. . . ."

Olivia sat next to her on the bench, picking at the fraying hem of her sister's long denim shorts. "I wish I could go, too." Olivia sighed.

Violet laughed and straightened out her long legs, crossing her ankles on the yacht's shiny white floor. "Too bad you don't have one of your dresses," she joked. "I'm pretty sure they'd notice you, no matter how drunk or blinded by love they are."

Olivia laughed and lowered her head onto Violet's shoulder, looking up at the stars.

"What about that one?" Violet asked, pointing up at the city skyline. A light was flashing at the top of a tower, and if you squinted, it almost looked like a flickering star.

"Nope," Olivia said quietly, as a strand of Violet's loose curls fell into her face, tickling the top of her forehead. "Not quite."

30

"No way." Calla laughed, reaching across the center console to scroll through Lark's iPod. "I promised myself I'd never eat at In-N-Out Burger again."

Olivia was squeezed in the backseat of Lark's ruby red Mini Cooper convertible. Lark had picked the girls up after school, and they'd made it over the Golden Gate Bridge before the worst of rush-hour traffic. Olivia hung her head out of the window, enjoying her first passenger ride along the water, and imagining where Violet was on her trip. She'd hugged her sister good-bye that morning for a full minute, suddenly more nervous than excited about spending a whole weekend alone with the girls.

But so far, the trip had been fun. Eve sat in the middle beside Olivia, busily knitting a stripy spring scarf, and at the other window was Austin, the pixie-haired girl from Olivia's art class, hungry and begging for fast food.

"Come on," Austin whined, running a hand through her

choppy blond hair and sticking a foot into the back of Calla's seat. "We're all the way out here and I never get to go. Animal! Animal!"

Olivia raised an eyebrow and Lark caught her in the rearview mirror.

"It's true," Lark said, flipping on her blinker and veering onto the exit ramp. "And I'm guessing Olivia's never had it animal style before."

The girls giggled as they pulled into the parking lot, an enormous yellow arrow pointing the way to a roadside restaurant, reminiscent of old-fashioned soda shops Olivia had only seen in the movies. "Animal style?" she asked, slightly afraid of the answer. But she was starving, and secretly hoped that whatever this animal style was, it involved actual beef and not meat-flavored, burger-shaped soy.

Austin dug in her overnight bag for her wallet, a handmade Velcroed billfold covered in pretty plaid fabric, and opened her door before Lark had even tucked all the way into the parking spot. "It's a burger fried in mustard, with pickles and grilled onions," she said. "It's part of the secret menu. You have to know to ask."

Eve and Lark piled out of the Mini while Calla crossed her arms in the front.

"I can't believe you guys are doing this," she pouted, and Olivia wondered if she should stay behind. "Lark, you brat. I thought you were going veggie with me!"

Lark shrugged and shut her door. "Special occasion," she said. "Coming, Olivia?"

Lark rarely offered invitations of any kind to Olivia, and Olivia felt it was in her best interest to accept if she wanted the weekend to go smoothly. Plus, she had to admit, this secret burger sounded pretty good.

And it was. Back in the car with little cardboard boxes open on their laps, the girls passed containers of ketchup and dug into their messy meals, the sticky orange sauce dribbling down their chins.

Lark waved her double burger under Calla's nose, but Calla refused to give in, though she did steal a handful of fries as Lark wedged them in the cup holder and turned the car back on.

"You and Farley are perfect together," Lark said, buckling her seat belt and stepping lightly on the gas. "He always brings one of those tofurkey things to Thanksgiving. Have you ever tried one of those? They literally taste like feet."

Eve washed down a mouthful of mushy fries with a swig of root beer and reached over Olivia to push Calla's shoulder. "I totally forgot you guys went out!" she squealed. "How was it?"

Calla flipped down the visor and began parting her hair in the mirror, a sly smile flickering into place. Olivia caught her own reflection over Calla's shoulder and willed her eyes to stay steady. Interested . . . but not too interested.

"Amazing," she said, sneaking a glance at Lark, as if asking for permission to go on. Lark shrugged and rolled up her window, a stuffy silence settling back around them.

"Spill it," she said. "It's not like he's my brother. I see him twice a year."

Calla smiled and flipped the visor back up, satisfied that her hair was sufficiently wavy and shiny. "He took me to this adorable little vegan place on Valencia," she said. "And then we just walked around for, like, two hours. We have so much in common, it's scary."

"Did he read you any of his poems?" Austin asked with a chuckle.

"No." Calla rolled her eyes.

"When are you going to hang out with him again?" Olivia asked, careful to keep her voice steady. Eve handed over her crumpled-up wrapper and gestured toward the trash.

Calla shrugged. "We'll see," she said with a smile.

Austin shook the back of Calla's chair as Eve danced in her seat excitedly. Olivia rolled down her window as they pulled onto a winding mountain road, the sweet smell of eucalyptus filling the car. Maybe she didn't have any reason to be nervous after all.

🦋 🦋 🦋

After passing through a pair of iron security gates and parking the Mini in front of a sprawling, shingled beach house, Lark flung the front door open and immediately began issuing a series of commands.

"Open every window you see," she said, dropping her silver Nike duffel bag at the foot of the crisp white stairs and waving a hand in front of her face. "It smells like a nursing home in here."

Eve and Austin scrambled up the wide staircase to claim guest rooms as Calla and Lark flitted around the first floor, drawing back white curtains and exposing floor-to-ceiling windows that looked out over the deck and the expanse of ocean and sky beyond.

Olivia stood frozen in the foyer, taking it all in. With every mile they had driven out of the city, Olivia had felt her eyes growing wider and wider. Suburban sprawl had given way to lush open spaces, taking them in and out of massive redwood groves as they made their way over the hills toward the ocean. Olivia couldn't believe all this had been just on the other side of the bridge the whole time she'd been in San Francisco, and she'd had no idea.

Her vision had just been starting to adjust, and now this.

The first floor of Lark's beach house was one giant room, all light wood beams and bamboo floors. The kitchen took up one far wall, separated from the rest of the space by a massive butcher-block-topped island, with shiny metallic appliances tucked against the built-in pantry. In the middle of the space was a semicircular cluster of pale blue and white striped love seats, surrounding a stone fireplace and chimney, all sandwiched by sliding glass doors leading out to the deck.

"Earth to Olivia," Lark called out from the downstairs bathroom, where she was standing on the edge of the tub and pushing open a long narrow skylight. "Open the doors to the patio, okay?"

Olivia left her suitcase—black and bulky with rolling wheels, it was the only thing she'd been able to find, and she didn't want to think about how ridiculous it looked next to the pile of gym bags and canvas totes—by the stairs and walked over to the sliding doors, pulling them open and welcoming the muted early-evening breeze.

The deck was split into two levels, the first a round stone patio with a grill in one corner, and down a few steps, a wooden dock that ended right at the water, so that you could sit and dangle your feet over the edge.

Olivia stood at the open door, breathing the salty sea air and closing her eyes. Aside from a few cliff-top views of the bay, it was the first time she'd been at the ocean since the Vineyard the summer before. The water was so much bigger and wilder here, and seemed to never end.

"Who wants red and who wants white?" Lark was crouching in front of a windowed liquor cabinet, taking out unopened bottles of wine. Olivia pulled the screen door shut and went to join the girls, now gathered around the kitchen island, unpacking a bag of groceries Lark's mom had sent up for the house.

"Put some white in the fridge," Austin suggested, twirling a hoop earring at the top of one ear. "And let's break out the hard stuff. Have you guys ever had a Greyhound?" Austin eyed a bottle of Grey Goose vodka in the cabinet and gestured to the plastic container of organic grapefruit juice Eve was lifting out of a wrinkled paper bag.

"Vodka and grapefruit?" Calla seconded. "My sister and I lived on those when I visited her in LA. Be careful, though. They go down easy."

Lark stood on her toes to reach a row of fancy margarita glasses on the top shelf of a built-in cabinet. "Be *very* careful. My parents are coming early in the morning," she warned. "No puking, no passing out in weird places, and *no* redecorating."

Eve giggled, twisting open the bottle of juice. "Oh, my God," she gasped, her tiny features squishing together as she struggled with the stubborn cap. "I forgot about that. The look on your mother's face when she saw all of the furniture upside down in the front yard . . ."

"Yeah, well, *you* got to go home the next day," Lark said dryly, opening a hidden door and revealing a state-of-the-art stereo system. She flipped through a pile of CDs and popped one in, something mellow, vaguely bluegrassy, and probably belonging to her parents. Olivia breathed a tiny sigh of relief, secretly happy for a break from the too-cool hipster bands she was always struggling to keep straight.

Calla metered out healthy slugs of clear vodka, and Eve topped them off with the pulpy pink juice. Austin slid a glass down the island toward Olivia, who was stationed on one of the high-backed stools at the opposite end.

"Cheers," Calla sang, lifting her glass. Olivia circled the thick stem with her fingers, clinking glasses one at a time with each of the girls around her. It all felt so grown-up, but not in a way that felt forced or fake. It was easy, and Olivia felt herself starting to relax.

"Shall we take these outside?" Lark asked dramatically, sauntering over past the couches and running her hand over a panel of light switches, illuminating the wraparound deck.

"Ahhhhhhhhh!" Eve shrieked, pointing through the window at a dark silhouette rounding the corner. The girls all ran to the glass as the shadow stepped into the light, lugging a case of Sierra Nevada and dropping it heavily on the round glass patio table.

"What the hell?" Lark screamed, pulling open the sliding door and stalking outside. "Logan! What are you doing? I told you I was using the house tonight."

Olivia followed Eve and Austin to the windows, watching as Lark seethed with her hands planted squarely on her hips.

Logan stood his ground while Lark threw her hands up and stormed back inside. Logan followed, keeping a careful distance behind. "Good evening, ladies," he said in his extra-low voice from the door. "Sorry about the interruption. We'll stay out of your way, I promise."

Lark froze behind a striped ottoman and slowly swiveled back to face her brother. *"We?"* she repeated. "What 'we'?"

Logan glanced across the open room toward the front door, behind which a muffled chorus of rowdy voices could be heard. The knob turned and the door flung open, revealing Graham, a six-pack of beer wedged under one arm, an acoustic guitar nestled inside the other.

"Surprise!" Graham shouted, careening across the room like a lunatic, plopping the six-pack down on the counter and lifting Eve up by her waist.

Eve squealed, unable to hide her delight, and Olivia took a few steps back so as not to be awkwardly hovering over their embrace. A couple of other guys Olivia recognized from school filtered in, including Austin's dread-headed boyfriend and some of Logan's sophomore friends. The sudden chaos was so overwhelming that Olivia didn't look back to the door until she heard Eve whispering beside her.

"What an asshole," she said. "He knew she'd be here. Why would he even come?"

Olivia's stomach lurched, and she felt herself frantically grasping for little strands of hope. Maybe Eve was talking about somebody else? Maybe Lark had a belligerent ex-boyfriend whom nobody liked?

But all it took was a quick glance to the door and Olivia knew her instincts had been right. She never should have come. She should have stayed home, with Violet, far from Calla, from the beach, and far from Lark's front door, where Soren was now standing.

31

"Hey, Lark." Olivia stood with her back to the refrigerator, her nearly empty glass sweating condensation into the palms of her hands. "Can I ask you something?"

Lark was taking a break from championship rounds of beer pong on the deck, and Olivia had found her by the massive stainless freezer, refilling her glass with chips of machine-made ice. It had taken two Greyhounds and about half of the new Band of Horses album (after Graham hijacked the stereo and hooked up his own iPod to the speakers), but Lark had ultimately forgiven Logan for crashing Girls' Night In. In fact, the siblings had partnered up and were in the middle of a three-game winning streak, tossing Ping-Pong balls into plastic cups of foamy beer from across the table on the porch.

"Sure," Lark said, refilling her glass with grapefruit juice and a splash of vodka from the quickly diminishing supply on the counter. "What's up?"

Olivia sipped lightly at her drink and leaned her back

against the kitchen's center island. "Is Calla okay with Soren being here?" she asked, gesturing to where Calla had just closed herself into the downstairs bathroom. She and Soren had said gracious hellos, and Calla had been busily helping Graham and Eve design a playlist for the evening, but Olivia accidentally kept catching her staring sadly off into space when she thought nobody was looking. "I mean, do you think things are going to get weird?"

Lark closed the refrigerator door and made small circles with the drink in her hand, the ice sloshing against the glass and swirling peachy pink.

"I have a feeling," Lark said, taking a long swig and cracking an ice chip between her back molars, "that *things* are about to get a lot better."

All of a sudden Eve appeared at Olivia's side, hopping up and down at her elbow.

"Lark!" she squealed. "Isn't that your cousin?"

Lark feigned surprise and scanned the room. "Farley?" she asked, sugar-sweet innocence coating her voice. "What would he be doing here?"

Olivia turned to see the front door closing behind a lanky, dark-haired guy, who had just taken off his black peacoat and was searching for a place to hang it up.

"I called him," Lark admitted. "I figured Calla could use a little distraction."

Eve beamed at Lark and squeezed her waist. "You're so bad," she giggled as they all turned to watch the scene unfold. Farley, Lark's cousin, was indisputably attractive, but in that brooding, intellectual, undercover-vampire kind of way.

"Hey, Cal," Lark called. The bathroom door opened and

Calla stepped into the hall, her hair freshly mussed and her full lips glossy pink. "Surprise!"

Calla looked up just as Farley was starting to cross the room, his coat now draped over one arm. "Oh, my God," she whispered. "What is he doing here?"

Lark and Eve laughed, pushing Calla from behind, and Olivia watched as they noticed each other from opposite sides of the fireplace. Calla took a single step forward, before twisting on her heels and snatching Lark's drink out of her hands. "I'll take that," she said with a smile, before knocking back roughly half of what was left.

Calla sauntered across the room, her hips swinging in tight black jeans, a pair of layered pastel racer-back tanks scrunching up around her waist, revealing a narrow strip of smooth, tanned skin. She put one hand lightly in the center of Farley's chest and leaned in to kiss him on the cheek, gesturing back toward the kitchen with her glass raised.

Eve held up her refilled glass in return as Lark smiled. "See?" Lark said through a glowing smile. "Problem solved."

🦋 🦋 🦋

As much as she liked grapefruit juice, Olivia was having trouble getting her second drink down. Partially because of the vodka (she'd never caught on to hard liquor—usually the smell of anything stronger than champagne was enough to make her gag), but mostly because her stomach was doing that thing again. That thing where it flopped inside out like she was stuck on a high-rise elevator every time Soren so much as laughed or entered the room.

Olivia opened the sliding glass door and elbowed her way

through a small crowd gathered on the porch. Graham was straddling a lounge chair, playing his guitar and singing softly as Eve cuddled up behind him. There was a small fire going in a fire pit in the middle of the deck, and behind it Olivia could make out the flickering shadows of Calla sitting Indian style between Farley's knees on the ground.

Olivia was searching for a place to settle when she spotted Soren in the corner, crouching over an open cooler of beer. Calla seemed distracted with Farley, and everybody else was swaying to the sing-along. It might have been the single drink going straight to her head, but Olivia decided it wouldn't hurt to at least say hi.

She crossed the wide wooden slats to the far corner of the deck and stood over the cooler and Soren's crouching frame. "Hey," she said, her voice shaky and loud. "Pass me one of those?"

Soren looked up and smiled. He was wearing a black-and-orange Giants hat, and his shaggy hair was sticking out in a perfect curl against his neck. "Sure," he said, handing her a frosty can and keeping one for himself.

Olivia leaned back against the side of the house, her hips settling against the angled ledge of a wide bay window. She glanced around at the party, the glowing profiles of smiling faces by the fire.

"I didn't know if it was okay to talk to you," Soren said quietly, shuffling his sneakers against the dock. "Are you having a good time?"

"Yeah." Olivia smiled. "I am." She didn't realize how true the words were until she'd spoken them out loud. She didn't have that old uncomfortable feeling of not knowing where to stand, or what to do. There was enough going on to keep everyone entertained, and as far as Olivia could tell, not a single fight had broken out; not a single girl was crying. "Are you?"

Soren shrugged and tapped the top of his beer, pulling it open with a pop. "It's okay," he said, then turned to her with a shy smile. "It's a lot better now."

Olivia blushed and looked away. The waves were crashing loudly against the high sea wall. She was imagining going for a walk on the beach with Soren, or maybe a midnight swim, when a flash of movement caught her eye on the other side of the fire. Calla had untangled herself from Farley's lap and was pointing toward the cooler, taking orders from the crowd for beers.

"I should go back inside," Olivia said quickly, and Soren glanced up. Confusion scrambled his features until he followed Olivia's worried gaze to Calla, slowly making her way across the porch.

"Okay," he said. "I guess I'll see you."

Olivia waved a subtle good-bye before ducking behind a row of rosebushes and crossing back over the deck, passing Farley in his chair on her way to the kitchen. It seemed silly that she and Soren had to sneak around while Calla was so obviously moving on. But it would have to do.

Bedtime sort of snuck up on people a little after one in the morning. Lark had already excused herself to her bedroom at the end of the hall; Austin and Dread Boy had snuck up to one of the guest rooms; and Graham had carried Eve threshold-style up the stairs, making a beeline for the other.

Soren was still outside somewhere, and Olivia was lingering

at the bottom of the steps, hoping he'd pass through and give her a good-night wave before she went upstairs to the trundle bed she'd been assigned in Lark's room. The living room was spooky and quiet, a graveyard of half-empty bottles and sleeping bodies. Logan and his friends were sprawled out on the floor, slumped on couches with their legs flopped over the armrests, and Farley was tucked into a sleeping bag next to the fireplace.

Olivia was about to give up when a shadowy figure outside caught her eye. At first she thought it might be Soren, climbing down the steps to the lower deck. Was he waiting for her?

She took a few steps toward the sliding doors and saw a long mane of dark hair flickering in the last reaching flames of the fire.

Calla.

If Farley hadn't been snoring at her feet, Olivia might have assumed she was sneaking off somewhere with him. But he was.

Olivia pulled the glass door open, silently crossing the deck in the dark. She climbed carefully down the dark and crooked stairs, the wooden planks creaking under her bare feet. At the water's edge, Calla quickly turned around, and Olivia could see by the orange glare of the nearby fire that her face was stained with tears.

"Oh," Calla said quietly, a relieved smile crossing her face. "It's you."

Olivia settled herself down onto the dock beside her. Calla's feet were swinging in the black water, making perfect round ripples around her slender ankles. "Are you okay?"

Calla sniffed and shrugged, lifting her chin to stare out

at the dark horizon. The moon was full and the sky around it was shocked with pale gray. It was exactly the kind of quiet Olivia missed on the Vineyard. It even smelled the same.

"It looked like you were having a good time with Farley," Olivia offered.

"I wasn't," Calla said, shaking her head with a sad smile. "I tried to. He's such a nice guy. But . . ." She trailed off.

Olivia curled her hands around the edge of the dock, gripping the wooden planks as if she might fall off. "But what?" she gently prompted, as Calla wiped her damp cheeks with the back of one hand. Even crying, Calla looked beautiful, and for some reason Olivia thought of her dad. She'd seen him cry only once in her life, at the funeral, and had been amazed at how calm and graceful he'd looked while doing it. Some people got all splotchy or did weird things with their mouth, trying to hold their emotions back, but not her dad. He looked exactly the same as he always did, strong and handsome, with small, silent tears gently falling down his face.

It was the same with Calla.

"It's not fair to Farley," Calla was saying now, pushing her feet through the chilly water. "I know I shouldn't, but I just keep comparing everything he does to Soren."

Olivia's stomach tightened, and she realized how hard she'd been hoping Calla was going to say something else. She took a deep breath and turned to the water.

"And it's not like Soren was *perfect*," Calla said with a little laugh. "He was just . . . there. And now he's not. It's hard to get used to."

Olivia nodded, feeling a hard lump growing in the back of

her throat. "I know," she said quietly. "It must have been hard to see him tonight."

Calla shrugged again and sniffled, wrapping her arms around her waist.

"Yeah," she said. "We spent a lot of time together here. We kind of officially started going out at this same party last year, and over the summer we were up here basically every weekend."

Olivia closed her eyes, trying not to imagine Calla and Soren together on this very deck, walking hand in hand on the beach, swimming at night under a different full moon. . . .

"There were a few really bad weeks in August, when my parents were always fighting," Calla said, tilting her face to the sky and squinting to remember. "My dad hadn't been home for almost a month. He's always traveling for work, but this was different, I could tell. And Soren would just sit with me out here, listening to me talk and talk and talk—not giving advice or anything, which I loved, you know? Just letting me cry. It was exactly what I needed."

Olivia nodded. The lump in her throat was bigger now, and throbbing. She felt a heavy pulsing behind her eyes, and her nose was starting to tingle and burn.

"He's great at that," Calla said. "I guess it's what I miss the most."

Olivia tried everything she could to stop them, but the tears were already pooling and dripping onto the tops of her cheeks. She had no idea where they'd come from, but once they'd started, there was no turning them off. Calla must've heard her sniffle because she turned and gasped.

"Oh, no," she said, hurrying to put a long arm around

Olivia's shoulders. "Not you, too! It's not that bad, I promise. God, I'm such a drama queen."

Olivia meant to laugh, and it might have started that way, but the sound caught somewhere in her throat and turned into a loud, ugly sob. Soon she was smiling and crying at the same time, and shaking her head with embarrassment.

"No," Olivia gulped. "It's not that."

Olivia hiccuped for air but the tears kept coming, and Calla rubbed her back in small, comforting circles.

"What's wrong?" she asked softly.

Olivia pushed the heels of her hands into her eyes, wiping them dry and taking a full, calming breath.

"It's just . . . my sister," she managed, before hiccuping again. She hadn't fully realized why she was crying until she'd said the words out loud.

Calla cocked her head forward and tucked a strand of Olivia's curls back behind her shoulder. "I didn't know you had a sister," she said quietly.

"I do." Olivia nodded. "I mean, I did. She died last summer."

As soon as she'd said the words, she felt another wave of sobs growing from the pit of her stomach. They sounded so real. So final. She couldn't believe they were true.

Olivia could hear Calla holding her breath, then exhaling in a long, full sigh.

"I'm so sorry," Calla said. "I had no idea."

Olivia nodded and squeezed her hands together in her lap.

"I totally understand if you don't want to talk about it," Calla said, squeezing Olivia's shoulder. "But if you do . . ."

Olivia smiled and took a deep breath. It felt like she'd

been living with a brick wall inside of her, holding everything back. And now, all of a sudden, the wall had crumbled to the ground. Everything came out in a flood.

"We were at our summer house on Martha's Vineyard," Olivia began. "It was late. My parents were out. A bunch of us went to go night swimming at the beach. There was this spot where a storm had blown over the peninsula. A breach. People said the current was so strong it could pull you out to sea in seconds."

Olivia squeezed the sides of her knees with her palms.

"She asked me to go in with her," Olivia continued, quieter now. "She begged me to. I told her I wouldn't and she shouldn't, either. I hate doing things like that. But I've always been the stronger swimmer. . . . I should have gone in, too. I should have been there. . . ."

Olivia trailed off, her voice disappearing into a cloud of buried memories. Violet standing ankle-deep in the water, the fraying bottom of her jean shorts getting wet, her green lace camisole clinging to her waist.

Violet up to her waist in the cold, angry waves, her arms flailing behind her, beckoning Olivia to come in.

Violet laughing, diving into the deep dark of the choppy sea. The water closing around her neck, pulling her down . . .

Violet's face one last time, her eyes wide, panic gripping her open mouth, her hair swirling around like floating seaweed as she struggled to the surface.

And then . . . nothing.

Endless seconds of terrible silence, before the flurry of activity.

People running, screaming, boys holding each other back,

everybody holding Olivia back, Olivia yelling that she had to go in, too.

Knowing it was too late. Knowing if she went in, she'd never come out.

Olivia gasped.

It was over.

Her face was now drenched and her shoulders shook, tiny, faraway whimpers slipping out from between her shuddering lips.

"That is so terrible. I can't even imagine . . ." Calla said, after a few moments of heavy quiet. "And here I am, all pathetic and crying over a stupid boy." Calla linked her arm through Olivia's elbow and pulled her in to her side.

"I'm sorry," Calla said. "I'm so, so sorry, Olivia."

Olivia allowed her body to melt. It felt good to be so close to somebody. It felt good to finally cry. Now that it had all been said, now that everything was out, even breathing felt easier.

"I'm glad I met you, Madonna," Calla said, looking up at the enormous sky, the moon floating high and bright overhead. "You really are True Blue."

32

*O*livia was quietly padding down the hall from the bathroom when she heard a soft whistling sound following
her from behind. At first she thought it was coming
from one of the guest rooms, but the doors were all closed and
the hallway was empty. She heard it again and leaned over the
cherrywood banister to find Soren standing at the bottom of
the staircase, tipped high on his toes and waving her down.

Olivia's pulse raced and her mind felt cloudy. Calla and
Lark had been asleep in Lark's queen-size bed when Olivia
remembered she hadn't brushed her teeth. The girls had hardly
even twitched when she'd tiptoed out of the room. Glancing
out over the railing, she saw that downstairs, the living room
was still blanketed in sleeping boys and silence.

Olivia carefully made her way down the steps, every tiny
creak sending a shiver up her spine. When she reached the bottom, Soren was leaning against the knotted railing, his hands
stuffed in the pocket of a cozy white hooded sweatshirt, a
purple NYU logo over his heart. He was smiling and his eyes

were hopping around her face, like he was trying to memorize her features.

"Hi," he said softly.

"Hi," she said back.

"What are you still doing up?" he asked. His breath smelled faintly of beer, and his eyes were glassy and light.

"Bathroom," Olivia whispered. "What about you?"

Soren shrugged and yawned, the little lines around his eyes crinkling. "Couldn't sleep," he said with a smile. "Want to go for a walk?"

Olivia raised an eyebrow and looked through the narrow rows of rectangular windows on the front door behind him.

"Now?" she said. It was at least two thirty in the morning.

Soren smiled and reached out for her hand, giving her fingers a gentle tug as he intertwined them with his own. "Come on," he said. "It will be an adventure."

Olivia's stomach swirled as she glanced back upstairs. Calla was sleeping less than fifty feet away. The same Calla who had just admitted that she wasn't over Soren. The same Calla who had been so comforting when Olivia had told her about Violet.

The Calla who was her friend.

Olivia took a deep breath and untangled her fingers from Soren's warm grasp.

"I'm sorry," she said. "I can't."

Soren's chin ducked a little bit closer to his chest and he buried his hands back inside his sweatshirt. "You can't?" he asked. He was looking down at his feet, and Olivia noticed that his muddy hiking boots were already laced up.

Olivia chewed at the inside of her lip.

"Soren, I—" *This sucks. This sucks. This sucks.* It ran like a mantra in her head, but she kept pushing forward, the words tumbling around in her mouth like heavy rocks. "I don't think we should do this anymore. It's not right. I like you . . . like, a lot . . . but . . ."

A rustling noise from the living room startled her, and they both turned to see Farley rolling over in his sleeping bag. Soren looked back at her, his green eyes dark and sad, before glancing back toward the door.

"Let's talk outside," he said, and after Olivia hesitated: "Just talk. I promise."

Olivia looked up toward Lark's room again. All of the lights were still off, and the only noise in the house was the muffled clanking of pipes in the bathroom.

Soren slowly and soundlessly pulled back the front door, quickly grabbing his heavy gray fleece from a pile on the ground and ushering her outside.

The night air felt warmer somehow, and the moon hung bright overhead, drawing the hulking, smudgy outlines of trees and mountains in the distance. Soren shut the door quietly behind them and took Olivia's hand, pulling her onto the grass and walking in the shadows down the hill, following the sloping edge of the driveway all the way down toward the gate.

"Soren," Olivia called, an urgent whisper, "wait, I don't think . . ."

But Soren kept dragging her along. His grip around her wrist wasn't strong or scary, and she knew she could pull away if she wanted to. But she didn't.

At the bottom of the driveway, they crossed a wide, two-lane road. It was the same road they'd driven through the mountains earlier that afternoon.

"Where are we going?" Olivia asked, but Soren just kept walking. The leaves in the trees rustled overhead, and Olivia whipped her head back around. "Aren't there . . . you know . . . *animals* out here?" she asked, following Soren down a narrow, winding path, her feet tripping over toppled rocks and a thick maze of roots.

Soren looked back, helping her over a fallen hollow tree trunk. "Don't worry," he said. "They're more afraid of you than you are of them."

Olivia huffed. "I doubt it," she said, hopping back onto the path and holding tight to Soren's hand. "Where are you taking me?"

"You'll see," Soren insisted. "You can keep talking until we get there, if you want."

"Oh," she said, her foot landing heavily in a pile of leaves and crunching through to the soft earth below. She kept her eyes on the backs of Soren's hiking boots, a narrow navy stripe crisscrossing his heels. "Well. It's just—it's Calla."

"What about Calla?" Soren asked, ducking beneath the low branch of an evergreen, its spindly needles brushing against his face.

"I just don't think it's right, for us to . . ." Olivia passed under the branch as Soren held it up and out of her way. "Thanks. I mean, I don't know. She's my friend, and I don't want her to get hurt." Olivia paused on the side of the path, waiting for Soren to catch up. Shouldn't they maybe stop to talk about this?

But Soren pushed right past her, following the trail around

a switchback turn. They were getting higher now, and Olivia looked up for the first time. All around them were clusters of gigantic redwoods, their trunks as wide as compact cars. Soren was getting smaller in the distance, and Olivia rolled her eyes, flopping her hands by her sides in reluctant surrender. This was not exactly how she'd imagined the conversation would go.

Finally, the path ended at a clearing. They had arrived at a vast, open field, at the center of which was a perfect circle of redwood trees, huddled together like a group of performers onstage.

Soren hopped over a few more rocks, pulling Olivia along until they'd landed on one with a flat, smooth surface. He stood completely still, taking in the open space around them.

"Is this—" Olivia started, but stopped when Soren grabbed her forearms from behind.

"Shh," he said softly. "Just close your eyes and listen."

Olivia closed her eyes, and for a moment all she could hear was the rushing of blood in her ears, the pounding of her pulse, and the whispers of the wind passing over the leaves. But all of a sudden, she heard it. A high-pitched moaning, like a muffled cry, or the slow creaking of an old rusty door.

"What was that?" Olivia asked, her eyes popping open.

Soren laughed and hugged her close. "It's the trees," he said. "They're so tall that they bend in the wind. My mom used to say it's how they talk to each other. Listen again."

Olivia closed her eyes, this time hearing past the leaves and the beating of her heart. Soren was right. From all around her, on every side, the trees were talking, a call-and-response chorus of sighs in the dark.

Soren swiped at the rock with the sleeve of his sweatshirt and gestured for her to sit down beside him.

"That was a good surprise," Olivia said, burrowing into his shoulder for warmth, the top of her nose pressed against the smooth, salty side of his neck.

"There's more," Soren said, and Olivia pulled her head back to see his face. He pointed up at the sky with one hand. Olivia sat back, craning her neck, and gasped.

The full moon was directly overhead, and all around it, like a blanket of shimmering light, the sky was dotted with a million tiny stars. There were too many to see at once, too many to organize into shapes or constellations.

"Wow," Olivia said. It was all she could say. The lump in her throat was back, and she knew if she tried to keep talking, she'd start crying again instead.

"You said you missed the stars," Soren said, leaning back onto his elbows. Olivia shifted closer to him, resting her head in the hollow of his chest. They lay like that, breathing together and watching the stars, until Soren cleared his throat.

"I was listening to what you were saying before," he said, picking up a few strands of her hair between his fingers, gently working his way through her curls. "It's not that I don't care. Or understand. I just . . . I have no idea what to do about it."

He heaved a hurting sigh, and Olivia could hear his heart drumming between the cover of his ribs.

"All I know is that I've never felt this way before," he said. "And I can't imagine losing you. For any reason."

Olivia's heart swelled, her lips tingling with a smile. She lifted her head from Soren's chest and leaned back on one elbow, squinting to make out the lines of his face. Even in the dark, she could tell his eyebrows were furrowed, his mouth drawn and severe. He looked nervous, and overwhelmed, and unsure. He looked exactly like she felt.

And so she kissed him. It was all she could do.

33

"Do you need help?"

Olivia glanced over at the front desk, where Bess, the pink-haired receptionist, was sitting at her post in the lobby. The last bell of the day was about to ring, and Olivia had asked her studio art teacher for permission to be excused early. She'd said she had a personal crisis.

Which was kind of the truth. If sitting in the lobby waiting for Calla so that she could finally come clean about her feelings for Soren didn't qualify as a personal crisis, she wasn't sure what did.

After the rest of the weekend at the beach with Lark's family (the guys had gone home early Saturday morning, just missing Lark's parents as they pulled up to the gate), Olivia had decided that she was done. She couldn't give Soren up, and she couldn't keep seeing him behind Calla's back. Things were getting too serious, and their circle of friends was too small. Calla was bound to find out.

The only option left was to be honest and break the news

to Calla herself. Even though it was sure to be painful and terrible, in the end, it would be worth it. She and Soren could be together without being afraid of getting caught. And Calla would be hurt and mad and maybe turn all of Olivia's new friends against her . . . but she wouldn't be able to stay mad forever. Right?

Olivia fidgeted with a button at the top of her short-sleeved, brown and white polka-dot dress and managed a tight smile in Bess's direction.

"No, thanks. I'm just waiting for someone," Olivia said, scooting farther down the bench and toward the window. If only the kind of help that she needed were as easy as a dismissal note, or a quick call for a ride home. Somehow, Olivia didn't think advising students on how to come clean to their friends while dating their exes fell under Bess's front-desk jurisdiction.

The bell rang and Olivia's temples throbbed, her hollow stomach churning as the lobby gradually filled up with students leaving class. Everyone looked disgustingly chipper and carefree. Like they'd been instructed to smile bigger and walk with extra pep, just to make Olivia feel crappier than she already did.

Olivia was keeping careful watch over the arched mouth of the hallway. Every dark-headed girl in skinny jeans was Calla, and Olivia felt her bones trembling in her skin, the backs of her ears burning red. She was staring so intensely, realizing that she was praying *not* to see Calla more than anything else, that she didn't notice Miles's mushroom loafers toe-tapping the lobby floor, directly in front of her face.

"Hey," a cool voice said from overhead, and she looked

up. Of course he would find her now. Miles was nothing if not a master of impeccable timing.

"Hey, Miles," she said quickly. "I'm kind of waiting for someone, so—"

"Oh, yeah?" he said, with a short, mean little laugh that shivered the hairs on the back of Olivia's neck. "That's cool. You must be really busy, huh?"

"Um, yeah, kind of," Olivia said softly, glancing back and forth from the hallway to Miles, his arms primly crossed. "Sorry, it's just . . . a long story, and I don't really have time to—"

"You don't have time for anything, do you?" Miles asked, dropping his hands to his sides. "You don't have time to talk, you don't have time to pick up your phone, you don't have time to go to Santa Cruz to film lighthouses over the weekend like we planned. . . ."

Olivia's eyes stretched wide open and she brought the flat of her hand to her forehead. "Miles," she said, rising to her feet and dropping her bag to the bench with a thud. "I am so sorry. I decided to go up to the beach at the last minute. It all happened so fast and I must've just totally spaced—"

"Spaced," Miles repeated, his dark eyes narrow and angry. "And what? You couldn't pick up your phone? I only called you ten to twelve times. . . ."

"I was at Lark's house in Stinson Beach," Olivia said quickly. "I didn't have any service all weekend long. I swear."

It was the truth, but even Olivia could hear how pathetic she sounded. She looked up from the ground at Miles's face. He didn't look as angry anymore, only hurt and disappointed, which was worse.

"Whatever," he said quietly. "I went by myself. I shot some great stuff. Maybe you can take a look sometime, if your schedule ever frees up. . . ."

Olivia felt her breath catching, and she wanted to say more, to apologize until she was out of ways of saying sorry, when over the top of Miles's shoulder she saw Calla.

"Miles," she said, putting a hand on the back of his bony elbow, "I'm really sorry, but I have to go. I'll call you later and we'll work on the project this week, I promise. Okay?"

She'd liked to have thought that she'd waited for Miles's answer, or at least looked him squarely in the eyes, but she didn't. Even before the last words were out of her mouth, she was pushing past him and edging her way through the lobby, arriving at the rounded corner of the desk just as Calla was turning around.

"Calla," Olivia said. "I'm so glad I found you. I really need to—" Olivia stopped suddenly and held her breath. Was Calla . . . crying?

"Olivia," Calla managed, before her features crumpled, her lower lip pouting, the tears welling at the corner of her eyes. She shook her head, her dark hair tumbling around her face like a curtain. Then she spun on her heels, running back down the hallway without another word.

Olivia stood frozen by the desk and looked up at Bess, who was staring back down at her, her silver-studded eyebrows knitting with concern.

"Maybe you should go check on her." Bess shrugged and gestured toward the girls' bathroom, just around the corner.

Olivia nodded, dumbstruck, and let her heavy feet carry her down the crowded hall. "Calla?" she called out quietly, after

258

pushing through the bathroom door and ducking her head to search for feet under the stalls. The bathroom was small, with only one regular stall and one handicapped one, and a long row of windows by a standing sink and mirror.

"Over here." Calla sniffed, standing over the sink as tears dripped down her face.

"What's wrong?" Olivia asked, her voice small and timid. *She already knows. Eve must've found out. She's crying and miserable and it's all my fault.*

Calla ran the water and held her palms underneath it, cupping her hands together and leaning down to splash her face. Olivia glanced up at her reflection in the fingerprinted glass. Despite Lark's constant reminders to reapply her SPF, Olivia had gotten too much sun at the beach on Saturday, and a fresh batch of freckles had cropped up, forming a crowded constellation on her nose and forehead.

Olivia held her breath until Calla turned the faucet off and leaned back against the brick wall beneath the window.

"Everything is wrong," she said slowly. "When I got back from the beach last night, my dad was packing his things. He's moving out."

As Calla was talking, Olivia felt her lungs slowly filling back up with air, her heartbeat settling into something that resembled normal human function. As awful as it was, Olivia couldn't help but feel relieved that Calla's tears had nothing to do with her.

"This time it's for good—I can feel it." Calla hiccuped, her eyes filling up again. "He already left for the office in Greece. I bet he won't even come back."

Olivia took a step closer to the sink and rested her hand on

Calla's shoulder, which was rolling up and down with gentle little sobs.

"And he definitely won't be back in time for the fashion show," Calla huffed. "Not that it matters. There's still so much to do, and I'm such a mess. . . ."

Olivia stretched her arm long around Calla's shoulders, pulling her in for a hug. Calla's body was shaking with little short-circuit quivers. How could she possibly tell Calla about Soren now?

"It's going to be okay," Olivia said quietly. "We have a whole week to make the fashion show happen. And that's exactly what we're going to do."

Calla looked up, her big doe eyes hopeful and warm, and nodded.

"Everybody's going to be talking about it," Olivia said with a smile. What Calla needed now was help. And after everything Olivia had done, she could at least give her that. "Your dad will be devastated once he realizes that he missed out on the social event of the century."

Calla leaned her head on Olivia's shoulder. She caught a glimpse of their reflection as Calla tried on a brave smile.

"You're right." Calla wiped the last wet tears from her cheeks. "You're totally right. We need to focus on the really important stuff." She met Olivia's eyes in the mirror. "Like what we're going to wear."

34

"Mommy's home!"

It was Friday afternoon and Olivia was kneeling on the Anthropologie circle rug in the middle of her room, elbow-deep in one of Violet's boxes, searching for the pair of gold wedge sandals she'd been hoping to wear to the event that night. She turned quickly to see her sister suddenly at the window, her arms held wide and a silly grin stretched from ear to ear.

Olivia hopped up and ran to the window, wrapping her arms around her sister's neck and burying her face in Violet's tangled, salty hair. "You're back!" Olivia breathed. "How was it?"

Violet flopped back on the bed, her long, freckled limbs spread out like those of a starfish.

"It was incredible." She sighed. "We went all the way down to these little islands off the coast of LA. There were sea lions everywhere—which, it turns out, are not all that cuddly."

"Really?" Olivia asked, trying to muster up all the

enthusiasm she could find. It had been a long, exhausting week of getting ready for the fashion show with Calla—collecting thrift-store donations, coordinating models and outfits, making sure the food and the drinks and the venue were all squared away—and Olivia had only that afternoon remembered to pick up a dress from Posey. To top it all off, she hadn't been sleeping, and had been missing Soren like crazy and wondering when Violet would finally come home from her trip.

"Totally." Violet nodded. "Like, don't put your hands anywhere near them. They look cute, but they will eat you."

Olivia managed a laugh, but it must not have been very convincing, because Violet sat up with a shock and slapped her knees with her hands. "Crap!" she exclaimed. "The fashion show! I forgot it was tonight. How was your week? How was the weekend at the beach? Tell me everything!"

Olivia smiled anxiously and opened her closet door, pulling out the hanging garment bag she'd picked up from Posey that afternoon. She hadn't opened it yet.

"The weekend was fun," she said, hooking the hanger over the top of the closet door and slowly pulling down the zipper. Without really paying much attention, she gathered open a hole in the soft, cool fabric and stepped her bare feet inside. "Soren was there. Things were really weird with Calla, so I decided to tell him that we should stop hanging out. But then he took me on this amazing midnight hike, and I just couldn't, so . . . I tried to tell Calla everything in school on Monday, but that was a bust, too. . . ."

Olivia wrangled her arms through the straps and heard Violet draw a sharp breath. "What?" she asked, quickly running her hands down the smooth fabric at her hip. "Is it bad?"

Violet jumped from the bed and spun Olivia around so that she was facing herself in the mirror.

Posey had done it again. This time, the dress was long and forest green, falling past her ankles and gathering in a shallow pool around her feet. The rich silk chiffon perfectly complimented the pink undertones of Olivia's skin, the light smattering of peachy freckles at her collarbone, her long, strawberry curls. The sleeves fell just to the outside curves of her shoulders, the easy, rolling scoop of the neckline meeting low in both the front and back, with little pockets of material ruffled and slimming her already narrow waist.

It was red-carpet material, and, again, Olivia felt like she'd stepped into a movie.

"You look like a princess," Violet said, shaking her head with a smile. "A princess with a wish to make . . ."

Violet smiled coyly and hopped back up on the bed, as Olivia sat down in a chair in front of the white, mirrored vanity.

"So . . ." Violet asked. "Any ideas? And don't tell me you haven't thought about it, because you had a whole week without me here to distract you, and you must have come up with—"

"I've thought about it," Olivia said quietly, opening the black-and-white Sephora cosmetic bag her mother had ordered for both girls two Christmases ago. She'd hardly ever used any of the pre-selected products inside, but she thought she remembered seeing a pale pink eye shadow that would be a perfect complement to the deep green of her dress.

Violet pulled one leg up on the bed and shook her knee up and down. "You sneak. Tell me! What are you going to wish for?"

Olivia took a deep breath, dipping a tiny brush into the powder and drawing it across the smooth crease of her upper lid.

"Well, I was thinking," she said, fluttering one eyelid and examining her progress in the glass. "Everything's going so well, you know? I have you back, and I have Soren, and Calla and I are getting to be real friends . . . and I realized that the only thing left, the one other thing that would make me really, truly happy . . . was if Calla could be happy, too."

Violet was still and silent for such a long time that Olivia eventually turned around.

"What?" Olivia asked. "You don't think it's a good idea?"

Violet cupped her knees in her hands and turned to face her sister, her blue eyes still and serious.

"Is this really how you want to use your last wish?" she asked.

Olivia sighed. She'd known Violet wasn't going to be on board with this one. Maybe she shouldn't have even told her.

"I don't know, Violet. It's the only thing I can—" Olivia suddenly paused, her hands falling down to the top of the bureau. "Wait, what do you mean? It's not my last wish. I have two left."

Violet stood from the bed and walked to the window, pulling back the curtain and peering outside. Dull yellow lights in the purple-painted town house across the street were just starting to switch on as the sky faded deeper and deeper blue overhead.

"Violet?" Olivia asked. "What's going on?"

Violet took a deep breath, the bony wings of her shoulder blades lifting and then settling down her back. "I have to tell you something," she said, turning around. Her eyes were jumpy and her fingers twitched at her sides.

Olivia turned from the mirror to face her sister. "What is it?" she said flatly. "Violet. You're scaring me."

"I really did want to tell you sooner," Violet said, pressing her hands against the glass. "But you were having so much fun. You were really *living*, for once, and I didn't want you to think that—"

"Violet . . ." Olivia closed her eyes and took a long, full breath. "Whatever it is you are trying to say, could you please just say it?"

Violet turned around to face Olivia, her eyes serious and sad. "I tricked you," she said. "At the gala. I tricked you into wishing for Soren."

Olivia stared at her sister, her face frozen and blank. "You did not. I never made a wish. I couldn't think of anything, remember? So I just didn't—"

"I wish you were right," Violet said quickly, cringing as soon as the hurried words escaped her lips.

"Right?" Olivia repeated. What was Violet talking about? "Right about what?"

Violet kneeled on the floor in front of Olivia, taking her sister's hands in her lap. "That's what you said," Violet started to explain. "After I got you to admit that it would be fun to be with Soren, and that it could happen, if you wanted it badly enough. You said, '*I wish you were right.*'"

Flashes of hot and cold were rippling in waves beneath Olivia's skin, and she kept her eyes trained on the floor. It was the same trick she used in public; if she directed all of her attention at something specific, something *real*, maybe she could get a little perspective.

No, there is *not* a ghost beside me. No, this is *not* my dead sister, telling me that the best thing that's ever happened to me only happened because of a wish.

"That's ridiculous," Olivia said finally. "Even if I did . . . say that. It's not a real wish. I was just . . . talking. It doesn't make sense."

Violet squeezed Olivia's hands. "It makes perfect sense," she said. "You don't think it's a little bit of a coincidence that Soren and Calla broke up that very night? Or that you had that perfect romantic afternoon with him the very next day?"

Olivia took a deep breath and shook her head, freeing her hands from Violet's grip and pushing herself to her feet.

"Think about it," Violet pleaded. "It makes sense. I wish it didn't, but it does."

Olivia just shook her head again, searching the top of the vanity for the gold clutch she'd borrowed from Calla. She picked it up, tucked it under her arm, and walked toward the door.

"Think about what you're doing!" Violet called after her sister as Olivia opened the door to the hall.

Olivia stood like a statue in the hallway. Her head was pounding; her heart hurt. "I have to go," she said, and closed the door behind her.

"Olivia, wait!" Violet called out from the other side of the door.

But Olivia was already at the landing, hurrying down the stairs and out into the night.

35

"There you are!"

Calla ran across the wide, dewy lawn of the Palace of Fine Arts. She looked stunning in one of the many designer gowns her mother had donated, a vintage Chanel cocktail dress, black with lace details and a low, scalloped neck.

"We're in the middle of a total meltdown." She sighed, catching up to Olivia by the reflecting pool. "Half of the evening-wear pieces Lark's mother donated are way too big for any of the models—I guess they're from her maternity collection or something. Who knew?"

Olivia tried to smile and picked up her pace down the cobblestone path. She had been lingering by the side of a long, narrow reflecting pool, and knew she was running late, but her conversation with Violet had made hustling a bit of a challenge. It was all she could do to keep from collapsing, or screaming, or at the very least sitting quietly alone in a corner, until she'd figured this whole Soren-wish thing out.

She'd spent the whole cab ride going over every minute they'd spent together, searching for some sign that what Violet had said couldn't possibly be true. Soren's feelings for her had been real. But the longer she thought about it, the more the coincidences were starting to add up. Everything had happened so fast, and she remembered how she'd felt at the beginning, that it all seemed too good to be true. Had it been?

"Earth to Olivia . . ." Calla groaned.

Olivia looked up and for the first time saw the open-air rotunda in the middle of the Palace greens, lit up like a Christmas tree with hundreds of twinkling white lights. Jutting out from its center was the long red runway Calla and Olivia had helped to assemble themselves. It was the first time she'd seen the whole thing put together, and at night. It was breathtaking.

"It's so beautiful," she said, staring wide-eyed at the cluster of round tables with matching gray satin cloths, dotted with bouquets of tall white lilies.

"Did you see the flowers?" Calla asked, beaming. "They're calla lilies. My dad had them delivered. I guess he isn't a *total* ass."

Calla smiled and took Olivia's elbow as they walked toward the pointed white tent, a raw-bar buffet set up on one side, a makeshift changing room curtained off on the other.

"So, I was thinking," Calla said, while Olivia scanned the gathering crowd mingling inside the ornate sculpture garden. "We could either use some of the men's ties we have, and loop them around as belts, or . . ."

As Calla continued to troubleshoot wardrobe malfunctions, Olivia's mind drifted back to the night at the Academy of Sciences. She remembered how cute and awkward Soren had looked in his suit. She remembered Violet teasing her, and then acting suddenly, weirdly upset. She even remembered, now, vaguely, saying the words *I wish* . . .

Olivia took a sharp breath, glancing away from Calla and back toward the lawn. As if she'd dreamed it, Soren was there, stepping out of a cab and walking toward the stone path. He looked even better than he had that first night, in a crisp white button-down shirt, dark denim jeans, and bright white sneakers.

Olivia's heart stung. Wasn't there a chance, however small, that it *hadn't* been a wish? That Soren really had fallen for her on his own?

There was only one way to find out.

"Calla," Olivia said suddenly, stopping short. She needed to talk to Soren. She needed to know if his feelings were real.

"I'm so sorry," Olivia said, shaking her head with bewildered regret. "I—I forgot my phone in the cab, and . . ."

Olivia stalled and Calla turned around from a few steps ahead, looking back with careful, worried eyes.

"Oh," Calla said lightly. "You could just call it from mine; it's in my bag over—"

"No," Olivia insisted. "I think if I run, I can catch him. I'll meet you backstage in a minute. I promise."

"Hurry!" Calla yelled as Olivia broke into an awkward little jog across the lawn. "We're up first, remember? The welcome speech?"

Olivia waved to Calla, stopping to step out of her gold leather sandals and holding them out between her fingers as she ran. All she needed was a minute. She'd meet Calla onstage with plenty of time to spare.

She caught up to Soren at the long round table set up at the edge of the driveway, glancing over a display of name tags and searching for his own.

"Hey," she said, tapping his elbow and catching her breath.

Soren spun around, his crooked smile glowing as soon as he realized it was her.

"Hey!" he said. "You look . . ."

Little patches of red appeared on his cheeks and Olivia tried not to think about how good *he* looked, dashing and comfortable at the same time. Before she could help it, Olivia felt her insides turn to mush.

"Olivia, these are my parents." Soren gestured to a cheerful couple standing at the table. He had been right; with almost the identical shade of light brown hair tinted with the same amount of gray, and the same tanned, smooth skin and familiar green eyes, they looked more like siblings than husband and wife.

"Hi," Olivia greeted them warmly. "It's really nice to meet you."

They smiled and shook her hand before excusing themselves toward the tent to search for their table. Olivia looked around the entryway for a quiet place to talk, spotting a tall row of pink plum trees next to a curved brick wall.

"Can I talk to you for a second?" she asked, nodding her head toward the shaded patch of grass.

"What's wrong?" Soren asked as they ducked beneath the canopy of pink-and-black speckled blossoms on the far side of the wall. "You're shaking. Are you okay?"

Olivia held out her arms, circling her fingers around Soren's wrists and squeezing them tight. "I have to ask you some-thing," she said. "It's going to sound strange, and random, and maybe kind of annoying, but . . . I need to know."

Soren's sandy eyebrows were catching the last low rays of sunlight, glistening yellow as they locked together at the bridge of his nose. "What is it?" he asked, his emerald eyes searching hers.

"I just really need to know," she said, taking a deep breath and pressing her eyes shut. "Why do you like me?"

With her eyes closed, she could hear Soren's laugh, quiet and raspy. She opened one eye and saw that a toothy, lopsided grin had spread across his face.

"Why do I like you?" he repeated. "That's the question? Why do I like you?"

Olivia stomped her feet in place, suddenly remembering the way she'd felt as a toddler, in those first few moments of a temper tantrum, just before sprawling out and kicking her gangly limbs against the tiled kitchen floor. She didn't have time for this. She needed an answer, and she needed it to be good.

"Yes," she said. "Why do you care about me so much? What is it that makes you want to be with me?"

That was it. That was exactly what she needed to know. Because if he could give her a reason, one reason, then she would know for certain that he didn't just like her because of a wish.

Soren's smile faded and turned into something quieter, something more aware. He freed one of his hands from the clutches of her trembling fingers and reached around behind her neck, burrowing his palm inside the tumble of her curls

271

until the soft part of his hand was pressed flat against her skin. He leaned down, bringing his face even with hers, and looked her squarely in her eyes.

"Olivia," he said, and Olivia felt her lungs expanding, the veins in her forehead starting to pulse. "I don't know what happened, but from the very first moment I saw you . . ."

Olivia swallowed and held her breath.

"I don't know how to explain it," he said, shaking his head, bewildered, a sideways smile lighting up his face. "It was just . . . magic."

Olivia's stomach dropped, a high-pitched ringing suddenly buzzing in her ears.

Magic?

She had her answer.

Soren loosened his hold on Olivia's neck, his arms hanging in quiet defeat by his side. He took a small step backward and glanced down at the grass. "What?" he asked, his voice wounded and afraid.

Olivia looked up at him, at his piercing green eyes, his strong jaw, the little row of scars beneath his chin. She'd never gotten to ask where those scars came from. There hadn't been time to learn all of his stories, and now she might never get the chance.

But she wasn't supposed to. He'd said it himself. They were only together because of the magic. His stories were supposed to be for someone else.

She had to say good-bye. She would use her last wish to free him from the spell, to take away the magic that had made him hers. It made her feel empty just thinking about it, but she knew it was what needed to be done.

Just one more kiss. All she needed was one more kiss, and then she'd wish the wish away.

Olivia stepped forward, reaching her hands around his face and drawing him in. She wanted to remember this feeling, the heavy weight of his chest against hers, the sweet-mint taste of his lips. She felt the blood rushing through her veins, filling her up like helium in a balloon.

I wish—she forced herself to say the words first in her head. *I wish I'd never*—

"Olivia?"

A sharp voice interrupted them from over Olivia's shoulder, and she untangled her arms from around Soren's neck.

Calla was standing at the foot of the path, her face drained of color, her eyes hard and cold. "It's time for our speech," she said, evenly and without emotion. "Everybody's waiting."

"Calla," Olivia said, turning her back to Soren, her hands gripping the sides of her head as if she were afraid it might fall off. Calla's eyes pooled with angry tears and she shook her head silently from side to side. "Calla, I'm sorry. I was going to—"

Calla gathered her skirt in her shaking hands and hurried back toward the stage.

"Calla, wait!" Olivia called, rushing after her.

But Calla had already taken off in a sprint, running down the stone path and away from the rotunda, away from the runway, away from the hundreds of people quietly sitting, waiting to be welcomed to the show.

36

"Get out of the road!"

Olivia looked up and realized she'd veered off of the sidewalk and into a bus lane, as a trio of angry mountain bikers zipped by, nearly tearing off one side of her wrinkled, dirty-hemmed dress.

She'd been walking for over an hour. The Palace was miles from her house, and she certainly wasn't interested in breaking any records for speed. It was enough of a challenge to keep her feet moving at all, let alone think about where they were going or how fast.

After a bit of a delay and a chorus of curious murmurs as to Calla's whereabouts, Lark had decided that the show must go on and had happily taken the reins. Olivia had passed off her thrift costume to Eve and scoured every corner of the Palace grounds, but Calla was nowhere to be found. Soren had hung around, trying to be helpful, comforting Olivia and telling her it would all be okay. But every second he was near her only made Olivia feel worse.

And so Olivia decided to walk home, back to the place where she couldn't do any more harm. Or where, even if she did, nobody would be paying enough attention to notice.

She finally trudged around her corner, but standing in her gown at the foot of her stoop, Olivia knew she wasn't ready to go inside. It wasn't very late, and her parents would probably still be up. The last thing Olivia was prepared to do was to put on a good face.

She walked back out toward the street, turning at the corner and crossing over to Dolores Park. In the distance, on one of the low wooden benches lining the perimeter of the lawn, Violet was already waiting.

"How did it go?" Violet asked, blinking like she was afraid of the answer.

"How did it go?" Olivia repeated. She couldn't hold the tears back any longer. They poured down her cheeks in endless sobs, her nose running and her cheeks red-hot. "How do you think it went? It was a disaster."

She slumped on the bench next to her sister, expecting Violet to wrap an arm around her shaking shoulders. When she didn't move, Olivia looked up to find her sister staring vacantly at the sidewalk.

"I told you so," was all she said.

Olivia froze, a sob caught in her mouth. "*You told me so? You're the one who tricked me into wishing for Soren in the first place.*"

"Of course I did," Violet whispered. "Sometimes being alive means taking risks, and sometimes things can get messy, but—"

"Risks?" Olivia asked, screaming now, totally beyond

275

caring what she might look like to random, late-night passersby. "You want me to take *risks*? Like the risks you took? Like the reason you're dead?" Olivia didn't know why she said it, or where it came from, but the minute the question escaped her lips, she knew the words had been building inside her for a long time.

Violet looked back toward the gravel walkway. Her eyes were cloudy and her cheeks flushed red. She shrugged sadly and looked back up at her sister. "At least I *lived,* first."

Olivia felt her body trembling with rage, her veins jumping, the blood rushing past her ears in hot, angry waves. "You're impossible!" She held the hem of her dress in one hand and spun on her heels, walking quickly toward the curb. "I wish you'd just leave me alone."

Olivia ran across the street, hurrying down the sidewalk.

It wasn't until she reached her front door that she realized what she'd said.

37

The dress.

Olivia reached her stoop and looked down at her gown.

I wish you'd leave me alone.

What had she done?

She sprinted back up her street, cutting between a crowded row of parked cars and crossing toward the park.

The bench they'd been sitting on was lonely and deserted.

"Violet?" Olivia called out into the night. "Violet, come back!"

She whipped her head in one direction, then the other, scanning the dark, empty streets for her sister. "Violet!" she sobbed. "I didn't mean it! I didn't mean any of it."

Olivia collapsed on the bench, her head falling into her hands. "Please come back," she whispered into her fingers, tears soaking her palms.

And that was when she saw it.

At first it was just a light, a blurry glow between clenched fingers.

She let her hands fall to her lap and turned to the other side of the bench, the side where Violet had been sitting.

There, fluttering its wings precariously at the edge of the armrest, was a fragile, shining butterfly.

Olivia gasped, her hands again finding her face.

"Violet?" she asked quietly. "Please. Don't go. Don't leave me again."

The golden butterfly flapped its wings once more, before lifting and gliding off into the night.

38

"Honey, I think there's somebody on our boat."

Olivia's eyes blinked open, a squeaky, high-pitched voice pulling her out of a deep and troubled sleep.

"What do you mean there's somebody—"

Olivia, still in her gown from the night before, wrapped the itchy blue blanket around her shoulders and stumbled to her feet. Too upset to go home, too heartbroken to face her empty room, she'd decided to hail a cab to Sausalito and spend the night on her grandfather's boat. She'd snuggled up under the shelter of the faded green awning and cried herself to sleep . . . completely forgetting that the boat now belonged to strangers. Strangers who were now standing across from her on the dock, seething in their tennis whites.

"This is private property," the ambiguously British man scolded. Olivia swung one leg over the ledge at the stern, quickly reaching back for her discarded sandals and hopping up onto the swaying dock.

"Hey!" his wife called after her as Olivia took off running. "Get back here!"

Olivia ran harder than she'd known she could, her bare feet burning on the gritty pavement. She didn't look back until she'd reached the main road, ducking inside a bait-and-tackle shop and peeking out from behind the door.

She flattened against the wall, a display of fishing lures flopping around her face, catching her breath until she was convinced she wasn't being followed.

"Sorry," she murmured to the befuddled shopkeeper, a salty old man in a black wool cap. "Do you think I could use your phone?"

Forty minutes and one silent cab ride later, Olivia was quietly letting herself in the front door of her house, hoping against all odds that her parents had chosen this morning as the first in their lives to sleep in.

"Where the hell have you been?"

No such luck.

The question came from Mac, who was rushing toward her with short, brusque steps, his face red and worn.

Over his shoulder, Bridget appeared in her bathrobe, her blond hair flattened to her face and her cheeks marked with drying tears.

"Sorry," Olivia said, so softly she wondered if she'd even said anything at all.

"What were you thinking?" Mac continued. "You can't just disappear. We've been up all night, calling anybody we could think of, trying to find out where you were."

Bridget joined them in the hall, silent for once, and Mac turned to her abruptly, as if he'd forgotten she was there.

He put a sturdy arm around her shoulder and hugged her close.

It was the first time Olivia had seen her parents touch each other in months, and for reasons she couldn't quite explain, it made her furious.

Who were these people? And who were they kidding? Her parents had hardly even said a word to her, let alone each other—unless it was four letters and screamed from behind a slamming door—in weeks, and now they were going to go through the whole worried-parent-tag-team routine?

Olivia rolled her eyes, exhaled a flop of tangled hair out of her face, and hugged the blanket closer to her shoulders, starting up the stairs.

"Where do you think you're going?" Mac called after her. "We're not done here."

Olivia turned on her heels, her heart pounding.

"Done?" she shouted back. "Done with what? What are you doing? All of a sudden you're *worried* about me? You want to know where I've *been*? Where the hell have *you* been?"

Mac and Bridget looked at each other, appearing to shrink back into themselves.

"You can't just decide to be parents when it suits you," Olivia said, before scampering up the two flights to her room, slamming the door behind her, and collapsing onto her bed.

39

*A*fter changing out of her dress and shoes, Olivia stormed back downstairs, pulling the front door open and slamming it shut behind her.

She started down the street, not entirely sure where her feet were taking her, but too exhausted to second-guess. A few blocks of trance-walking later, she found herself under a familiar awning, peering in through cloudy windows at a small girl hunched over a sewing machine.

Olivia pushed through the doors, the metallic, ear-piercing chimes causing her to jump.

"Back so soon?" Posey greeted her without looking up.

Olivia walked slowly across the uneven floorboards, her eyes drifting from one expressionless mannequin to another. Suddenly, she recognized herself in their faces: blank, sullen, empty.

She sank into a heap on the ratty sofa without saying a word.

Posey switched off the machine, a thick silence hanging in the room. She spun around on her low swivel stool.

"What happened?" she asked. Olivia could tell by the hushed tone of her voice that she already knew it was bad.

"I need your help," was all Olivia could manage, before falling apart into a now-comfortable rhythm of labored breathing and rocking sobs.

Posey sat beside her, not so close that their bodies were touching, but close enough so that Olivia could feel her gaze, wide with careful alarm.

Once Olivia had caught her breath, she started again. "I used my last wish for something terrible," she said, "and I need you to help me take it back."

Posey started to say something, but Olivia cut her off.

"I didn't mean it," Olivia said. "I said I wanted her gone, but I don't. You have to believe me."

"Your sister?" Posey asked quietly. "You wished your sister gone?"

Olivia looked at the floor and nodded.

"Why would you do that?" Posey asked, her eyes bright and concerned.

"I wasn't thinking." Olivia sighed. "But there has to be something you can do. I know I'm out of wishes, but—"

"Technically," Posey interrupted, "you're not."

Olivia tugged on the sleeve of her faded cotton sweatshirt. "What does that mean, *technically*?"

Posey scratched the back of her head with one finger and turned her back to Olivia. "Well," she said, "there's good news and there's bad news. Which do you want first?"

Olivia took a deep breath. "Good," she said. "If I don't hear some good news soon, I might not make it."

Posey nodded. "Remember the dress you wore to the charity event? When you made your second wish?"

Olivia thought back. The gala. The Accidental Soren Wish. "Yes." She nodded. "I wished for a guy to like me, but I didn't—"

Posey licked the corners of her mouth. "Okay," she drawled, "and do you remember if anything . . . happened . . . right after you made the wish?"

Olivia sighed. "Yes," she said sadly. "A lot of things happened. The wish came true."

Posey spun around and looked at Olivia long and hard, as if considering the features on her face for the first time.

"What?" Olivia asked impatiently.

"Interesting," Posey said.

"Why is that interesting?" Olivia asked. "I made a wish. The wish came true. Isn't that kind of how this works?"

"Sure," Posey allowed, "when you're wearing a magic dress."

A narrow smile snaked across Posey's lips.

"Wasn't I?" Olivia asked quietly.

"Did you see a glowing butterfly come out of it?" Posey countered.

Olivia's eyes stretched wide. *The butterfly.* She might have forgotten making a wish, but she definitely would have remembered a fluorescent bug flying around her ankles. "No," she said slowly. "There wasn't a butterfly that time."

Posey lifted her dark, thin eyebrows and stared into Olivia's eyes.

"So the dress wasn't magic?" Olivia asked, the words

jumbling together and racing out of her mouth. "But why not? I mean, you made it, didn't you? "

Posey's smile vanished and she shrugged. "I made you a dress," she said. "But it was only a dress. You broke a rule. You told your friend about the shop."

Olivia sat sharply back. "But I didn't tell her anything about *you*," Olivia insisted.

"I know you didn't," Posey said, "which is why I only faked the dress that one time."

"So last night's dress was real?" Olivia asked, a heavy sadness returning to her voice.

"Afraid so," Posey said.

"But," Olivia said, beginning to work things out, "if the dress I wore at the museum wasn't *really* magic, then that means I still have one dress left."

Posey nodded.

"Exactly," she said, the word hardly out of her mouth before Olivia had hopped up to her feet.

"This is perfect!" Olivia shouted. "I can wish for Violet back again!"

Posey sat quietly, her gaze shifting to the ground.

"What's wrong?" Olivia asked.

"There's still the bad news," Posey said. "Remember the rules?"

Olivia closed her eyes, remembered that morning with Violet and the dusty diary.

"Sure," Olivia said. "No telling anyone about the dresses, no wishing for world peace, no wishing for more wishes . . ."

Posey sat patiently and Olivia felt her face falling. They spoke at the same time:

"No wishing the same wish twice."

"You already wished for Violet once," Posey explained slowly. "I'm sorry."

Olivia scanned Posey's face, her small, doll-like features, as if searching for a clue.

"Wait," Olivia gasped. "What about the wishing-from-the-heart thing? Wasn't that a rule, too?"

"Yes." Posey nodded uncertainly. "But—"

"But in my heart," Olivia continued eagerly, "I never would have wanted Violet gone."

Posey shrugged sadly. "I'm sorry, Olivia," she said, "but in that moment, you did. Or else the wish wouldn't have come true."

Olivia's eyes were frantic, her fingers trembling in her lap.

"Maybe," she said quietly. "But I was so upset. And everything she was saying was just making me feel worse."

Posey smiled, her eyes warm and sympathetic.

"Nobody knows how to push our buttons better than family." She smiled.

Olivia sat back onto the couch, her eyes glazing over. She felt as if she'd been punched in the gut, her breathing choppy, her knees wobbling and falling in toward each other.

Posey stood and crossed the room to an old armoire. She opened the door and pulled out a garment bag, identical in shape and color to the others Olivia had received. She laid the bag gently over the back of the couch. "Here you go," she said. "Your third and final dress."

"I don't want it," Olivia mumbled under her breath.

"What's that?" Posey asked.

"I'm sorry," Olivia said. "I don't mean to sound ungrateful. It's just, if I can't wish for Violet back, there's nothing else worth wishing for."

Posey shrugged. "Well, it's up to you whether you use it or not," she said, settling behind the desk, feeling for something in a low drawer. She pulled out the faded leather journal and opened it in her lap. "But the dress is yours. I said three dresses, and I keep my word."

Olivia scooped the bag into her arms and started for the door.

"Olivia, wait," Posey called out to her.

Olivia turned back as Posey ducked under the table, rummaging through a collection of shopping bags and holding one out for Olivia to grab.

"What's this?" Olivia asked.

"Something else that belongs to you," Posey replied mysteriously.

Olivia opened the bag and reached inside, catching a familiar handful of satiny fabric. The colorful kaleidoscope of Violet's secondhand dress peeked up from between the bag's rope handles, and Olivia's breath caught in the back of her throat.

"I'm sorry I've kept it so long," Posey said. "I didn't know if you still wanted it mended or not."

"That's okay," Olivia said, her fingers landing comfortably on the still-torn seam. "I like it the way it is."

Posey smiled and nodded, settling back into her tattered armchair and taking the journal from the desk. She uncapped a pen and scribbled something on one of the worn yellow pages.

"Thanks, Posey," Olivia said softly as she opened the door. "For everything." She stepped out into the bright afternoon sunlight and headed for home.

40

*O*livia stared at the blinking numbers of her alarm clock on Monday morning, the first rays of morning light peeking through the blinds and falling in narrow stripes across her swaddled frame.

She had spent much of the night chasing sleep, tumbling in and out of memories and dreams, her mind catching and turning over recent events: the fashion show, the fight with Violet, the fight with her parents, and everything that Posey had said.

The alarm went off, a sudden, staccato series of beeps, and Olivia slapped at the clock with her hand. Earlier, she'd heard her mother's footsteps on the stairs and felt Bridget pause on the landing. She'd done the same thing the night before, standing outside of Olivia's door, the shadow of her high heels hovering in the narrow strip of light above the floor.

Olivia had held her breath both times, waiting for the knock that never came.

From the kitchen, she could hear Mac shuffling around,

making coffee, the refrigerator door suctioning open and shut. She knew she'd have to talk to her parents eventually, but had no idea what she would say. Where would she start? Where would they?

She let one arm flop down over her tired eyes, red and puffy from the lack of sleep and crying. The idea of getting up, of even moving her legs to get out of bed, knowing that she wouldn't see Violet today, or tomorrow, or ever again . . .

Violet.

Just thinking her sister's name sent waves of grief through her arms and legs, as if pieces of her were missing, her body aching for lost, phantom limbs.

How was she supposed to go to school? She'd had enough trouble getting people to notice her in the first place, and now she was somehow expected to show her face again, after what had happened at the fashion show? Calla would never forgive her, and had undoubtedly already spread the word. Olivia suspected that most of the Bay Area was aware of her scandalous affair with Soren by now.

Olivia's heart tightened. In all of the drama with Violet, she'd practically forgotten all about Soren. She'd heard what Posey had said: The second wish never came true. Soren had truly cared about her all along. But what did that mean now? What *could* it mean, now that Calla, and probably everyone else, knew about them?

The window was open a crack, and a sharp early-morning breeze gusted across the room, rattling Violet's door against the frame. Olivia groaned, dropping her heavy arms back down to her sides and heaving herself up on the bed. She untangled her legs from the sheets and lowered her feet to the floor, each movement feeling separate and exhausting. Walking slowly to the door, she pulled it open, and took a few tentative steps inside, half hoping to find Violet waiting for her at the windowsill, as she'd been that first early morning, weeks before. She closed her eyes and tried to feel her sister in the room, tried to smell her shampoo, or hear her rolling laugh. But all she smelled was stale, trapped air, and all she heard was stuffy silence.

She lunged for first one window, then the next, throwing them open and welcoming the cooling cross-breeze as it whooshed around the room.

At least there was some air in here now.

Back in her own room, Olivia's eyes landed on her curtains, billowing white clouds in the corner by the window. She could barely make out a strange noise coming from behind them, a hollow fluttering sound, and she followed it across the room.

Propped between a pane of glass and the screen was Olivia's favorite photograph, the family shot on the boat that Violet had been looking at that afternoon.

"Huh," Olivia said out loud, wondering how the picture had gotten there. Hadn't she put it back in her desk?

Olivia forced the window shut and lowered down in the chair behind her desk, the bordered edges of the photograph curling up in her palms. She studied the smiling faces on the water, the girls arm in arm, sandwiched between their parents on the back of Mac's boat, remembering back to that warm summer day.

Her father had been driving the boat, her mother sitting beside him in her navy and white striped one-piece, the big straw hat she always wore in the sun covering one half of her face. Not long after the automatic timer had gone off, the hat had blown out across the water. Mac had swung the boat around to retrieve it, dragging his hand along the surface until he scooped the soggy hat back up, holding it high over his head, their hero.

He'd asked who wanted to drive the boat home, and for some reason, Violet had been adamant that Olivia have a turn. Olivia had insisted she didn't want to—they were nearing the harbor and she was nervous about being so close to the other boats. But Violet wouldn't let it go.

Olivia remembered the way her sister's features had changed, darkening as her voice grew louder, her stubborn pleas more intense.

Just do it, she'd coaxed. *Come on. Live a little.*

Olivia could feel how mad she'd been. How frustrated and spent, fuming at her sister for making her do something she was afraid to do. It was exactly the same way she'd felt after Violet had pushed her into admitting she had a crush on Soren. And exactly how she'd felt the night before, after Violet had said all of those horrible things.

At least I lived.

Olivia looked back down at the photo on the boat, remembering what had happened next. Tired of listening to Violet's nagging, she'd grabbed the wheel and guided the boat home, into the harbor and all the way up onto the landing, all by herself, all on her own.

Olivia smiled, shaking her head clear of the memory.

Nobody knows how to push our buttons like family. . . .

Posey's voice was suddenly ringing in Olivia's ears. Then she heard Violet, that evening on their grandfather's yacht.

291

You're going to need friends, after . . .

Olivia pressed the photograph between her fingers.

Violet had known.

She'd known Olivia could never make the wish on her own, even if it was time. She'd known her sister needed that little extra shove to start living on her own. And maybe, just maybe, she'd pushed Olivia on purpose.

Olivia leaned back on her bed, her head heavy, her eyes tired and raw. Was she really ready to be on her own?

There was only one way to find out.

Olivia found a pushpin rolling around in her top desk drawer, and tacked the photo up onto the wall beside her bed, smoothing the edges and pressing it in place.

41

*O*livia stood lingering outside the People's Republic, anxiously checking her watch as the minutes ticked by. She didn't have much time before the homeroom bell, and she had been hoping to catch Miles on his coffee run before class. There was a chill in the early-morning air, and Olivia was back to wearing her old favorite fleece, the soft gray collar zipped high under her chin.

That morning on the bus, Olivia had considered her options for dealing with the disaster that was sure to await her at school. The idea of using her last wish to straighten everything out—with Calla, with Soren, with Miles—crossed her mind once or twice. But she knew that Violet had been right: Olivia needed to face her own problems, even when those problems were piled so high that she could hardly see beyond them, or begin to imagine a potential road across.

Olivia was about to give up and head toward school, when the glass door, plastered with flyers for local bands and art openings, swung open. Bowie skipped out onto the sidewalk, a vegan no-cheese cheese Danish in one hand and a steaming thermos of fragrant black coffee in the other. Her hair was loose and much longer than Olivia had expected, flipping up in a little curl at her shoulders. She looked uncharacteristically cute, and Olivia had the sudden urge to pick her up and hug her.

"Bowie," Olivia said quickly, her voice fake-chipper and high. "I'm so glad you're here. Is Miles inside? I stopped by your house but your mom said you'd both left early."

Bowie shifted her weight from one metallic green combat boot to the other, unwrapping the wax paper from her sticky pastry and nibbling at one corner.

"Yeah," Bowie said quickly, offering the Danish to Olivia as an afterthought. "I think he said he was going to the computer lab to do edits on your scene. He's been at it all weekend. I had to lend him one of my wigs, you know, so he could read the rest of your lines convincingly."

Bowie glared at Olivia dramatically before taking a sip of her coffee, gasping as she burned the pink tip of her tongue.

"I know," Olivia said, talking more to herself than to Bowie. "I feel awful. I can't believe I did this."

Bowie stared at her, her round blue eyes blinking behind the thick rims of her retro glasses.

"Did what?" she asked innocently.

"I don't know," Olivia said, hugging her arms to her waist against a sudden gust of wind. "Flaked out on something for school. I never used to do things like that."

"Oh," Bowie said, nodding with exaggerated empathy. "You mean, have *fun*?"

Olivia stalled for a moment, before realizing that Bowie's

painted red lips were stretching into a wide, teasing grin. The way the sun was bouncing off the mischievous little twinkle in her clear blue eyes reminded Olivia suddenly of Violet. She couldn't believe she hadn't seen it before.

"I wouldn't worry too much about it," Bowie said. "It's just school. And Miles is kind of a control freak. He's probably happy he got to do the whole thing by himself."

Olivia smiled gratefully as Bowie lifted her bag, a worn men's briefcase that appeared to weigh more than she did, over her shoulder and waved to one of her friends on the corner.

"I gotta run," she said to Olivia. "Come over for dinner again sometime. Caroline's always looking for another sous chef."

Olivia nodded and picked up her own bag from where it had been resting on the tops of her feet.

"Thanks, Bowie," she said, stepping off the sidewalk and preparing to cross the street.

"Godspeed," Bowie called, tossing Olivia a wink from over her shoulder.

🦋 🦋 🦋

Olivia found Miles holed up in one of the far cubicles in the upper-school computer lounge, dragging his finger over a mouse pad and scanning images of choppy ocean waves on the flickering screen of a shiny MacBook Pro.

"Hey," Olivia started gently, touching the shoulder of his moth-eaten brown and tan striped sweater.

Miles jumped at her touch and recoiled into the cubby, his long legs knocking clumsily against the underside of the desk.

"Sorry." Olivia smiled. "Didn't mean to scare you."

Miles looked quickly back to the glowing screen and shrugged as fingers of blushing rage crawled up both sides of his neck. Olivia settled awkwardly into the adjacent cubby, leaning her head over and around the woven partition separating the two plastic chairs.

"Listen," she whispered, the corners of her eyes peeled for the computer aide, a student teacher with colored contacts and a fauxhawk, expecting a disciplinary hush at any moment. "I'm really sorry about the way I've been acting."

"Don't worry about it," Miles said automatically, clicking the mouse pad and dragging images with exaggerated effort, his eyes unmoving and attached to a spot in the center of the screen.

"I just wanted you to know that I feel horrible," Olivia said quietly. "Really. There's no way to really explain it, but I haven't been totally . . . myself . . . since I moved here. And I don't want to bore you with all kinds of excuses, but if you're ever interested in hearing them, or, I don't know, maybe even being my friend again . . ."

Suddenly, the student teacher's birdlike head appeared from over the top of his desk.

"Excuse me," he stuttered, indicating a sign hanging on the back of the door. "This is a noise-free zone."

Miles's eyes drifted back down toward Olivia's face, and they shared a quick, eye-rolling smirk. "Really," he said. "Don't worry about it. I'm sure you had a lot of family stuff going on."

Olivia nodded and looked down at her hands, remembering when Miles had tried to talk to her about Violet, and wishing she had let him.

"I remember what it was like when my parents split up,"

he said quietly into the cubby. "And then when my mom and Caroline got together . . . I didn't want to think about it. I just wanted it all to go away." His profile was lit up by the glowing screen, his eyes blinking and faraway. "I was convinced it was just a phase, you know?" He laughed. "I thought everything would go back to the way it was supposed to be."

Olivia smiled. "Did it?" she asked.

Miles stared at her with mock frustration. "Clearly, no," he deadpanned. "But it did turn into something else. We're not the family we were before, but we're definitely a family."

Olivia thought back to chopping vegetables with Miles and his family in the kitchen. Everything had seemed so happy and comfortable, it was hard to imagine a time when things weren't so easy.

"Besides," he said, "family's not family unless it's totally messing you up. I'm pretty sure that's the point."

Olivia smiled. "I guess that's why it's so nice to have friends," she said. Miles hunched forward, red patches growing underneath the smooth dark skin of his cheeks.

"True," he agreed. "But I didn't want to just be your friend. You know that."

Olivia sat up a bit straighter, surprised to hear Miles be so abrupt. As awkward as it was, it was also the first time he'd really said anything so direct, or with this much authority. It looked good on him, Olivia thought.

She looked down at her hands in her lap, searching for something not totally lame or meaningless to say.

"Please." Miles smirked. "Spare me the *I'm just not that into you* speech."

"Okay." Olivia nodded. "But, I do want you to know that

297

it's not that I'm *not* into you, it's just—well, I was kind of already into someone else." Olivia braced herself for more questions, but Miles only tucked a cowlicky tuft of thick brown hair behind his ear, tapping the eraser side of his mechanical pencil against the keyboard.

"I know," was all he said.

Olivia raised an eyebrow. "You do?" she asked.

Miles leveled her with an obvious stare. "Let's just say your little rendezvous with Soren at the Palace this weekend is basically in the public domain by now," he explained. "Seriously, I think somebody's making a musical about it already."

Olivia tried to smile, but her stomach was already somersaulting. Miles must have read the panic on her face, because the skin around his eyes softened as he looked back her way.

"Things don't always work out like they do in fairy tales." Miles shrugged before leaning back in his seat just slightly and gesturing toward the screen. "Anyway . . ." He sighed. "I just finished editing the footage. When I cut the scenes we shot of you painting in the backyard with some of the lighthouse stuff, I think it turned out pretty good. Want to take a look?"

Olivia smiled gratefully and leaned over the keyboard, taking in the broken images of sea and sand. "These are beautiful," Olivia said, as short clips of rolling water and gusting wind played on the screen. Miles typed frantically and dragged the mouse back and forth, images rotating and snapping darkly shut.

"Look at this one." He played another clip, this one starring a beautiful old lighthouse, clinging to the side of a crumbling rock jetty. "It's actually a hostel outside of Santa Cruz," he said. "It was incredible. Check out all those sea lions."

Olivia smiled to herself, remembering Violet's warning, and leaned in closer to the screen. Out in the water, beyond the shining beacon, there was a glimmer of green, and when she squinted she could see that it was a boat, a yacht similar to her grandfather's. Olivia inched her nose even closer to the screen and felt her pulse racing as the image came more into focus, before the camera zoomed back out, blurring everything but the lighthouse again.

It could've been her mind playing tricks on her, but for a moment she was fairly certain about what she'd seen. It didn't just look like her grandfather's boat. It *was* his boat, complete with the calligraphy *Sybil* on one side, and there, leaning over the bow, a wild tangle of strawberry blond curls blowing in the rough sea breeze.

"What is it?" Miles asked. "Don't you like it?"

Olivia shook her head, swallowing heavily and smiling back at Miles.

"No," she said softly. "I love it."

42

"Very nice," Mr. Whitley managed through his stern, locked jaw, switching off the flat-screen TV that had been temporarily propped up against the dry-erase board. Olivia and Miles were squirming in the "hot seats," two folding director's chairs set up at the front of the room, awaiting critique by Whitley and the class.

"Olivia," Mr. Whitley intoned. It had taken a few weeks, but he'd finally started to call her by her real name. "I'm wondering if you can tell us a little bit about why you chose this scene, the scene of Lily finishing the painting at the end of the novel?"

Olivia's thoughts swirled. She hadn't realized they'd have to defend their projects, and she didn't have anything prepared. Not to mention the fact that *Miles* had been the one to choose the scene. But she couldn't flake out on him this time. Not again.

"I'm only curious," Whitley continued, rapping his red pen against the inside of his wrist, "because you seemed not to identify very much with the character at the beginning of the unit. I'm wondering how your feelings might have changed."

"That's not true," Olivia said suddenly, clearing her throat and shifting forward in her seat. She wasn't exactly sure what she was going to say, but she suddenly felt confident that the right words would find her. It was an old, familiar feeling, kind of like relearning how to ride a bike. Once the wheels started turning, the mechanics took care of themselves.

"I never said I didn't identify with Lily," she went on, her voice clear and her own. "I think in some ways she's the heart of the book. And her transformation at the end, when she's finally able to finish her painting, after she doesn't have anything holding her back . . . it's one of the most important scenes in the novel. It's when she finally realizes who she is."

Mr. Whitley nodded vaguely, pacing the length of a square-paned window overlooking the courtyard below.

"And what was it?" he asked deliberately. "What do you think was holding her back all that time?"

Olivia looked down at her feet, feeling every pair of eyes in the class burning holes into the top of her head. Miles's mush-room loafers were fidgeting under the chair beside her, and she felt him holding his breath. Her heart was pounding, but this time it was different. Everybody in the room was waiting for her, and that was okay. This time she had things to say.

"The past," Olivia answered finally. "The past was holding her back."

🦋 🦋 🦋

Olivia hurried down the crooked maze of hallways toward the gym, her heart skipping an erratic beat inside her chest.

The last bell of the day had finally rung, and she knew that if she wasted any time, the gym—which was doubling as Calla's thrift-store donation center—would be teeming not only with volunteers and people dropping off donations, but also the boys' basketball team, stretching before practice. It was going to be horrendous enough to try and find the right words to apologize to Calla. She couldn't even imagine how mortified she'd be if it had to happen in front of a captive audience.

Olivia peeked her head through the open red doors and was relieved to find Calla sitting alone in the far corner of the empty court. She was carefully separating items of donated clothing into piles, placing them gently in cardboard boxes arranged at her feet.

Olivia stole a deep breath of musty gym air and started across the shiny floor, her old sneakers squeaking against the clean parquet.

She had originally been hoping to catch Calla after Whitley's class, assuming they could lighten the mood with a few jokes about how bad her on-screen performance had been. But Calla had been mysteriously absent, presumably in order to hang signs for the clothing drive that was now officially under way.

Maybe it would be better this way, after a full day at school had passed. And after the relative success of the Miles apology, Olivia couldn't help but hope that Calla maybe wasn't as furious as she'd been the night of the fashion show.

"What do you want?" Calla barked from across the clean lines of the court, without looking up.

Then again, maybe not.

Olivia paused, fiddling with the zipper of her sweater. She took another steadying breath and kept on.

"I have nothing to say to you." Calla bent over a pile of boxes stacked inside of each other, wrangling the top one free and slamming it onto the table.

Olivia stopped in front of the makeshift donation center, her hands jammed low in the back pockets of her worn corduroys, rescued from underneath her bed where Violet had insisted they remain in a trash bag for eternity.

Calla had uncapped a Sharpie and was writing *Evening Wear* in tiny, perfect print on the top flap of the box.

"Calla," Olivia said, her voice small and uncertain. "I'm so sorry."

Calla held up a pair of satin wide-legged women's trousers, examining the tag and folding them neatly across her elbow.

"Unless you have something to donate," she said, placing the pants inside the appropriate box, "would you mind leaving me alone? I don't really have time to relive being totally humiliated right now, as thrilling as that sounds."

Olivia sighed and shifted her weight from one foot to the other. "Okay," she said. "I just . . . I've been trying to find you all day, and I really wanted to apologize—"

"What's done is done." Calla shrugged. "Nothing you can say will change what happened. Why bother?"

Olivia chewed the dry corner of her lower lip, feeling a lump forming in her throat and willing it to disappear. Her eyes burned and she blinked furiously at the hot tears threatening to escape down her flushed cheeks.

"I mean," Calla continued, tossing aside a pile of pastel-colored cashmere shells in search of more dresses or skirts to add to the box, "it would have been one thing if you'd talked to me first. You had plenty of time to tell me that something was going on between you two." Calla snapped a long pencil skirt free of wrinkles, sending a sharp gust of air in Olivia's direction and ruffling the hairs on her arms.

"I really didn't mean for it to happen this way," Olivia said, her voice growing stronger and more confident. "I had no idea he was going to break up with you. And after he did, and we started hanging out . . ."

Calla made a sound like she was choking on something, waving her hands in front of her face. "Stop," she said quietly. "Please. You've made your choice. I really don't want to hear details, okay?"

Olivia watched in silence as Calla tucked her long dark hair into a bun and went back to sorting a pile of pants.

She tried to speak but her mouth was dry and no words came.

Turning back toward the door, Olivia started the seemingly interminable walk of shame back across the gym, her back burning under the weight of Calla's hurt and angry eyes.

Violet had been right. *Life was messy.* Too bad she hadn't said anything about how to clean it up.

43

Olivia pushed through the lobby doors and onto the street, her teeth clenched to hold back the sobs that had been brewing inside her all afternoon. She gathered her fleece around her waist and walked toward the corner, her steps heavy and deliberate against a bitter wind whipping her hair back from the creased lines of her forehead.

"Hey." She heard a familiar voice behind her, and then felt a warm hand on the small of her back.

She turned to see Soren, a checkered wool scarf waving wildly around the collar of his brown leather coat, his blond hair tousled and his eyes swimming red.

Olivia looked immediately to the sidewalk, shimmying out from under his touch and taking another step toward the curb. "Hey," she said, her voice curt and cold. "I'm actually in kind of a rush."

"Wait." He steadied his hands on her elbows, searching her face with his soft green eyes. "I've been calling you all weekend. What's going on?"

"I'm sorry," she said, the lump in her throat thickening, the burning fire back behind her eyes. "I have to go home."

Soren let his arms fall heavily to his side. "Okay," he said uncertainly. "So that's it?"

Olivia whipped her head around, glancing hurriedly up and down the street.

There they were, standing together in plain view of school, and just around the corner from People's. Anybody could turn that corner and catch them at any time. *Anybody.*

"Soren, please," Olivia said. "I really have to—"

"Why are you doing this?" Soren pleaded. "What are you so afraid of?"

Olivia crossed her arms, hugging warmth around her waist.

"I don't know," she said. "I just don't want to make things worse."

"For who?" he asked.

Olivia raised her eyes quickly to meet his, the glaringly obvious answer on the tip of her tongue.

Soren shrugged. "Yeah," he said finally, "but Calla was going to find out eventually. And okay, it will be hard for a while, but things will settle down."

Olivia looked up at Soren's face, open and optimistic. She wanted so badly to fall into his arms, to let him make it better, to run away with him and never deal with any of this again.

Suddenly, Olivia felt something brushing past her shoulder. She turned her head quickly, expecting to see Violet, *hoping* with everything inside of her to find her sister standing there, arms crossed, ready with deadpan instructions for Olivia to follow.

But it was only the wind.

Olivia took a deep breath, the realization that she was more alone than ever hitting her like a rusty screw turning in the center of her heart.

Soren shuffled his feet and looked down at a crack in the sidewalk. "I've been thinking," he said, his voice kind of crackly and unsure. "When you asked me, at the fashion show, why I liked you . . . I didn't really know what to say, and I'm sorry it came out so lame."

Soren was blushing now and he refused to look her in the eye, talking directly to a pair of tire marks on the pavement, scuffing the tops of his sneakers against the side of the tar-spotted curb.

"I guess I just wanted to say something that sounded important and big." He shrugged, stuffing his hands deeper into his pockets. "But the truth is, I don't really have a reason. Even that first day I skated past you in the courtyard, it was like I was running into someone I hadn't seen in a while. Somebody I already knew."

Olivia smiled and nodded, remembering back to all of the stops and starts in their first few awkward conversations. It had felt a lot like they both already had so much to say, and were tripping over themselves not to let it all out too soon.

Soren glanced up from the street and caught her eyes. "And I know that it's right, because . . . it's right."

Olivia laughed, losing his logic but not wanting him to stop.

"Right?" he repeated, smiling and nudging her with the outside of his elbow.

Olivia felt her features softening as Soren untucked one hand from his pocket. He reached carefully out for her hand, his fingers timid and curious as they grasped for hers.

She let her palm flop motionlessly inside his hand for a moment, before tightening her grip and giving his knuckles a cozy little squeeze.

There it was: the perfect fit.

Another gust of wind ruffled the waist of Olivia's coat, and although she didn't have to look to know that Violet wasn't standing nearby, she couldn't shake the feeling that she wasn't really alone.

🦋 🦋 🦋

Despite the damp cold, Soren and Olivia took the long way home, huddled close together and taking slow, coordinated steps. In front of her house, Soren kissed her and promised to call that night. She watched him disappear around the corner, a warm, easy calm floating up from inside of her.

It wasn't until Olivia had turned her key in the lock that the fluttering in her stomach returned. She pushed the door quietly open, hoping her father would be drilling somewhere in a far corner of the house, lost and buried in one of his many projects of distraction. But all that greeted her was a homey silence, the familiar clanking of old pipes and the hum of the new refrigerator.

That was surprise number one.

Surprise number two was her mother's long wool coat, hanging lazily over the banister, her patent leather pumps lined up directly beneath it, the discarded costume of an after-hours professional. What was her mother doing home in the middle of the afternoon?

Suddenly, into the quiet chorus of home appliances, low, friendly voices drifted down through the floorboards. Olivia craned her neck up toward the ceiling, slowly taking the uneven stairs up to the third floor.

Violet's door was pushed open into the hallway, and Olivia could feel a cool breeze tickling the tip of her nose, rushing inside from the windows she had left open that morning. She was almost to the end of the hall when she heard a sound so foreign it made her stop short, the top of one sneaker stubbing against the newly laid hardwood floor.

It took her a second to place it:

The short, choppy baritone.

The singsong soprano sigh.

She took one more careful step and peeked around the corner.

There, in Violet's room, settled between the bay windows, with the contents of open boxes spilling around their tangled limbs, were Olivia's parents.

And they were laughing.

Mac, his broad shoulders hunched back against the love seat, saw Olivia first. He lifted his eyes to hers and she noticed right away that they were moist from crying. Olivia hesitated in the door frame, her tote sliding down the length of her arm and landing on the floor in a deflated heap.

"Hi," she said uncertainly, feeling like an intruder or unwelcome voyeur.

Bridget turned quickly, her eyeliner smudged into the wet creases at the corners of her eyes. "We were just going through some of Violet's things," she said softly. "We thought it might be time to give more away."

Olivia crossed her arms and leaned back into the door, half out of stubborn resolve and half because she suddenly felt off balance.

Mac cleared his throat and levered his weight against the sill, hoisting himself up to his feet. "And I finally finished those bookshelves I've been working on," he said, approaching Olivia slowly from across the room. "I was thinking about putting those in here later. We could make this a library. Another room of your own, if you want."

Olivia felt her eyes brimming and quickly looked at the tops of her boots.

"Honey," Mac said, reaching out and lightly resting his rough, calloused hand inside the crook of her elbow. "We're really sorry you've been feeling so alone. But you have to know it's been hard on us, too."

Before she could control it, a slow wave of hot anger burst up from the pit of Olivia's stomach, and she lifted her gaze toward her parents' hopeful eyes.

"Hard?" she quietly repeated, the tears already starting to flow, her nose running and her face on fire. "But all you do is work! At the office, or on this house! You never even *talk* about her."

Bridget looked toward the window, a single teardrop careening off the strong silhouette of her chin. Mac needlessly cleared his throat again and took a step back.

"And guess what? All that working?" Her voice was high and cracking now, the tears welling up behind her burning eyes. "It's not *working* for me."

Olivia's eyes darted wildly back and forth before she covered them with her shaking hands, sliding down the wall and landing in the corner with a muted thud.

Her father crouched low beside her, smelling like he always did of sawdust and aftershave, and pulled her head into the solid curve of his shoulder, just as he'd done when she was a little girl.

Too exhausted to argue, Olivia sobbed against his sweat-shirt.

"We miss her, too, hon," Mac said into the cold mess of her hair.

Olivia felt a warm push against her open side, Bridget's voice echoing Mac's in soft, soothing tones.

"We miss her every day," Bridget said.

Olivia pushed both of her parents away and sat back against the wall, wiping the backs of her hands against her cheekbones. "You do?" she sniffed.

Bridget reached out and pushed a wispy link of curls back away from Olivia's damp cheeks. "Oh, Olivia," her mother said quietly. "I think about your sister first thing every morning."

"And I talk to her before I go to bed every night," Mac said, his voice fading into a cough. This time he was unable to stop the clumsy tears that were dropping onto his sleeve. Bridget reached across Olivia's lap, taking Mac's hand and squeezing it.

Olivia's heart ached to see her parents cry, but it was the kind of ache that felt important and real, like she'd been underwater for too long and was finally coming up for air.

As they sat there, the three of them huddled in a corner

of a room that would have been Violet's, Olivia knew that something had changed. Violet was gone, and she was never coming back. Things were pretty messed up, and her family would never be the same.

But they were definitely still a family.

44

The next morning, Olivia did something she hadn't
done since she was ten years old:

She let her parents drive her to school.

Bridget and Mac rode up front, while Olivia sat crushed in
the back by the piles of boxes and bags full of Violet's clothes,
things they'd decided to give away.

Olivia had told her parents about Calla's clothing drive
while they were painting the walls of Violet's room—which,
no matter what color it was, or how many books it held,
would always be Violet's room.

"Are you sure you won't want them someday?" Bridget
had asked, as they sat down to a meal of green-pepper-and-
onion pizza in front of a marathon of *Seinfeld* reruns on TV.

Olivia helped herself to another slice and nodded. "They're
not me," she said plainly, pretending not to notice her parents
eyeing each other carefully.

It had been an evening of sideways glances, tiptoeing questions, and accidental affection passed between the three of

them, steadily back and forth. At times, it was so quiet that Olivia wanted to scream, but she knew it would be a while before things were totally normal again.

The early-morning donation drop-off was more crowded than after school, with trendy mothers using carpool as an excuse to flaunt last year's fashions and fawn over what a sophisticated set of leftovers the shop would receive. Olivia stood patiently between her parents in line, trying to smile pleasantly as her parents passed reassuring glances back and forth.

Finally it was time to lay their goods on the table, and each of them presented a box to Calla, who was checking items off on a clipboard and smiling gratefully from one charitable parent to the next.

The change in Calla's welcoming expression was so slight when she registered the Larsens that Olivia was certain neither of her parents suspected that anything was amiss. But Olivia felt a pointed coldness from across the table, a hard look of stubborn resignation settling in the whites of Calla's hazel eyes.

Mac took the clipboard and leaned over the table, scribbling his name and address as Bridget prompted him with her social security number.

Avoiding eye contact with Olivia, Calla pulled one box toward her with both hands, beginning to rifle through its contents. She slowly uncovered a pair of Violet's favorite Joe's jeans, a cashmere tunic, a chunky leather belt. The bridge of Calla's nose wrinkled as she glanced across the table.

"But a lot of this stuff looks pretty new," she said to Olivia. "Is it yours?"

Olivia shook her head slowly, clearing her throat and about to explain, when slowly, like an injection, a wave of understanding passed over Calla's face.

"Are you sure you want to do this?" she asked quietly. "I mean, this stuff . . . it was hers, wasn't it?"

Olivia nodded solemnly. "I'm sure," she insisted. "It's time."

Calla looked back at the box and pulled out the torn secondhand dress, running her fingers over the swirls of bright orange and red. "This is beautiful," she said, just as Mac and Bridget were handing over the clipboard.

Bridget put her arm on Olivia's shoulder, and for the first time, Olivia didn't try to wriggle free.

"I can't thank you enough," Calla said to the three of them. "This is very, very generous."

Mac and Bridget nodded and said their good-byes, and Olivia started to follow them across the crowded gym floor.

"Olivia, wait."

Olivia froze, turning slowly to see Calla reaching for her bag on the floor.

"I have something for you," she said, digging through notebooks and binders in her bag until she'd found a crumpled pile of neon yellow flyers. She found a pen and leaned over the table, scribbling something on the back of one and handing it to Olivia.

"It's for a reading Farley's doing at this café in the Haight this weekend," Calla said quickly, and Olivia recognized the familiar sound of excitement in her voice. "I've read some of his stuff, and it's actually not so bad."

Olivia took the flyer and folded it in her hand, looking back to Calla with a smile.

"Come," Calla said, before nodding once and hurrying back to her post behind the table.

Olivia hustled through the crowd to catch up with her parents, the flyer warm in her palms. As she reached the doors, she stopped, turning the crumpled yellow paper around in her open hand.

There, written in familiar, perfect script, was the one word she'd most hoped to see:

Madonna.

45

ater that night, Olivia crawled into bed, too spent to wash her face or pick out her clothes for the next day. She'd even forgotten to do her homework, and for the first time since kindergarten, she truly didn't care.

Her heavy head hit the pillow and she pulled the comforter up under her chin, eager to drift off into a much-needed full night's sleep. But as the minutes slowly ticked by in neon beside her, she tossed and turned, her body restless and her mind racing, uneasy and confused.

She flopped over onto her back, sighed heavily, and reached over to switch on the lamp. Her eyes landed on her closet door, open just a crack. Angled through one corner was the edge of a familiar garment bag, the forgotten parting gift from her last visit to Posey's shop.

Olivia threw back the covers and tiptoed over the cool wooden floor panels, pulling the door open and unhooking the bag from the top of the door. She kneeled back on her bed, a messy tangle of sheets and blankets, and pulled the zipper down.

The dress, cradled inside the curves of the musty vinyl bag, was spectacular.

Before she knew what she was doing or why, Olivia whipped her pajama top over her head and fed her arms through the gown, the strapless top hugging her torso, the long skirt flaring gently at her hips.

She toed the closet door shut and smiled at her reflection in the mirror.

In addition to the expertly flattering cut, the flowing fabric of the dress was dyed a deep, warm shade of purple.

A shade commonly known as *violet*.

In the mirror, she saw the reflection of the curtains swaying in a gentle breeze behind her. She went to the window and heaved it all the way open, swinging her legs over the damp sill and crawling to the small wrought-iron balcony outside. She hadn't been out there since that first morning with Violet, when she'd all but given up on trying to see any stars from her new roof.

She settled back onto the cold brick of the windowsill, tucked her bare feet under her body, and craned her neck up toward the sky. The darkness felt heavy as it closed in around her, and she liked how small and anonymous it made her feel.

As she had come to expect, the blue-black sky was distanced by a low layer of thick fog. But for the first time, she didn't mind. She was starting to like the cushiony ceiling, the way it hung heavy over the city at different times of day, as if reminding her to pay closer attention for those rare, special moments of flawless sun.

Olivia took a deep breath, her lungs opening to the cool night air.

Posey had told her she'd know what to wish for when the time was right, and that she should wish from her heart. That night, when she'd seen her last dress for the first time, she hadn't known what her wish would be, but she knew she was ready to make it.

Now, out here on the balcony, leaning back against the house that was finally starting to feel like home, she closed her eyes and listened.

First, she heard the wind, the lulling breeze crashing softly around her, like rolling ocean waves.

Listening deeper, she felt the steady rhythmic thud of her pulse, the whoosh of blood rushing in her veins.

And then there was a voice. Her own voice—small at first, but growing louder, speaking from somewhere deep inside of her, a place she hadn't even known belonged to her.

I'm ready, the voice said. *I'm ready to live a little. The way Violet taught me. My only wish—*

Olivia's eyes snapped open.

Here it was. Her last and final wish. What was the only thing left to want, the only thing she needed to let go?

I don't want to wish to forget, she thought. *I don't want to wish the hurt away. I want to be real. I want to live. I just wish I'd been able to say good-bye.*

Olivia looked around, holding the skirt of her dress, pressing the little fabric butterfly between two fingers.

"Good-bye, Violet." She spoke softly into the darkness. "I wish you could hear me."

Olivia held her breath for what seemed like an eternity, waiting for something to happen. Would Violet come back? Would she hear her sister's voice, her clear, strong laugh, one last time?

Finally, the pressure in her lungs was too much to bear, and she exhaled, her shoulders dropping. Disappointed, she let go of the seam of her dress, her hands dropping to her sides. Olivia unfolded her legs from beneath her, about to climb back inside, when she felt something moving.

There, inside the pile of purple fabric gathered in her lap, was the little butterfly, beating its wings against the material, desperately trying to take flight.

Almost without thinking, as if she were helping a wounded ladybug from the tip of her nail, she lifted the dress and shook it gently in the air, giving the butterfly just the extra push it needed to fly away.

Olivia ran to the edge of the balcony, watching as the glowing, fluttering light circled around her, striking out over the rooftops and floating up, higher and higher.

For a moment, she thought she would lose it to the thick sea of fog overhead. She squinted her eyes, trying to follow the blurry light for as long as she could. And then, as if parted by a brushstroke, or a pair of helpful hands, the clouds separated and the golden glow returned, attaching itself to a clear patch of night sky and streaking into place.

Olivia gasped.

At last, there it was, shining bright against the darkness, a tail of dusty starlight fading in its wake:

Violet's shooting star.

Epilogue

"**E**xcuse me?"

Calla looked up from under the desk, where she'd been buried to her knees in donations all afternoon. It had been a quiet day at the thrift shop—Saturday mornings were always fairly slow—and she jumped when a small voice called out from the bargain bin.

"Could you tell me how much this is?"

The girl was tall and lean, with fine blond hair cut short to her chin. Calla had never seen her before and was pretty sure she wasn't a student at Golden Gate. She felt a quick twinge of excitement sparking in her belly. She'd known that the thrift store had been an instant success, but she'd never imagined it would spread beyond the walls of school.

"Everything in the bin is ten dollars," Calla replied. She could hardly remember what she'd thrown into the blue recycling box she'd borrowed from the art room. Mostly it was the stuff with major flaws—stains, missing buttons, a pair of Louboutin stilettos with one broken heel.

The girl nodded and stared at the dress in her hands, holding it out from her body as if she were weighing the fabric on a scale.

"That one has a pretty bad tear on the side," Calla offered. "The zipper's totally busted. It's too bad, it's an amazing dress."

The girl looked up and smiled before digging in her purse for her wallet. "I'll take it."

Calla shrugged and accepted the crumpled twenty from the girl's outstretched hand. "Do you want a bag?" she asked, searching for change in the drawer.

But the girl was already halfway back into the hall, shaking her head. "That's okay," she said. "And you can keep the change. It's worth it."

Once outside, the girl took the dress in both of her hands and held it out to admire. She'd never been drawn to anything so bold—she couldn't remember the last time she'd even worn a dress, let alone one so colorful—but something about the pattern, the bright, interlocking circles, and the background of slippery cool satin . . . she knew this dress was supposed to be hers.

As she was folding the cool material back up into her bag, she felt a tiny prick on her finger. A safety pin had fallen open and was sticking out near a seam by the zipper. It was holding the torn fabric shut, and on the inside of the zipper was a small cardboard card.

The girl angled the card through the tear and freed it from the pin. It was graying and creased in the middle, with one small line of typed print at its center:

Mariposa of the Mission.

And next to the words, a simple indented graphic, a tiny floating butterfly pressed into the paper.

The girl looked at the card and shrugged, before folding it carefully into her pocket and running to catch the bus.

Acknowledgments

During the time it took me to write this book, I had a number of part-time employers. I would like to thank (most of) them for not-firing me, even on the countless occasions on which I was caught doodling and dreaming, when I had More Important Things to Do.

I would also like to thank (though thanking is never enough): my parents, Maria Krokidas and Bruce Bullen, for reading to me, writing with me, and cheering me on all the way. My brothers, George and John, for being ridiculous and golden-hearted friends. The entire island of Martha's Vineyard, especially the Coutts family, for giving me a home. Frances Evens and the Urban School; Mary-Katherine Menikheim and the Marin Country Day School, and the many kind souls who took the time to show me their San Francisco. And the most brilliant, patient, and thoughtful pair of editors a girl could ask for, Sara Shandler and Joelle Hobeika. I couldn't have wished for a better team.

WISHING FOR MORE?
TURN THE PAGE FOR A SNEAK PEEK AT

THE NEXT WISH NOVEL
BY ALEXANDRA BULLEN

"We're closed."

Hazel Snow stood on the inside of a heavy glass door, squinting in the musty dark of what appeared to be an abandoned dry cleaner's shop. She had a funny feeling about this seamstress situation, pretty much right off the bat. First of all, a seamstress? The word made her think of a plump old lady with full skirts and a mouthful of needles. But this seamstress, the one hidden in the back of a grimy storefront, lounging on an old, ratty sofa and reading a glossy paperback, was neither old nor plump. No, she was young, though it wasn't immediately clear how young— maybe Hazel's age, maybe a youngish-looking thirty—and she looked to be in dire need of a cheeseburger.

It had been three months since Hazel discovered the name of her birth mother, and almost exactly as long since the Google search that changed her life. Because, according to the Internet, not only did "Rosanna Scott" live in San Francisco, she was an active member of an elite group of artist/ philanthropists, and hosting a fundraising event at a restaurant in the Ferry Building, on Sunday, March 26, at seven o'clock in the evening. Tonight.

This, Hazel knew, was where she would meet her mother. As if the decision had already been made for her, she knew she would have to go. And just as clearly, she knew what she would wear.

It's not like she had a closet full of options. Hazel owned one dress, and it was a fluke that she even had it. She'd found the dress over a year before, in a thrift store attached to a fancy private school in the Haight. She had been, at the time, living with a foster family on Oak Street. On her walk home from her own, boring public school, she would pass Golden Gate Prep, and often stare in through the glass at the fashionable students, each toting their personalized laptops and climbing in and out of expensive-looking cars.

One spring day, she noticed the school's thrift store. She hadn't even gone in looking to buy anything. But the dress found her, from under a pile of broken shoes in the Bargain Bin. It was definitely brighter than anything else she owned (mostly because everything else she owned was black) and she wasn't even sure it would fit. But something about that dress just wouldn't let her leave it behind.

She'd known about the dress's torn seam when she brought it home. But it wasn't until this morning that Hazel realized, unless she wanted to meet her mother with six inches of torso hanging out, she would need to have the dress fixed. Which was when her eyes had landed on the business card. Hanging from a thread and safety-pinned to the tag, it read: "Mariposa of the Mission." And under the address, a single word: *Seamstress*.

And that was how she ended up in the Mission on a Sunday afternoon, standing in the doorway of a dusty shop that smelled like mothballs, crowded with sewing machines and headless dress dummies, and which was, apparently . . .

"Closed," the girl on the couch said again. "Sorry." But she didn't sound sorry. She sounded annoyed.

Hazel wanted to scream. Of course something would go wrong. Learning her mother's name may have changed every fiber of who Hazel was on the inside, but in the outside world, exactly nothing was different. "Great," she huffed. She leaned into the door, and took one last look at the strange and empty shop. Business didn't exactly appear to be booming.

"You know," she started, angry words backing up in her throat. "Keeping regular business hours might go a long way. I mean, if you ever find yourself interested in any actual customers."

Hazel started to push through the door, but her bag's strap caught on a brass hook and tugged her back into the room. The dress spilled out of her tote. *Perfect*, she thought as she bent down to stuff it back into her bag. *Just perfect*.

"Wait." Two clunky clogs were suddenly making their way to where Hazel was crouched by the door. "That dress," the girl said, pointing one long, spindly finger at Hazel's tote. "May I see it?" Hazel slowly held the dress out towards the girl's open hand. "Where did you get it?" she asked, spreading the material and holding it out to one side.

"In the Haight," Hazel offered. "A thrift store. I guess I just liked the colors. . . ." She let her voice trail off. Why was she defending her fashion sense to a grumpy girl with weird bangs who, until recently, was primarily interested in getting her to leave?

The girl was staring at her with eyes that looked more

feline than human: small, piercing, and almost golden. "What do you need it for?" she asked slowly.

"I'm going to a fundraiser," Hazel said. "It's at this restaurant in the Ferry Building." She took another full breath before adding, "I'm meeting my mother tonight."

It was the first time Hazel had said it out loud, and the words felt like sharp explosions in her mouth. She looked at the tops of her checkered, slip-on sneakers.

The girl was quiet. Finally she turned, her heavy clogs scraping the floor, and walked slowly back to the couch. She took the dress with her. "Can you come back in two hours?"

Hazel stared at the girl's small back, the arch of her spine curving beneath her thin sweater. "Two hours?" she repeated. "Yeah—I mean, yes. Are you sure?" She waited for the girl to turn back around, to say something more. When she didn't, Hazel put her hand on the doorknob, afraid that another word would make her change her mind.

"Hey," she heard from behind her with one foot on the sidewalk. "What's your name?"

"Oh, sorry." Hazel blushed. "I'm Hazel."

"Nice to meet you, Hazel," the girl said, landing heavily on each word like she was sharing a secret. "I'm Posey. See you at three."

DON'T MISS

Wishful Thinking

AND MAKE YOUR WISH COME TRUE AT
WWW.WHATWOULDYOUWISHFOR.COM

To Do List:
Read all the Point books!

♡ 📖 ♡

Airhead
Being Nikki
Runaway
By **Meg Cabot**

Wish
Wishful Thinking
By **Alexandra Bullen**

Top 8
What's Your Status?
By **Katie Finn**

Sea Change
The Year My Sister Got Lucky
South Beach
French Kiss
Hollywood Hills
By **Aimee Friedman**

Ruined
By **Paula Morris**

Possessed
Consumed
By **Kate Cann**

Suite Scarlett
Scarlett Fever
By **Maureen Johnson**

The Lonely Hearts Club
Prom and Prejudice
By **Elizabeth Eulberg**

Wherever Nina Lies
By **Lynn Weingarten**

To Die For
By **Christopher Pike**

The Vampire's Promise
By **Caroline B. Cooney**

Clarity
By **Kim Harrington**

Girls In Love

Summer Girls

Summer Boys

Next Summer

After Summer

Last Summer

By **Hailey Abbott**

*And Then
Everything Unraveled*

*And Then I Found
Out the Truth*

By **Jennifer Sturman**

Hotlanta
By Denene Millner
and Mitzi Miller

Hotlanta

If Only You Knew

What Goes Around

In or Out
By Claudia Gabel

In or Out

Loves Me, Loves Me Not

Sweet and Vicious

*Friends Close,
Enemies Closer*

Love in the Corner Pocket

The Comeback

By **Marlene Perez**

*This Book Isn't Fat,
It's Fabulous*

*This Girl Isn't Shy,
She's Spectacular*

By **Nina Beck**

Kissing Snowflakes

By **Abby Sher**

Breakfast at Bloomingdale's

By **Kristin Kemp**

Secret Santa

Be Mine

Spring Fling

By **Sabrina James**

21 Proms

Edited by **Daniel Ehrenhaft**
and **David Levithan**

Point

www.thisispoint.com